Tales from Tellis
Book One

The Fall
from
Lunathal

By Christopher S. Carlone

Prologue
700 years ago...

On the highest peak of the tallest mountain in all of Tellis, the last Elves of Evaria settled.

The world around them was desolate and flooding. Otherworldly waters seemed to pour endlessly through the forests and valleys. Soon, even the Evarian Peaks would be part of the sea.

The Elves performed a desperate ritual using the last might of their arcana to commune with their Goddess. They sent her a plea for her aid against the rising tide. The Goddess answered them with a single tear, which fell from the Moon and landed on the

1

highest point of the mountain. Where it fell, it left a small shimmering pool of water.

At first, the Elves believed they had been betrayed. Many felt their deity had forsaken them, and they would soon be swept away by the great flood. Some of the most devout of the Goddess's followers questioned their faith, while others took it as a test of loyalty. Many of the most loyal drank from the waters in the pool, and their skin began to change colors. The non-believers who did not drink pleaded to any other Gods or Goddesses who would listen.

The sea continued to rise, threatening to overtake the mountain. No answers came from the heavens other than the small shimmering pool atop the peak. As hope began to fade for the survivors, the dawn of the winter solstice brought the sprouting of the Willow.

The solstice shrouded the land in moonlight, and from that moonlight, the sproutling found its nourishment. The sprout grew from the center of the pool, each day multiplying in size until it was the tallest tree in all of Tellis.

The Willow began to bear silvery leaves, and its limbs grew out in large platforms, so wide that two Elves could walk abreast across them.

The last Elves gathered their belongings and began to climb the tree. They wove town squares from the bark and limbs, crude houses from the branches and moss that the Willow provided. They brought their supplies, their livestock, and their books. They ate the assortment of fruits and fungi that grew from the tree and drank from the growing wooden basins that filled with wells of fresh water. The Willow grew so tall, it pierced the cloud sea above them. The clouds orbited around their colony like a small contained globe. The cloud wall protected them from the harsh atmosphere of the altitude, allowing the folk of the Willow to breathe freely and live comfortably.

The tree provided for them, and those that drank from the pool developed arcane properties to assist their new civilization. The great city of Lunathal was founded, and the world on the surface of Tellis was soon forgotten.

These Elves, over the generations, began to forget their own history. They started to refer to themselves as "Moonfolk" in reverence of the Moon Goddess who had saved them. The tree provided sustainability and safety for the citizens of Lunathal. They began to focus on astrology and art.

A hero amongst them, holding unforeseen power, saved the Old Willow from any threats of destruction. He was revered, an unlikely and powerful savior, before he vanished. Two hundred years passed, and the Hero of Lunathal never returned. The folk of the Willow continued to live peacefully above the cloud sea, blissfully unaware of the beauty and danger that had awoken on the surface of Tellis.

Chapter I
Fruit fly

The letter had finally come. Theryn could feel his excitement mount as he leapt from his window perch and landed on the wooden platform that held his Bub's house. These moments of anticipation were few and far between for folks in Lunathal.

"Afternoon, Theryn! Academy assignments here already it seems. I've been handing them out all day."

The courier handed Theryn the tightly wrapped parchment and gave him a smile. "Good luck to you, hope you get put with the couriers, we could use you."

"I don't think so, my time trials around the districts weren't fast enough for that," Theryn responded, slipping the thin twine off the letter and unraveling it. He had thought to wait for Bub to open it, but he couldn't contain his excitement, he had to know.

With bated breath, Theryn read the thick inked letters.

And his heart began to sink.

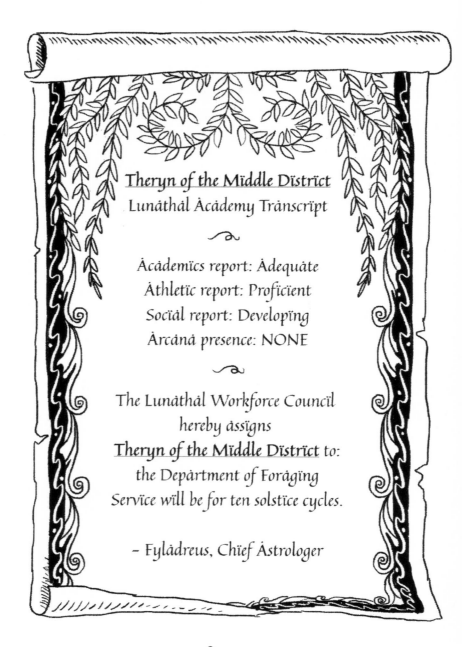

Theryn of the Middle District
Lunáthál Ácádemy Tránscrïpt

~❧~

Ácádemïcs report: Ádequáte
Áthletïc report: Profïcïent
Socïál report: Developïng
Árcáná presence: NONE

~❧~

The Lunáthál Workforce Councïl
hereby ássïgns
Theryn of the Middle District to:
the Depártment of Forágïng
Servïce wïll be for ten solstïce cycles.

— Fyládreus, Chïef Ástrologer

It had happened, Theryn was a rotting *fruit fly*.

He tried to shake off the disappointment from being assigned to the Department of Foraging. Part of him was glad his parents weren't around to see this. He felt guilty for thinking that way, but he was just so disappointed; it was hard to contain his dismal attitude. He had barely noticed how hard he had been clenching his fists as he read.

Theryn hadn't done very well in the Academy, he had always known that. He was glad when it ended; he wouldn't have to deal with being teased by the Summerborn again. Yet, there was a part of him that had always expected to at least end up working with livestock or in the Rookery.

"Good news?"

Bub had hobbled over and begun to read over Theryn's shoulder. Theryn handed him the letter with a sigh and collapsed on the moss cushions kept on the porch.

His grandfather held the letter out at a distance in front of him, measuring the angle until he found the perfect spot where his aged eyes allowed him to read. He began to mutter the contents of the letter to himself as he read. Theryn looked up at his grandfather with glazed eyes. Bub was a slender man, hunched over and wrinkled… evidence of a lifetime of labor in Lunathal. Theryn rolled his head back in dismay letting out an audible groan.

7

"You have always loved climbing branches, Theryn," Bub finished the letter and set it down on his lap, "and now we can have all the omela fruit and choice mushrooms the Old Willow has to offer. This is good news."

Theryn's face scrunched up, trying to fight back his sorrow.

"I guess I was still holding out hope they might sense arcana in me." A part of him felt childish for dreaming that he had arcana even after all the years at the Academy had proved he was far from holding any magical potential. All Winterborn were. That was just the way it was in Lunathal. They would never shape ice or wield sparks like the Summerborn.

"It doesn't run in our family, Theryn. I'm sorry, *keeko*."

Theryn hated when his grandfather called him *keeko*, it made him feel like a kid again. He loved Bub and was grateful the old man had saved him from being an orphan, but Bub had a way of spinning things with optimism that Theryn loathed. His grandfather always tried to remind Theryn that life was a gift. Deep down Theryn knew that, but he certainly did not feel like acknowledging it right now.

Bub watched Theryn gather his things with those cloudy brown eyes, his lips tight with concern. He placed an aged but firm hand on Theryn's shoulder.

"Oh Theryn, I know you wanted to be assigned to the Rookery like your parents were. Time will fly, and who knows, you may like being a forager. Give it a chance."

Theryn shouldered his pack and turned to face Bub, not even trying to conceal his disappointment.

"I don't have much of a choice, do I?"

Theryn strode out the door. It was already rather late in the afternoon. It was his last day of freedom before he became a rotting *fruit fly*. He wasn't going to waste it sulking about on the porch.

Theryn made his way across the spiraling platforms that connected the limbs of the Old Willow. He kept his head down, avoiding the potential for conversation with his neighbors in fear of having to explain his assignment to them.

A part of him just wanted to lay in bed for the rest of the day. Another part of him wanted to get out of the house and away from Bub's attempts to cheer him up. His grandfather meant well, he always did; it could just be a bit smothering.

Theryn found the energy to keep climbing to the far end of the Middle District, only stopping occasionally to pick up any grubs he spotted sticking from the bark of the branches.

Late afternoons in Lunathal's Middle District were always a hurried bustle. The pale-skinned Winterborn, dressed in traditional green ponchos and moss woven britches, hurried home from their workforce assignments. Most headed back to the Lower District while others closed their council approved shops. Elderly Winterborn swept the fallen willow leaves from the platforms and walkways, while chatting with their neighbors. Not many of the Winterborn lived in the Middle District. Most said the difference between the lower class and middle class was just an illusion, something to give Winterborn hope of a better life from crowded small rooms of the Lower District.

Theryn entered the Rookery, which was a small two-story building carved into the side of the Willow's main trunk. Once inside, he greeted the Ravenmaster. The balding man had fair skin tinged with a sky blue hue.

Summerborn. And he was a bitter one at that.

Ravenmaster was one of the lowest jobs the upper class could be assigned. The man had a chip on his shoulder about it. He never much liked Theryn. It was possible this man had requested Theryn to be placed elsewhere for work. Perhaps this man was the reason Theryn had been assigned to be a *fruit fly*.

He wanted to hate the Ravenmaster, but he didn't blame him. Theryn's parents had been assigned here, and they had gone crazy. The man was probably just being cautious, and Theryn could hardly blame him for that.

The Ravenmaster waved him on with a dismissive hand as he leafed through post and parcels the rooks would have to send tomorrow. The Summerborn man let out a nasty cough. It was hoarse and dry and sounded rather painful. Theryn had observed more and more Moonfolk getting sick each season. It seemed now, even the Summerborn were no longer immune. Theryn hurried his way up the ladder to the Rookery's balcony.

Several Winterborn workers were finishing up the day's work of feeding and cleaning the birds. Theryn joined in to help them, reaching into his satchel for those small grubs he had collected from the bark of the trunk. The Rookery was alive with the chorus of the very social birds' chirps and calls. He approached his favorite rook who was nesting on one of the long perches that extended upwards. Theryn pet the rook, running his fingers along the top of the dark-feathered bird's head.

Theryn enjoyed being here, it was one of the few places in Lunathal he felt he fit in. These birds had black feathers, and when he was around so many of them, his black hair didn't seem so different.

For a moment, Theryn forgot his worries, the world seemed to zone out around him as he watched the bird pick hungrily from his palm. Its sharp beak picked up each of the bark grubs with precision and agility. This was when he felt most at peace in Lunathal, when he could just tune out from the rest of the world and try to imagine himself as one of the critters that inhabited the Old Willow with the Moonfolk.

The large dark-feathered bird finished its snack, and Theryn gave it a scratch on the head. After he fed the rooks, Theryn usually grabbed a broom to help sweep up the fallen moss and fern stems that made up the Rookery's nesting. He found that if he helped out on occasion, the Winterborn who worked there didn't mind him being around.

Theryn made himself busy by working on assembling another roosting post for the remainder of the afternoon. The other workers began to leave, finishing their work assignments for the day and heading back to their homes, mostly located in the Middle and Lower Districts.

As they filed out one worker, Falla, stopped to speak with him. She was an older woman and Winterborn like himself, with that characteristic porcelain skin.

"I heard Academy assignments were going out today. Did you get assigned to the Rookery like you hoped?"

The teal haired woman had always been kind to Theryn. He assumed it was forced sympathy given the fact she had worked with his parents. Whether it was pity or genuine kindness, Falla had a soft spot for Theryn where others usually did not. Because of this, he tried his best to keep a cheery disposition as he relayed his assignment.

"Seems they think I am more fit to be a *fruit fly*."

The words came out far more bitter than Theryn expected them to. Falla gave him a sympathetic smile.

"Oh lad, I know you must be disappointed; you've been coming here since you were a kid, but don't call yourself a *fruit fly*," Falla said. "Foragers play an important role, without foragers we wouldn't have food here in Lunathal. I heard it's not as bad as everyone says."

"Yeah, for those who don't slip and fall below the cloud sea," Theryn said with an uneasy look.

Theryn could tell Falla was trying her best to put on a positive face, for a brief moment she faltered before regaining her optimistic smile. He shouldn't have said that, she had known his parents. She knew what happened to them.

"Few Moonfolk fall each year, Theryn, and you have always been sure-footed. You will be ok. Come on, you didn't expect to be assigned Chief Astrologer or the Hero of Lunathal reborn, did you?"

She gave him a light-hearted laugh and a pat on the shoulder as she exited the Rookery. Somehow all this reassuring by Bub and Falla had made Theryn feel even more uneasy about his assignment.

Theryn spent an hour or so tidying up around the Rookery. At one point, the Ravenmaster had poked his blue head up from the ladderway. He grumbled under his breath as Theryn worked, claiming the boy would have to climb down from the outside when he left. Theryn was used to this, the Ravenmaster usually let him stay after he locked up, but it always meant exiting from the balcony.

Eventually, Theryn set down the broom and hoisted himself onto the edge of the rooftop where he sat, legs dangling over the Middle District.

He sat for a long while, watching the sunset through the slender branches of the Old Willow. The Moonfolk of Lunathal returned to their hanging homes and hollowed out apartments scattered around the Willow's many limbs and branches. He marveled at the ice bridges and spiraling frozen staircases that connected the districts and how they twinkled in the sunset. The final rally of the evening was ushered in by the emergence of the light bugs. They dotted the branches of Lunathal with shining purples and oranges that danced around the leaves of the Willow branches.

The moon began to glow in the night sky and cast a deep purple light over the cloud sea. He liked to sit here at night when he could. The lanterns placed around the city rippled with a gentle arcane light. The night sky was filled with an endless sea of stars, and he swore he could see figures flying around and occasionally blotting them out. Theryn imagined they were large rooks or eagles that had come up from the desolation on the surface to seek refuge. Much the same as the first Moonfolk had when they climbed The Old Willow to avoid the flooding.

Theryn gazed out at the ocean of clouds that blanketed the landscape and dreamt. In his dream, he was his best possible version. He was optimistic and brave in the face of danger. He loved himself when he was like that. Theryn wished he could be like that more, but sometimes he just didn't have the energy. When he looked at Bub, he saw himself in a hundred or so years… lethargic and aged from a lifetime of overwork on the branches of their city. It was enough to drain the optimism from him like a moonfruit having the juice squeezed out.

The dreams overtook Theryn as he laid back to stare at the stars. In them he was no longer a *fruit fly*, he was a hero, riding magical creatures, weaving fantastical arcana. In his dreams he didn't have black hair and dark eyes. His hair was like everyone else's and his eyes were blue. In his dreams, he belonged, and he had friends. Friends who understood him and loved him for how he was different. At the end of his adventures they would come home and show Bub all the treasures they had discovered. In Theryn's dreams, *he* was the Hero of Lunathal.

Chapter II
Bird boy

Weaker hearted folk might have been nervous for their first day as a *fruit fly* in Lunathal. For Lyra, however, it was just another rotten day working another rotten job. Only this time, it was just a bit different. This time, she was doing something so simple, even someone with moss-for-brains couldn't mess it up.

Lyra was tall, lanky for a Winterborn and had long arms, which would be perfect for grabbing omela fruit and earning her some quick amber. It was a pretty foolproof plan by her estimates. No one actually *wanted* to be a *fruit fly*. Because of that, she determined it wouldn't be too suspicious for her name to appear on that list. The Summerborn probably wouldn't even take a second glance.

Lyra stopped at one of the gnarled, dark wood water basins that grew upwards from Fiddler's Square. The resin coated basin was covered in a layer of bark with tiny pinprick holes at the bottom that bubbled with a small pool of fresh water.

It was practically empty again. She had overslept.

Lyra scooped a meager palmful of water into her mouth and made her way across the Lower District. The scene around her was like any other morning in Fiddler's Square. Musicians who had been denied council workforce assignments were rolling up their packs and crude tents. She didn't mind being around the homeless musicians and performers that made up most of the Lower District's population. They were kind, honest folk... and easy for her to blend in with. Most would be headed to the upper districts to busk for amber chips or a spare hunk of mossbread.

Normally, this is what Lyra would be doing. But not today.

She was officially employed. The forgery had worked. She had snuck into the Academy and put her name right on the applicants' list. The foppish Summerborn professors hadn't even noticed. She even gave herself some decent grades for classes she never took.

Lyra left her wooden flute at home, it was unneeded today. She would say goodbye to her musician's lifestyle of begging for amber and petty thievery. Stealing was too risky in such a contained space like Lunathal, anyway. Also, it simply wasn't yielding enough results to pay for the expensive medicine she needed. Lyra would have to make amber the good old fashioned way from now on.

Today, she was a *fruit fly*.

By the time Lyra reached the Middle District, she was out of breath. Her lanky build equipped her with long legs, but she rarely used them for athletic purposes. All around her, hoity toity "middle class" walked about, their clothes still crudely woven but devoid of holes and stains. They were Winterborn like her, but they didn't know the struggle of the Lower District. They were middle class, whether they believed it or not.

Must be nice not smellin' like rotten sap and rook droppings.

She stopped at another of the wooden wells and was pleased to find the Middle District basin had more water. She cupped the cool liquid into her mouth and let out a refreshed sigh of relief. Pushing some of her pale curls out of her face, she strode across the walkway to the staircase below the Forager's Headquarters. The crude wooden apartment had been carved into a particularly large limb jutting out from the main trunk of the Old Willow. Lyra tried to gauge if she was on time or not using the trajectory of the sun in the sky but gave up quickly. She didn't remember how to check the rotten time anyway. She wasn't some fancy Academy graduate.

As Lyra entered, it dawned on her that she was later to work than she had presumed. The man at the front desk had made that clear by his disapproving expression. The short-haired and spectacled man spoke with a frown and a tired tone, "You're late. I'll give you the orientation."

Lyra put on her most apologetic face and approached the desk. She would have to work on that, she rarely had to act sincere. The clerk explained the requirements for the day, and Lyra tried her best to concentrate.

"You missed the introductory meeting this morning, so I will just summarize. Foragers pair up. One wears the basket, the other climbs and picks. At noon, you switch if you wish to do so. When your basket is full, you destone the fruit and drop them in a depository. This week you are on omela fruit. Next week, you will get a new assignment, probably jelly lichen. Everyone's already paired up. Looks like you will have to work alone today."

Lyra sighed and grabbed the long wicker backpack that was on the table. She put the twine straps around her shoulders and had to steady herself as the weight settled.

Why was it already so heavy? She really should have been doing some exercises before this.

Lyra dismissed the flourish of doubt and smiled at the clerk.

"No worries, *keeko*. I'll have this filled in two shakes of a willow branch, and I'll even bring you back an omela as pretty as you for a little snack."

The pasty clerk, seemingly a bit uncomfortable at being spoken to so informally, awkwardly handed Lyra a pouch.

"Erm… bring this back with the omela pits to prove you hit your quota. After a clerk has signed off, you will be paid. We have to dock your wage today for your late arrival… Hmm? Oh, it seems like you won't have to work alone today after all."

The dull-voiced clerk beckoned forward a young man who had rushed in through the entryway. Lyra turned around to see a disheveled looking Moonfolk about her age. The young man was rather short and more than a little scrawny looking. He had pallid skin like hers, but his hair was dark and a bit of a mess. That was uncommon in Lunathal. Most folk had curly hair streaked with brighter colors. His was straight and it stuck up in multiple directions as if he had slept on something oddly. He had pieces of moss and a couple feathers sticking from his bark-colored poncho and britches.

"I am so sorry I'm late," the young man said, as he tried to catch his breath. "I-I accidentally overslept at the Rookery. I read the Academy boards though, I know what to do. Theryn from the Middle District, yeah, there's my name, right there." The young man dragged his finger across the forager roster to find his name for the clerk.

The clerk narrowed his eyes on the boy. The young man only smiled back awkwardly. Finally, with a sigh, the clerk handed the newcomer a small pouch before repeating himself in the same slow, monotone manner. "Fill this with omela pits to prove you hit your quota. After a clerk has signed off, you will be paid a reduced day's salary because of your tardiness. She'll be your partner. Head to the Academy District and do the branches on the western limbs."

The young man didn't seem upset by the fact their wages would be docked. Lyra, however, felt it like a pit in her stomach. She was counting on that money. She needed that money.

Lyra unstrapped the backpack and handed it to her messy partner to carry. Instead of showing any signs of annoyance, he actually put it on. Once it was strapped onto him, the messy looking lad gave her a nervous smile, brushing off a feather that stuck out of his poncho. She rolled her eyes, "Come on, *bird boy.* Let's try not to fall to our deaths."

The pair ascended the bridge of ice some arcana wielders had created to allow ease of travel between the districts. It was slippery and crowded with other Moonfolk making their way to work. Her assigned partner, Theryn, who had finally finished brushing all the moss off his clothes, spoke up as they walked.

"I think I recognize you. Have you ever played the flute outside the Academy? I've seen you play once or twice when classes are released."

"Gotta do what you gotta do for money, kid."

Behind them, two sorcerers worked at repairing the cracks and hairline fractures in some of the ice bridges. They were Summerborn, and they waved their sky blue hands in the air in graceful arcs. Water vapor from the air crystallized and wedged into the cracks. Lyra ignored them. She didn't care for the upper class, and all the Summerborn were upper class.

The pair continued climbing the icy staircase to the Academy District. Lyra noticed that sections of the Old Willow's trunk near the stairs had been carved into for decoration. Most of the statues were of past Chief Astrologers. There weren't many of them, the Summerborn lived a long time, and the current Chief Astrologer had been around for over two hundred years. There was a statue of the Hero of Lunathal. Long flowing hair, an icy sword in hand, booted foot atop a dead ogre.

"Love this statue," Theryn chimed in through huffed breaths. "I think he looks so regal."

Lyra ignored him, she wasn't here for a history lesson. The pair reached the halfway point up the wide stairs that spiraled around the tree trunk. To their side was the largest statue of the bunch. It was of Seluna, the Moon Goddess, the mother of the Moonfolk.

Not a mother to me.

Lyra had a real mother, who had always been enough for her. No Goddess of the moon or the stars or the sun was necessary. Sure, she respected the sun, in the kind of way you respect something that could burn you to a crisp. But the moon? It just kinda sat there in the sky, sparkling as if to say, *hey look at me, aren't I so pretty. Oh, you are starving and sick? Have you tried looking at how pretty I am?*

It was clear to Lyra that the Goddess only cared about the Summerborn. Nothing divine or heavenly ever happened in Lunathal to prove her otherwise.

They were about to crest the top of the crystalline staircase when a group of three young carpenters strode down the opposite side just before them. All three were light blue of skin.

They gawked at the sight of Theryn carrying the wicker backpack.

"Look lads, Theryn is making his way up to the Academy. Maybe he's the new Chief Astrologer."

"*Seluna Above*, Theryn, they made you a *fruit fly*? I gotta give it to them at the Academy, they know what they are doing. They really mapped out your full potential."

Lyra glanced at Theryn. His pale face was red and he quickened his pace up the stairs. Theryn tried to pass them, looking embarrassed. The two taller young men in the front joked back and forth a bit more before the one in the back descended past and stepped in front of Theryn, blocking his side of the stairway.

The last carpenter had a pointed nose and high cheekbones. He wore finely woven clothes you could only buy in the Upper District. That meant three things to Lyra–he had arcana, he probably grew up wealthy, and that meant he was a rotten moron.

"Theryn, don't take what they say so seriously," he started. "*Fruit flies* are important to Lunathal."

Theryn looked up, hopeful.

"Otherwise, how would I get rotten omela to throw at the delivery birds whey they fly around in the mornings?" the carpenter leered.

His friends sniggered a bit behind him as they continued their descent. Calling jabs about Theryn's hair and teasing him to try not to fall on his first day.

Lyra could see Theryn's grip on his pouch tighten and his face redden. The words had upset him, that was plain as the bark on the branches in the morning sunlight.

"Come on kid, we don't have time for this," Lyra said as she grabbed Theryn by the basket and pushed him up the final steps.

Lyra wasn't sure what was worse, being the one who was holding the wicker backpack or the one who was climbing the narrow branches. Most Moonfolk were used to climbing, you had to be when you lived in a city built on a giant tree. She got pretty comfortable with it at a young age; the branches in the Lower District sometimes grew jelly lichen she could pick. But this... this was different.

Climbing willow limbs in the upper districts, suspended in the air on flimsy branches, was truly dangerous.

Lyra held her breath as she walked toe to toe with her arms extended beside her. She stepped carefully across the shaky limb, eyes locked on a cluster of the plump purple and cyan moonfruit. The omela fruit grew in twisting stalks that traced the branches all the way from the trunk of the Old Willow. This particular cluster was growing right over the Academy platform, dangling above the cloud sea lazily.

"You are doing great, almost there!" Theryn called encouragingly from below.

"Would you shut it, moss brains? I am trying to concentrate!" Lyra almost lost her footing as she snapped at her partner, but she regained her concentration and dropped to one knee, carefully extending her long arms and grabbing the bunch.

The pair had been at it all day, but they were still only halfway to the quota, and they were losing daylight fast. Theryn had proved to be as useless as he looked. The short middle classer was too stubby to reach the high spots and a bit too weak to hold the pack and pick at the same time, so he had resorted to putting the basket down and rolling the fruit into it like some sort of strange children's game. The two had worked mostly in silence, save for Theryn's occasional encouraging statement. Lyra had just been focused on finishing the day, getting the money, and getting back to Fiddler's Square.

She held the omela cluster out and made her way back, one careful step at a time. Once at a safe trajectory, she climbed back down towards the platform. As the sun set, the songbirds stopped their chirping, and the treefrogs and crickets took up their chorus. Light bugs began to flash around them. Lyra deposited the omela she had picked. Theryn approached the basket and dropped in his own cluster of omela.

"So, you from the Middle District? I don't think I've seen you around except when you perform. Did you graduate from the Academy?"

"No and no, bird boy. Now, less talking and more picking, please."

"We don't have to work in silence, you know," Theryn mumbled under his breath resuming his picking.

They harvested a bit longer and soon had enough of the omela to begin their next task. They found a flat place on the edge of the district platform and sat down to begin removing the pits from the fruit. By now the sun had almost completely set, and the moon and stars shone brightly in the sky, bathing the Academy District in twinkling light.

Lyra set each fruit between her knees and drove the pointed wooden tool through the stalk of the omela. The stone hit the wooden platform below her, covering it in a syrupy juice. Omela juice was sticky, tart, and used in practically every dish and drink in Lunathal. Lyra placed the stone in her pouch and licked the blue nectar from her fingers. Wines and liquors, juices, and desserts all were made from the omela given the lack of other options in Lunathal. She was sick of the stuff as surely others were too, but when you were part of a civilization stuck in a tree for seven centuries, you learned to deal with it.

After a while of working in silence, Theryn spoke up again. "What did you want to get? For an assignment?" He removed the pit from an omela in his lap and placed the stone in the pouch. "I can tell you aren't thrilled about being a *fruit fly.*"

Lyra turned to face him, "How can you tell? I *am* thrilled to be a *fruit fly* for your information, and I will be more thrilled when I get paid. Not everyone shows excitement by shouting encouraging statements to folks who are trying not to fall to their deaths."

Theryn's face flashed with momentary guilt. "I was only asking…"

"Of course I don't want to be a *fruit fly,*" Lyra interrupted, more than a bit irritated. "You know who gets chosen as *fruit flies*? The Winterborn who the council don't mind falling to their deaths. The folks who least resemble the Hero of Lunathal, that's who! Because *we* are the furthest thing from great sorcerers or wise astrologers. We don't have arcana, and we don't matter. No one from the Middle District does and no one from the Lower District does either. So, we are expendable. All Winterborn are. That's why we're up here."

For a moment, Lyra felt a twinge of regret when Theryn turned his gaze back to his work after her rant.

Perhaps she had been too harsh?

Lyra brushed away any guilt she felt. She was in a sour mood.

Why shouldn't she be? The job she had thought would be easy amber had turned out to be brutal. Her arms were sore from a day of climbing and extending. Her legs burned with exhaustion from the careful balancing. At the same time, the front of her head all the way to the curved tips of her ears were throbbing from a day of squinting in the sun. The air was even thinner up here in the Academy District, and she hadn't thought how it might affect her. On top of all this, her pay was being docked for the day.

A long awkward moment passed before Theryn spoke up again. This time his tone was hushed and timid, almost confessional.

"Well, I didn't want to be a *fruit fly*. I thought maybe, just maybe, there was a chance the professors and astrologers missed something. That maybe when they tested my blood at the Palace it *did* show some arcana, and they were just waiting to tell me in the letter. At the very least, I thought they would put me in the Rookery, like my parents had been."

Lyra could hear the disappointment in his voice as he spoke. She recognized that his cheery disposition had been an act, and in reality, Theryn must have been feeling much the same as her. For reasons she couldn't explain, that made her dislike him more. He was from the Middle District, his life had been easy compared to hers. They were so delusional up there; this guy had even held out hope he had arcana.

Lyra finished up the final fruit and stood. "We're Winterborn, bird boy, look how pale our skin is. Seluna ditched us long ago, she only cares about those blue-skinned zealots. Winterborn can't have arcana. Sheesh, didn't they teach you that in your fancy Academy?"

At this, Theryn stood up quickly. Lyra raised her eyebrows in surprise as he took up an angry tone.

"I know that," he snapped, totally abandoning any shred of niceties he had displayed earlier. "I was just *hoping*, that's all! Moon Above, you really are a rotten partner. Don't worry, I will make sure to come extra early tomorrow so I don't get stuck with you again."

Lyra watched as he grabbed his pouch and the wicker backpack. He teetered for a moment as the basket full of fruit threatened to send him backwards. With both hands extended he was able to steady himself and began to stalk off towards the depository.

"Nice of you to finally show some hustle when the job is done, kid! Better late than never!" Lyra called after him.

She would make sure to come a bit late tomorrow and hopefully get someone who didn't try and get a free therapy session out of her. She wasn't here to make friends. She was here to make money.

When Lyra was alone and sure no one was looking, she grabbed a fresh omela from a nearby branch. She closed her eyes and focused on the fruit. Her mind became totally clear like an empty canvas. Her fingertips went numbingly cold.

She had it today.

With total concentration, a sliver of arcana burst out from her fingers into the fruit. With a smoky flash, the color drained from the thick purple fruit, and its solid form vanished with a sound like a snuffed out lantern. Only the fruit's faint shadow remained in her palm. She stuffed it in her pocket for later and smiled as warmth returned to her fingertips.

Lyra picked up her pouch and made her way back to the Forager building. It was time for her to get paid. Her mother depended on it.

Chapter III
Watcher in the Starlight

Theryn awoke to a sharp pain that crawled up his back and extended through his arms. The previous day's work had been strenuous, and it was now taking a toll on him. He had been so exhausted after the difficult task of collecting omela, he actually hadn't dreamed. He couldn't remember the last time that had happened. Usually, his nights were wracked with all sorts of interesting fantasies of some sort.

He recalled groggily making his way home after completing his deposit and picking up his wages for the day. The last thing he remembered doing last night was trying his best to finish eating Bub's homemade mushroom stew. Theryn had set his hard-earned amber on the table and collapsed into bed, with no dreams to be had.

Theryn rubbed his eyes as his grandfather appeared in the doorway. The elderly man had the same round face as Theryn, but his body was all sinew and aged muscle from his time as a livestock caretaker.

"I am not going to let you oversleep today, *keeko*. Up and at 'em. There is fruit to be picked! Nice amber you came home with last night, although a little less than I expected."

Theryn groaned loudly and dropped his head back onto his pillow. The bed had been woven from animal hide and willow moss, a bit scratchy but comfortable. "Come on now, with all this amber you made yesterday, we will eat good tonight. I'll head to the Upper District and see if I can buy some duck eggs from the herding platforms."

Theryn ate a simple breakfast of mossbread covered in jelly lichen. The dark green grain was thin and crunchy and mostly bland, but the translucent magenta jelly lichen added a hint of sweetness. He washed it down with some tart omela juice before he bid Bub farewell. Bub waved him goodbye with a smile.

"Try to get done before sundown today, Theryn. They are putting on a magician's show in the Academy District tonight, and the walkways are sure to be crowded."

"I'll try my best," Theryn replied.

Bub was overly cautious of the crowded walkways and staircases in Lunathal. The elderly man had been that way ever since his son and daughter-in-law had toppled to the surface. It wasn't the crowded walkways that made them do that though. They had just been crazy. At least that's what everyone said about them when they thought he wasn't listening.

His grandfather must have sensed his apprehension because he offered another encouraging statement as Theryn departed. "Do your best to enjoy today, *keeko*. Stay positive— Remember, life is a gift."

Usually, on mornings like this, Theryn had time to stop by the Rookery before heading to his classes. Those days were now gone. He tried to see past the branches towards the main trunk and the balcony resting place of the birds. The silvery willow leaves were growing too thickly, and they obscured his vision, so he kept moving. It would be odd not to visit the rooks in the morning anymore. He would have to make his visits at night after work now, if he had the energy. Luckily, the Foraging office was located rather close to his home and the Rookery in the Middle District. From his home, he only had to climb one wooden bridge to the adjacent willow limb and up one residential branch. He passed small circular homes that dangled in the wind and others that were built on the limb itself.

Squeak!

An odd noise caught Theryn's attention. Something was hanging from the twigs overhead. A small creature with rodent-like eyes stared back at him. In some ways, it was like the wood rats that plagued the lower areas of Lunathal. In other ways, it looked rather different. It was bigger, and it had a large bushy tail and hands it could hold things with. The tiny creature was carrying a seedling nut it had plucked from the Old Willow.

Theryn bent down, just an arms length away from the creature, and held out his hand. For a moment, the bushy-tailed critter looked as though it would bolt away. Theryn felt a flash of white panic in his mind. It slammed into him, making him feel as if a large monster was going to eat him. Theryn stepped back and observed the critter. It was as if, for one fleeting moment, he had understood how the creature felt being confronted by someone so much bigger. That was odd. He hadn't really considered how smaller things may feel when confronted by something larger.

Theryn had to hold back an audible gasp of surprise as the creature extended its arms and legs and leapt into the air. The webbing under its arms allowed the critter to soar over a lower branch in a graceful arch. It landed and scurried away without so much as a glance backward.

Peculiar…

Theryn had never seen a wood rat like that, especially one with long arms that could glide in the wind. It seemed like more and more strange critters had been making the treacherous climb to Lunathal lately and slipping through the cloud wall cracks. Just last week, he had spotted some strange varieties of salamanders he had never seen before. The fiery desolation on the surface of Tellis must have been getting worse.

Theryn stayed a bit longer on the branch, trying to spot the critter again. After a few moments, he gave up and continued towards the Foraging office.

Another pair of seasoned *fruit flies* were exiting the office with their wicker backpack. The man and woman's eyes looked tired. Their limbs looked strong with muscle and sinew, and they had wrinkles on their face from sun exposure.

Looking at them gave Theryn a brief moment of panic, as if he was looking at himself in the future. Is this what life in Lunathal held for him for the next one hundred and forty solstices? No, he wouldn't let it. He would finish his ten cycles and reapply for the Rookery. He had to, for his own sanity.

Theryn let out an audible groan as he entered the building. Standing at the desk was a lanky, lilac-haired girl. The girl's skin was the typical cream color all Winterborn had except for the handful of peach-colored freckles that dotted her cheeks and nose. Her shoulder length curls jutted perfectly in line and was about the only orderly thing about her. She wore cheaply sewn musician's clothing. This was the same rude girl Theryn had worked with yesterday. The same girl who hadn't even introduced herself and had called him bird boy all day. Along with Theryn, she was the only one in the building other than the clerk.

"Perfect timing, who were you again? Ah yes, Theryn. Ok, yes, I see it here. Please, assist Lyra again today." The monotone clerk handed them each a pouch. "Today you are assigned to the upper branches of the Astral District."

Sudden panic fluttered inside Theryn's stomach and it distracted him from his disappointment in his partner assignment. The Astral District was the highest in all of Lunathal. It was off limits to Winterborn, unless you were working or summoned by the council.

The girl named Lyra tied her pouch to her belt. She was scrappy looking, her clothes too worn and too loose. Then again, Theryn wasn't exactly a model of upper class fashion either.

"Stuck with me again, bird boy. Are we going to get done before nightfall today, or are you going to slow me down again?"

Not expecting an answer, the porcelain skinned girl grabbed the wicker backpack, and without so much as a glance to Theryn or the clerk, strode out the door. Theryn gave the clerk a pleading look. He tried his best to shape his face in a way that conveyed, *please sir, I'd rather be paired with a diseased wood rat.*

The clerk, however, had begun tallying out the payroll and was ignoring him. Theryn would have to suffer another day with the girl named Lyra. With no choice, he followed after her.

The Astral Palace was built with finely carved white marble and was the only building in Lunathal not made of wood and twigs. Theryn had learned at the Academy that when the flood had threatened to wipe out the first Moonfolk, they quickly gathered stone from the mountainside to bring with them up the growing tree. Using some sort of arcana or craftsmanship Theryn wasn't familiar with, the astrologers and sorcerers had been able to expand the stone and shape it into the domed observatory now known as the Astral Palace.

Theryn had been in the palace once, for his arcana test. He remembered marveling at the glassy ceiling some Iceshapers had formed to cap the marble building. On that day, they had pricked his finger and asked him odd questions about what he did in his free time and about his family history. The council members had also questioned Theryn about his dreams. Bub had warned Theryn not to say too much, especially about his dreams. Bub always acted rather wary when it came to matters regarding the council. Theryn didn't tell the council much anyway, those dreams of flying through the clouds were a bit embarrassing to say out loud. It was an odd day, and he tried not to think about it often.

Once they reached the palace square, the day's work toiled on. Theryn dangled from the branches across from the palace, trying his hardest to keep his grip and extend his hand towards an omela. The branch began to bow under his weight, and Theryn found himself sliding down rapidly. In the last moment before he fell, he was able to reach out and grab the omela. Theryn landed on the moonfruit, squashing it under himself. His poncho and britches were covered in sticky, dark blue juice.

"What were you thinking climbing that far down on a flimsy limb?" Lyra called from a branch above him. "You had better get down on your knees and kiss that platform because without it, you would be a flat piece of burnt-up moss bread on the surface right now."

Theryn ignored her, face red with embarrassment, and brushed himself off. Around them, the finely robed astrologers and sorcerers were walking up the marble staircase of the palace. They ignored the *fruit flies*, deep in their own discussions.

Theryn's hands were sticky with blue juice, so he made his way over to a basin to wash himself and his clothing. A thin layer of water bubbled in the basin, and Theryn tried his best to scoop it out and onto his clothing. Next to him, a glasswing butterfly fluttered around, its translucent wings sparkling in the daylight. It looked so serene to Theryn, so carefree. He was a bit jealous, wishing he could flap around instead of picking fruit.

They worked a bit longer, mostly in silence except for the occasional mumbled complaint from Lyra. Theryn stopped to have a snack, biting into an omela and enjoying a jelly lichen he had found on the way over. Soon the sun was setting, and Theryn realized they had been at it all day. His arms were burning from hoisting himself from branch to branch and extending to reach the clusters of moonfruit.

Luckily for both of them, Lyra had made it clear she didn't intend to take so long today. She had insisted on holding the basket and had climbed the narrow branches on her own with it on her back. She plucked the bunches and tossed the moonfruit over her head into the basket with surprising skill. Because of this, they were done with the gathering quicker than yesterday and ready to destone.

The pair sat on the edge of the Astral Square, destoning the fruit in their laps. Their feet dangled over the ledge as they overlooked the Academy District to their east. The Academy courtyard was swirling with activity as hundreds of Moonfolk had come out for the evening's show. Down below them a light blue-skinned magician was weaving magical sparks with his fingers. The sparks were dancing in figures of Moonfolk and monsters. The depiction was one of the Hero of Lunathal, who had saved them almost two hundred years ago from countless beasts that threatened to destroy their home.

To Theryn's surprise, Lyra actually spoke up first.

"You ever wonder why folks like that gather so quickly to watch light shows and lightning tricks?" She stopped what she was doing and eyed the omela in her hand. "It's because their lives are so bland from working so hard all day. Winterborn will do anything to entertain themselves, so they line up to hear the same three stories every week told in different ways." The pale girl shook her head in disapproval and drove the wooden tool through another omela. The pit of the fruit hit the platform below her with a *plunk*.

"I've been to those shows… they aren't so bad," Theryn replied. "The arcana is fun to watch and pretty impressive."

The crowd was taking their seats on the long stacked benches placed in the Academy courtyard that made up the amphitheater.

"Sometimes they tell a version of the Hero of Lunathal where he brings back a living ogre from the surface which he tries to train," Theryn recalled out loud. "It's actually pretty funny."

That one was Bub's favorite. Theryn had loved sitting next to him as a child and watching the old man cackle when the Hero discovered the ogre had raided his pantry.

"*Pfft*, it's all made up stuff, kid," Lyra scoffed. "If you want real stories, you should come down to the Songbird in the Lower District. It's the only place you can get a stiff drink and a good ballad in all of Lunathal. They don't tell pandering Summerborn stories down there. They tell it like it is. Stories and songs about the surface when we were all equal. Not made up drivel."

Theryn shot her a warning glance. "It is not made up… and I have no interest in going to the Lower District. They eat wood rats and rooks down there." Theryn shook his head at her, as if she was eating one in front of him right now. The thought of eating an animal bothered Theryn, and he was glad he and Bub had never had to do it.

"When you're hungry, you're hungry, bird boy, we don't have omela growing all over the place down there, and folks are getting sicker and sicker. Astrologers, sorcerers, magicians, they don't help, so us Lower District folk just make due with what we got." Theryn could tell she was being sincere about that, but it didn't stop the words from bothering him.

"Well, you don't have to eat innocent rooks, they are just doing their jobs. I heard you guys throw pointed sticks at them when they perch to deliver parcels."

Lyra shook her head, "Nah kid, we don't do that." She paused, "That wouldn't be efficient. Usually, we just grab them and snap their necks real quick like. They don't feel a thing, and we've got dinner for the night."

That was too much. Theryn shot up from the wooden platform, the omela in his lap spilling over the side and hurtling down.

"That's terrible! Those poor creatures did nothing wrong to—"

Something flashed in the evening sky behind the Astral Palace and distracted him. Theryn squinted his eyes, trying his best to make out the figure in the distant clouds. The moon cast a faint ray of purple light on a huge hovering figure just barely visible from inside a large cloud. The creature slinked back and forth with flowing motions as it hovered in place.

What is that thing? And what is it doing?

The figure kept hovering, just barely obscured by the cloud wall. It seemed to be observing. Observing... Lunathal? Perhaps observing the Astral Palace?

Theryn strode across the platform and began to hoist himself over an extended limb to catch a better look.

"Hey, get back to work, we're almost done!" Lyra shouted after him. Theryn ignored her demand, instead, inching his way forward and brushing a cluster of leaves from his line of sight.

The figure was still shrouded by the clouds, but now, Theryn could see it was massive, even from this distance. The long, dark body that snaked between the cloud cover was accompanied by two slender wings and a massive ornamented head. Perched on the head was a smaller shadowed figure. Robed... and holding a glimmering blade of what looked to be ice or crystal.

"Do you see that?" Theryn said in a soft hush.

"What now?" Lyra had come up behind him and was peering into the distance.

He repeated himself in a whisper, "That thing in the clouds, what is that?"

"What are you talking about?" she replied. "Go out a bit further, I can't really see past you."

The pair carefully balanced towards the edge of the limb, which now extended over the platform. When near the end, they stopped and Theryn could see the figure had begun to hover upward and over the Astral Palace. Lyra's breath exhaled sharply next to him as she caught sight of it.

"Moon Above, what is that rottin' thing?" Lyra asked curiously.

Theryn narrowed his eyes, hoping to get a better look. He focused on the creature. The world seemed to zone out as he did. The more he seemed to stare at it, the more his head flashed with a funny feeling.

A feeling of wanting. No... perhaps a feeling of needing?

The creature wanted something in the Astral Palace. It wanted it desperately, and it couldn't get it. He felt the despair in the creature's heart. He felt its anger as well.

For a single moment, Theryn felt like he understood the distant figure. Theryn could sense that its life was being predetermined for it, much like his was in Lunathal. He must have been imagining all this, but it felt so real.

With a sudden jolt, the creature snapped its head so its gaze focused on Theryn. Even through the clouds, Theryn could see the giant silvery eyes lock onto him. Like large oval moons, they centered on his own dark eyes.

The world seemed to zoom out in one dizzying motion. The disorienting sensation of being ripped back to reality overtook him. Theryn had been so focused on trying to catch a closer glimpse that he had been leaning forward, and now he overcompensated by stumbling back in surprise.

"Hey!" Lyra cried as he crashed into her.

The force sent them sprawling. Theryn fell back and hit the limb. He frantically tried to grab hold. He gripped something tight in his panic and held as best he could. Lyra let out a yip of surprise as Theryn realized in horror that he had grabbed her leg. The pair was sent hurtling past the Astral Platform and sliding against the vertical trunk of the Old Willow. Theryn tried desperately to grab at chunks of bark. The rough outer layer of the tree scraped against his body as he bounced from it. The tree trunk began to curve away from him. There was nothing left to grab onto. The Lower District whizzed by him.

Theryn was now free falling towards the cloud sea.

Chapter IV
The Shade

One second Lyra had been peering into the distance at what looked to be a giant noodle hovering in the dark clouds, and the next moment she was spiraling to her death. Sure, she had always been a bit curious about what it would feel like to jump from Lunathal to the cloud sea, but now that she was actually doing it, she was less than thrilled.

The wind whistled in her ears, and her hair and clothes were plastered back as she plunged belly first down to the clouds. Theryn fell screaming in front of her, arms outstretched and flailing frantically. This is what she got for getting partnered up with a stupid bird boy. The moron probably thought he could fly, and now his clumsiness was going to get her killed.

Cynical thoughts aside, Lyra was seriously panicking. How could she survive something like this?

She tried to slow herself by outstretching her arms, but it was no use. She was traveling fast, and the clouds were getting bigger and bigger. Lyra's vision went white as she pierced the cloud sea. A blue flash slowed her slightly, as if she was going through a big bowl of jelly. There was a sound like shattering glass, and in an instant, she was submerged in the cloud wall. Lyra tried to scream, but the breath to do so wouldn't come. Her lungs and face burned as the sky rippled around her. Her large pointed ears popped as the shock of leaving the contained atmosphere of Lunathal hit her. Lyra's vision went blurry, and water vapor filled her lungs as she finally caught her breath. In about three heartbeats, she was through the clouds.

Her eyes adjusted and although wet with tears, she could see a sprawling landscape curved around her. Lyra tried to look all around, but her vision was foggy and unfocused. She could only make out colors in the moonlit evening. Where she expected to see the raging reds and blacks of scorched earth, she saw the greens of little trees and the blues of bodies of water. Lyra felt her consciousness swim for a moment as the realization struck her. The pair would end up as piles of jelly when they hit the surface if she didn't do something quickly.

Theryn was falling just a bit in front of her, screaming at the top of his lungs. Another blur appeared alongside her. Lyra watched in horror as a massive cobalt colored creature snaked around them in the sky just below Theryn. It glided in line with them, its scaled face revealed a mouth full of fang teeth of varying size and color. The snake-like beast beat its wings and made a swipe to grab at them with short talons. Lyra increased her speed by wrapping her arms tight against herself and tilting her body downward. The air whistled around her as she picked up speed. It was just enough to bump into Theryn and send them sprawling away from the creature's massive jaws that bit down where they had just been.

"Grab hold of my waist!" Lyra tried to scream, but the words wouldn't come. The air pressure of their plummet made it impossible for her to do anything but scream breathlessly. Instead of grabbing hold of her, Theryn tried to kick away from the monster. His flailing ended up sending them flipping backward. The pair careened through the sky together as the beast reared its head back. Its huge silver eyes were locked onto them, totally pupilless. The monster exhaled columns of cold air, spraying splinters of ice into the sky. Lyra made herself as narrow as possible and the misty torrent passed over them. As she did, she managed a glance at the monster through her cloudy eyes. She could have sworn someone was riding that thing. The beast let out a screech so ear-shattering, Lyra thought she would black out from its volume. The winged monster presented double-layered rows of awful teeth and prepared to strike at them again. Lyra looked down, they were running out of time, in a few seconds they would hit the surface and be done for, or worse, digested. Theryn broke from her grip and covered his eyes.

For a moment, Lyra had resigned. It was hopeless, there was nothing she could do. She wasn't the rottin' Hero of Lunathal, and she definitely wasn't some sort of great sorcerer or astrologer.

Then an image of her mother flashed in her mind.

Her poor, sick mother, the woman who had raised her and sacrificed everything to keep her safe. The woman who would be alone in this world if Lyra became a flattened pancake.

Lyra pushed forward with all her might and crashed into Theryn again, this time gripping him tightly around the torso. The monster flew forward, its mouth opened wide. Lyra closed her eyes and tried her best to concentrate.

Come on…

She couldn't feel the tips of her fingers from the fall. The beast was getting closer. She furrowed her brow and focused harder. Lyra tried to make her mind a blank canvas, completely destitute of thoughts or emotions. Around her, Theryn screamed and wriggled in her grip.

Come on…

She took a slow breath and a shiver went up her spine. The screaming and the air droned out around her. A surge of purple smoke billowed from her hands where she held Theryn. A noise like low thunder rang out in her mind and with a puff the pair vanished in thin air.

The world's colors inverted and all vibrance became dampened. She was a trail of smoke, vaporous and shrouded in shadow. Next to her, Theryn's form shifted, and the breath was sucked from his screaming lungs as they entered a world of silence. The deafening wind went completely mute as their mass dissipated and their speed slowed. The pair floated downwards with the same grace as two falling leaves. The beast passed right through them. Lyra expected to be pierced through the chest by one of those massive fangs. Instead nothing happened, she felt a tingling sensation, but no pain. Lyra continued to focus, her mind still tense with a burning migraine.

Next to her, Theryn gripped at his face in horror. The hands passed through his swirling, insubstantial form. Lyra saw him try to call out, but no sounds could be heard in this void. Above them, the beast had stopped in its pursuit and was searching the skies frantically for the falling pair. Lyra's head throbbed with pain as she focused. It took a tremendous amount of mental effort to keep them as shadows.

After a short while, they were only a few meters above the ground. The intense concentration made Lyra feel as though she was going to black out. She couldn't hold it any longer, she had to let go and relax her mind. Lyra felt her body begin to materialize, starting with a tingle of warmth returning to her fingers. Her ears regained equilibrium, and her body became heavier. The world around her flooded with color. Sound met her ears as the wind raced through her hair. She and Theryn popped back into solid form and knocked violently against a narrow tree.

Theryn landed on his arm with a sickening crunch and let out a sharp cry. Lyra had been luckier; she landed on one leg and a knee in a crouched position. She held it for a moment, thinking she might look kind of graceful… then her muscles gave out, and she dropped to the surface with her hands sprawled outwards. The pair was a duet of exhausted moans and shallow breaths.

After a minute of fatigued panting had passed, Lyra rolled over and lifted herself upright into a seated position. She was mentally and physically drained, and her head throbbed like she had spent the day banging it against her uncle's old drum.

Lyra lifted her hands in shock as they brushed some tiny plants growing on the ground. Even in the dusk, she could make out the thin stalks of green littering the forest floor with the occasional yellow flower poking out through its blades. It looked like the moss that grew on the bark of the willow, only it was like little individual sections.

She plucked one of the yellow flowers and lifted it to her nose. It had a similar and sweeter smell to the jelly lichen that grew all around Lunathal. She popped it in her mouth and began to chew.

"You good, kid?" Lyra called through her chewing. The flower was bitter and probably not edible, so she spit it out and surveyed her surroundings more carefully. The land swelled and dipped around them as if they were on the side of a mountain.

Theryn didn't respond. He was still trying to catch his breath and was lying face down on the forest floor. He looked like a mossy lump, his only movement the rising and falling of his chest with labored breaths. Eventually, he tried to adjust his position only to accompany it with a pitiful whine.

Lyra's own muscles screamed as she tried to rise. It took all her effort to stand and approach him.

All around them were thin trees. They were odd looking, different from the Old Willow that held Lunathal, not just in size, but also in shape and design. These trees grew up in a point and their leaves were tiny emerald colored needles. The forest floor was littered with these needles that had fallen and dried up. Animals chittered around them.

"Come on, get up," Lyra bent over to make an effort to raise Theryn, and she noticed a long gash extending from her elbow to her shoulder. The sudden realization of her wound made it flash with pain. She had hit the trunk of the Old Willow pretty hard, and then hit the surface again, but she had no recollection of getting the gash.

"Hey, get up will ya!" Lyra urged.

Finally, Theryn rolled over and spoke, gripping his arm. "What was that thing? Are we dead? Why does being dead hurt so much?"

Theryn hoisted himself upright, staring all around them with wide eyes. "My arm is broken, and I twisted my ankle. I don't know if I can walk."

"Can you stand?"

"Maybe."

That was good enough for her. Lyra grabbed his good arm with all her strength and heaved him up. Theryn winced as he rose, letting out a sharp inhale of pain and gripping his injured arm. Lyra helped steady him. He was a frazzled, bruised mess, like he usually was but somehow worse. Lyra wasn't much better off. The gash on her elbow was throbbing now, which paired with her headache, made her feel as though she was a smashed light bug.

"What is this place?" he asked, eyes darting around wildly. "Where is all the ash? The volcanoes and seas of fire?"

"No clue, but we can't stay here, kid. That monster looked pretty focused on making us his lunch."

Theryn's eyes went wider as he turned his attention to her.

"You... you did something. You turned us into smoke!"

He tried to take a step back from her and almost stumbled. It was as if he was just now remembering how they had made it down without being flattened.

"You lied to me. You said Winterborn can't have arcana. You're a sorcerer or a magician or... or something. Who are you?"

Lyra held out her hands in a diplomatic way, in her best attempt to reason with Theryn and get him to stop making so much noise.

"Would you relax? I ain't none of those things. I'm just a *fruit fly*. Same as you."

"But you saved us! You said you didn't have arcana because no one in the Lower District has it. You... you didn't even go to the Academy... you're Winterborn. Can you use it to get us back to Lunathal?"

"I *am* Winterborn and I *am* from the Lower District, but that doesn't mean I don't get lucky every now and again." Lyra searched the skyline for the Old Willow. She spotted it, a bit of a ways up the mountain. "I've never done anything like that before, but I can try. Let's find the trunk and see what I can do about getting us back up."

About an hour's ascent upward, the massive Old Willow's trunk was sprouting into the sky and disappearing in the ball of clouds that surrounded their home. Somewhere in the distance, a roar sounded out and echoed through the valley. Lyra handed Theryn a curved stick for walking and led him forward.

The pair made their way through the steep forested area. Lyra tried to focus on walking, but her ears were ringing from the fall. She felt like a carpenter was hammering inside her head. Beside her, Theryn didn't look much better. His short, messy hair was frazzled, and he had a tense expression on his round face. One of his pointed ears was bleeding a bit. Lyra's own gash hadn't been deep, but she had wrapped it tight with her handkerchief to keep it from stinging in the open air.

"Look at that," Theryn said in a hushed voice, pointing towards a peculiar looking creature.

The brown animal standing in the treeline before them had a long narrow face and a bushy white tail. It had a thin layer of nut-brown fur over its four-legged body. The creature was munching happily on some plants and smacking its lips together in a way that Lyra thought made it look a bit stupid. It raised its head and observed them, still chewing. Theryn took another step forward.

The creature turned and bolted off. Its hind legs kicked with majestic leaps as it bounded away. Theryn turned back to her, his face carrying an expression of awe.

"What was that thing?"

Lyra shook her head. "Do I look like I know? Who do you think I am? A grand explorer? I didn't even go to the Academy, kid. I ain't exactly a rottin' professor of all the surface life of Tellis."

"It didn't seem like it wanted to hurt us," Theryn replied, still trying to catch sight of the fleeing creature.

"Yes, yes, we've encountered two creatures since we have fallen from the cloud sea, and one hasn't tried to kill us. *Love* those odds. Keep walking, bird boy, the trunk ain't far."

Spiraling roots the size of Lunathal homes rose from the ground as they trudged forward in the settling twilight. The closer they got to the Old Willow, the more the dirt around them became tightly packed. Soon, their meandering hike in the forest turned into an acrobatic training course. The pair had to hop from root to root and sometimes climb through the gnarled foundation of the tree. Eventually, they reached the final stretch to the peak of the mountain where the tree sprouted from.

Lyra decided a couple things–first, scaling a mountain was hard; second, finishing a day's work, falling a couple thousand meters, escaping a giant flying beast, and *then* scaling a mountain was even harder. She tried to focus on just putting one foot in front of the other. They took time to rest every couple minutes, but the cliffside had too many exposed patches for Lyra's liking. If that winged monster returned, she didn't want to be sitting out in the open like sweet treats in the window of a shop. They would occasionally hear the deafening shriek of the beast in the distance. Luckily for them, each time it sounded, it seemed the noise was getting further and further away.

After what seemed like an eternity, but was probably only a few hours or so, they reached the peak. The air was surprisingly easy to breathe under the cloud sea and had a fresh, sweet smell. Lyra looked out down the cliffside and took in the scenery. The mountain was huge, and it was surrounded by smaller hills and rocky highlands. Each was littered with clusters of those green needle trees. Small rivers flowed down, displaying more water in one place than she had ever seen before. She observed the sprawling landscape of green and blues… it was all so disorienting. The vibrance of colors, even in the moonlight, made her head swirl. Ahead of them, the Old Willow of Lunathal sprung from the rocky mountaintop.

Theryn was just as awed as her. He took in the vista just a moment longer before rushing to the tree trunk. Lyra hurried after him, wasting no time on any more sightseeing. She began searching for anything that looked out of the ordinary. The problem was the trunk was so wide, it took a lot of energy to scale the final massive roots and walk around the entirety of the trunk.

"There has to be some sort of arcane lift or hidden frozen staircase. Why don't we see it, where is it?" Theryn argued with himself under his breath as he joined in the search. "Lunathal wouldn't exactly be a hidden city if we had signs with directions posted everywhere. I can't even remember the last time someone went to the surface and came back. The Hero of Lunathal did often, he must have figured it out back then. The stories said ogres climbed up, but that would be impossible. There must be another way to get up."

He tapped his head in thought before he turned and pointed expectantly at Lyra.

"Turn us into smoke again."

"I can't."

"Why not?"

"Because I turned us into shadows, not smoke, bone head." Lyra replied. Taking a seat on an extended root, she began to massage her sore feet with her hands, despite the pain coursing through her wound.

"Ok…" Theryn began, "So, turn us into *shadows* and float us back up to Lunathal."

"It doesn't work like that, kid."

Theryn's face went red with frustration, and he threw up his hands. "What do you mean it doesn't work like that? One minute we are falling to our death, the next we are foggy wisps, and now you can't do it again?"

"Listen, bird boy, I ain't never done anything like that before, and frankly, it wasn't exactly the easiest thing to pull off." Lyra tried to show him her arcana by extending a hand, but her fingers stayed warm and her vision blurred with pain. She was totally drained.

A sudden realization must have hit Theryn because he raised both hands at her as if to ward her away. "You're a *Shade* aren't you! Shades are supposed to be outlawed in Lunathal. I thought the sorcerers weaved away anyone with that arcana."

"They do, if they can find you."

"Ok, well, turn us into shadows and we can float back up or something!" he said excitedly. Lyra sighed, bird boy just didn't seem to get it. She wasn't practiced in this arcana stuff on account of her needing to keep it hidden her whole rottin' life.

"Listen, bird boy, I'm no expert at this. I barely know how to make an omela disappear. The fact that we survived is pure luck!

Usually, I can only turn small objects into shadows," she tried to explain. Her headache worsened as fatigue hit her. "I was warned to never use it on myself or others," Lyra buried her head in her hands and began to massage her temples, "and I don't think I could if I tried. I feel like my brain is going to explode."

She took a minute or so to rest her eyes. When Lyra felt some of the aching pressure in her head subside, she looked up. Theryn was heading back to her from the other end of the cliffside. His face had softened, and he was back to his normal, meek disposition. "There is a cave just below this ridge. We should head in there for shelter."

Not having the energy left in her to argue, Lyra rose and brushed herself off. Her stomach gurgled audibly, enough for Theryn to hear. "Maybe we can try and find some food later," he offered, clutching his own stomach. Lyra realized they had missed almost a full day's meals to try and finish their shift faster. Moon above, what she wouldn't give for even a rotten omela or hunk of mossbread right now.

A hug from her mother would be even better.

Before the duo disappeared into the craggy cavern mouth, they both took a final, longing gaze at the Old Willow for the night. The moonlight cast a dark glow over the dome of clouds that surrounded Lunathal. Somewhere up there, her mother was worrying about her, sick and alone. Every moment on the surface was another she lost with the only person in the world who mattered to her. Lyra needed to figure out how to get back, and she needed to do it fast.

Chapter V
The Beast

P rey rarely escaped the predatory gaze of the Winter

Wyvern. The ancient beast sat perched atop its temporary resting place on the parapet. Its sharp sapphire talons scratched against the dark stone of the stronghold in its contemplation.

The beast could barely control itself around prey. It had to strike; it was in its nature. Yet, the Rider was very particular about what it could hunt and what it couldn't. Once, many centuries ago, the Wyvern could have free choice of all the livestock, creatures, and even Humans of the valley. Now, it was a servant, and this evening, it had failed its master.

The Rider was not pleased. The beast could sense it.

Then again, the Rider was rarely pleased.

The beast exhaled in its frustration. Long columns of frost erupted from its nose, littering the air with fragments of ice. The crystalline shards drifted to the ground like falling snow. It sniffed the evening air, catching wind of an alluring scent.

Hooded Elves who served the Rider approached the stronghold tower. They had brought with them only two dead animals to eat this evening.

So much less than usual.

Anger surged inside the winged beast like a winter storm. The Wyvern snapped at the servants, threatening to gobble them up to complete his meal. The beast wanted to cover them in its winter fury... Leave them as frozen statues and then feast on them.

And why should I not?

They would be juicy, and their bones would crunch nicely between its fangs, but the Wyvern knew it was not permitted to eat these ones. Temptation burned inside it regardless.

And why should I not?

It was the Great Beast of Evaria, the Terror of Tellis.

The Ancient Winged Blizzard.

In the many centuries of flying through these skies, the Wyvern had never been forbidden a meal. Surely, such an ancient creature could forge its own rules? The beast eyed a particularly plump servant and slithered towards him. The hooded Elf yelped and stepped backwards. The Wyvern opened its great jaws.

A sudden wall of suppressive power slammed into the beast's emotions. The power subdued its ferocity and made the beast recoil. The temptation for food dissipated. Its mind went blank, its will docile and submissive. The Wyvern bowed its head and rested it on the cold stone wall.

The Rider approached from behind, laying a single gloved hand on the scales of the Wyvern's back vertebrae and stroking softly. His hand was cold to the touch, reflecting a shred of the power he had taken from the Wyvern.

An uneasy feeling settled inside the beast. Its scales shuttered and prickled slightly; the Rider must have that wretched *thing* on him. That unnatural ball of light that the Wyvern hated so much.

"Come now, what did I say about eating the Acolytes?" the Rider said in a soothing voice. "You test the tethers of our bond too strongly. For that, and for your fight against our Soulbridge today, I will allow you the opportunity for redemption."

The Wyvern's mind flooded with thoughts of justice and pride. The beast had trouble remembering which were its own memories and which were being subjugated upon it by the Rider.

Visions of former glory, of battles fought and won, raced through its head. In them, it saw the mangled corpses of the Duke's men littered around the courtyard. The Duke's own head, crushed into fragments under the weight of its armored tail.

"You will make up for your small dinner tonight by collecting the one who was able to penetrate your mind."

The Wyvern's senses ignited with a burst of white hot anger. It was filled with a sudden and compulsory urge to hunt.

"You will be rewarded three times your normal dinner portions and a night on your favorite snowtop hoard if you bring him to me unharmed."

The Wyvern let out a determined shriek. The hooded master turned to the robed Elves and dismissed them. "Leave us, lead the evening's training without me tonight."

The men scurried down the tower stairs. When they were gone, the Rider reached into his dark jacket and produced that ball of light the Wyvern hated so much. The beast recoiled from it, flicking a dangerous tail upward in defensive thrashes. The orb was unnatural, its rings orbited in a way that made the creature uncomfortable. That *thing* didn't belong to Tellis and had caused the Wyvern kind much pain.

"I understand why you loathe this thing so much, it has caused so much pain to this land," the Rider said delicately. "The ancient Wyverns went all but extinct in the flooding because of this otherworldly rock. Those that survived were driven from their mountain perches by retreating Men and Elves… We are similar in that way. I hate it too."

The Rider held the luminescent orb closer. The Wyvern wanted to slam its spiked tail onto it and destroy it, but the Rider wouldn't allow it… not yet.

"That is why we had to seize this place, do you understand now? To ensure this meteorite never falls into the hands of those that would use it again. Follow my orders, and we will destroy it together. Only after I am sure it is of no further use to us… Only after you find the boy."

The hooded man gave the beast's scales a soft pat.

"Our prize in the Astral Palace will have to wait. Go now, and find him. Find the Moonfolk who fell from Lunathal. I have more research to attend to here. Find him, and bring him to me here in the Stronghold."

The beast ripped from the parapet, crumbling pieces of the stone turret as it lifted off. The Wyvern extended slender wings and took to the sky. It had no choice but to serve. The Rider was in control today. The hopes of gorging itself on meat and returning to its old winter lair amongst its treasures in the north was motivation enough to obey. Finding the ones who escaped would please the Rider. As long as the Rider was pleased, the beast could live on. As long as it remained useful to the Rider, its life was safe.

It had to find the boy...

The survival of the last Winter Wyvern on Tellis depended on it.

Chapter VI
The Cavern

"What is all this junk?" Theryn asked. This was the third hovel carved into the caveside they explored since waking up. They had stopped in the first concealed space they had found the night before, blissfully unaware of the many other ancient homes the cave held.

The stone carved tables and furniture in each had been abandoned for years yet still held all sorts of ancient trinkets. There were stone-tipped arrowheads, ornate clay pottery, and destroyed parchment scattered all around. Many of the walls had etchings in characters Theryn didn't recognize. They were so worn out, it would have been hard to read them even if he did know the symbols. The only legible carvings were of crude depictions of people. The cave drawings seemed to resemble a group of pointy-eared figures which had been scraped into the cavern walls. A group of them circled a small orb with rings around it, almost like a tiny distant planet. They found the remnants of cookware and tools that looked far from primitive. Lyra took a seat on a flat gray stone surface and began rebinding the gash on her arm.

"Hard to believe we slept on the ground when we could have had these lovely rock mattresses," Lyra stated with an air of sarcasm.

The night's sleep in the cavern had been lackluster for the most part. Although Theryn had fallen asleep easily, he had been jostled awake with multiple dreams. Sensations of the fall and the panic of the beast's pursuit controlled his first dream; however, that had been the lesser of his nightmares. His second was of his parents, memories of their faces before they left for work on the day they jumped.

In his dream, he had followed them.

He had thrown himself right from the treetop of Lunathal, just to remain with his parents. They floated through the cloud sea together, and as they did, his parents' visage changed. Their flesh grew gray and gaunt, tearing away from their bones in heaping chunks as they fell. In Theryn's nightmare, he landed right on their skeletal corpses—still decomposing at the trunk base. Theryn had jolted awake, drenched in a chill sweat. There was a feeling of instant relief that he had not truly seen his parents' remains. Although it was a fleeting relief. Most of his nightmare wasn't some sick joke. He was truly trapped on the surface.

His roommate hadn't exactly slept like a log either. Lyra had been curled in a ball and muttering to herself in her sleep for most of the night, occasionally screaming and sitting upright with haunted eyes. The two had probably woken up half a dozen times before the surface birds began to usher in the rising dawn.

"Look at all this rope. This would be worth a few amber back home." Theryn eyed a particularly frayed chunk that had been severed at the ends. He put himself to work winding it around his arm. His elbow and shoulder stung with pain, but it wasn't as bad as yesterday. In fact, his ankle felt surprisingly sturdy as well. It was a strange sensation since he had fallen pretty hard. Perhaps he was still in shock. Regardless, he tried to tie the rope to keep his arm upright. He held one end with his chin and attempted to grab the other end from behind.

Lyra sighed and rose. She came around behind him and began tying the rope off. She pulled tight and he felt a sharp pain as his arm raised towards his body. The pain receded as Theryn's arm held in place, now in a workable sling that kept it elevated.

"Thank you, and I'm not sure I thanked you yesterday… for saving us."

"Yeah and how about, I dunno, maybe… maybe, a *sorry*?" Lyra said, her tone full of resentfulness.

Theryn was surprised at the annoyance on her pale face. The few specks from the sun that riddled her nose and cheeks were now covered with a flush of red. "If you hadn't been sightseeing on a dangerous branch and you hadn't grabbed my leg, I would still be in Lunathal right now. I wouldn't be lost on the surface and stuck in this rottin' cave with some Middle District fop."

The words stung, but at least Theryn was being teased about being middle class for a different reason than usual. Usually, it was the Summerborn students making him feel inferior; it felt strange to hear someone consider him to be privileged. Guilt twisted inside him as he recounted frantically grabbing what he could to try and steady himself, only to bring Lyra down with him in the process.

Theryn was thinking of an apology while Lyra crossed the cave and took a seat on a stone slab, looking defeated. Before he could respond, she spoke up, her voice empty of its usual thorny tone.

"When you were asleep, I went back to the trunk at sunrise." She gave a rock at her feet a feeble kick across the cavern floor. "The morning light didn't help…" Lyra hesitated, as if searching inward for the right words. "There is no way up. Summerborn can probably make steps from ice, but us? We aren't supposed to get back up. Winterborn aren't supposed to live through the fall. They didn't build a way back up…" She turned to face him. Despite her melancholy tone, her eyes burned with a suppressed rage. "Because we are expendable."

They sat in silence for a bit, the faint dripping of water in the damp cavern the only distinguishable noise. The words hurt to hear, but deep down Theryn knew them to be true. Theryn searched his mind for the right thing to say… for any shred of optimism he could find. Finally, Lyra stood up and turned on him, the usual thorns in her voice restored.

"You got us in this mess, and now you expect me to get us out. Well, I'm done kid, time for you to pull your weight a bit. Make yourself useful for once since I've made your rotten acquaintance."

Theryn realized then that Lyra was probably just the same as everyone else. She thought he was useless, dead weight, a burden.

His confidence wavered for a moment. He wanted to run away from her, to be anywhere but this cave; however, Bub had always encouraged him to stand up for himself and not let anyone treat him poorly for being different. The old man had urged Theryn when he was teased to hold his head high and stay optimistic.

Just as Theryn was finding the confidence to slam back a retort about her bad attitude, a scurrying noise sounded from the main cavern. It echoed in the chamber, and they fell quiet. The sound continued, seeming to originate from the entrance of the cave and ricochet down into their chamber. Theryn and Lyra pressed against the cave wall, hoping to hide if something passed the doorway. The scurrying became louder, headed in their direction.

Theryn held his breath and closed his eyes, listening intently.

Claws on stone. Closer, almost upon them. But these were too light and small to be the giant beast that had attacked them. Theryn opened his eyes as the scurrying loudened outside the entryway.

Instead of a giant winged monster, a small and sleek furry creature poked its head into the doorway. It had slick fur, a wet button nose, and two black beady little eyes. The critter had a faint streak of gray going down its belly, but other than that, it was completely white in fur. It held two padded hands close to its body nervously. The creature and the pair stood completely still, locked in awkward eye contact. The long silver whiskers on its cheeks and eyebrows twitched slightly as it cocked its head to peer directly into Theryn's eyes. It let out a squeaky chitter and held its hands close to its mouth.

Theryn was more than a bit frightened, as he had never seen something like this peculiar animal before. Although the slender creature looked rather harmless, Theryn was still scared, nonetheless. They didn't move, only continued to stare. As he stared into the void of the creature's black eyes, Theryn felt a twitch. Something scratched at his mind. Like a little spasm, but deep in his brain. He felt emotions pop into his head.

Fear, curiosity, a bit of sadness (but also happiness), slight hunger.

For a moment, he became lost in these thoughts.

Sure, Theryn felt most of these things on a regular basis, but these particular emotions didn't seem his own. He realized, after a while, these were not initially his own thoughts. Of course, he shared some of the same feelings, but these thoughts had been presented to him from a different origin. They blended together in his mind, swirling and mixing with his own thoughts.

There was a snapping sensation as the critter broke free from Theryn's gaze with a shake of its head. Theryn would have fallen backwards if he hadn't been leaning against the cavern wall. He relaxed suddenly, no longer feeling any imminent threats.

"Oh great, they have giant white wood rats here, just like at home," Lyra said in a whisper.

The critter had begun chittering loudly and rolling around on the ground in an apparent attempt to scratch its back.

"They have these in the Lower District?" Theryn asked, carefully extending a finger towards the critter.

"Of course not, moss brains. What are you doing? Don't touch the rottin' thing, it could bite you!"

Theryn continued to slowly extend a pale finger forward. The critter shuffled back to its feet as the finger approached, locking eyes with Theryn in the process. Again, the world around Theryn fizzled away as he felt his mind tether to the animal's.

Soon it was just Theryn and this creature. Everything around them had faded away.

Theryn reached out with his thoughts, searching for any hint of the creature's intentions. Its thoughts darted around wildly much like the rooks' had in Lunathal. The difference was he had only been able to faintly sense their emotions; this was so much more complete. In Lunathal, he had always believed he was imagining it, that the birds had just liked him because he fed them. Unlike the rooks, when he connected with this fuzzball, its thoughts flooded into his mind and vice versa.

Theryn could sense it was still uncertain about him but also bursting with curiosity. He wanted to show the creature that he meant it no harm. Theryn jammed his feelings forward into the front of his mind in an effort to convey this to the creature.

With another shake, the creature wrenched itself apart from Theryn's mind. It gave him an expectant look and darted through the doorway. Theryn felt the urge to follow it.

"Let's see where it's going," Theryn said, gathering himself.

Lyra was staring at him as if he had three heads.

"You just had a staring contest with that big rodent, and now you want us to follow it?"

"Yeah, it just seemed like it wanted us to go that way. You didn't sense anything weird from it? Like feelings?"

Lyra gave him a look similar to the dismissive one most girls offered him whenever he entered a room.

She really does a great job of making me feel like I'm right at home, he thought sarcastically.

"I am *not* following that thing deeper into this cave! We need to get back up to the trunk and find a way back to Lunathal," Lyra insisted. Theryn was about to protest when the slender critter popped into the doorway again. Its head swiveled back and forth between them before scurrying back down the path. Theryn started after it.

"Seriously?" Lyra called behind him, gathering her things and following. "Are we really going to follow a wet rat down a dark path?"

The cavern began to slope downward, and the sunlight leaking through the ceiling cracks diminished. They descended the damp cave path, the slender white creature always staying a few meters ahead of them. Water trickled in thousands of tiny streams down from the stone columns that lined the pathway. It formed a thin waterfall leading downward. The echoed sounds of rushing water crescendoed in the distance.

"Oh no you dont. I am *not* going down there. Don't you realize we are headed *away* from Lunathal right now?"

The constant arguing was getting annoying, so Theryn tried to blot her out of his mind and focus on his new four-legged friend. The curious animal had stopped right in front of them on a rock. It gave Theryn a quick glance, and then it dove from the rock and landed on its stomach. It slid with surprising grace, sliding all the way down the smooth stone into the shadows. Theryn sat down to slide after him.

He felt Lyra grab at the rope sling dangling behind him. It made his shoulder stretch, which did not tickle.

"No way, kid. We are not going down that. We'll drown and there's no light down there. This has to be your dumbest move yet if you think I am going to—"

Lyra cut off as a whole swarm of the creatures appeared in the path. These ones were assortments of browns and grays with the same black beady eyes and button noses. Lyra let out a yelp as they rushed in around them and started sliding down the stone tunnel.

Theryn felt her grip release, and he took the opportunity to push himself off to follow. There was no explaining why he felt the urge to do this, it just felt natural, like the right thing to do. He slid into complete darkness, letting out a whoop of excitement.

Theryn slid for what seemed to be a dozen heartbeats in the winding tunnels of the dank cavern. His stomach rose with the thrill, like a child being lifted between the handholds of two parents. The current was strong, and it threatened to sweep him away. There wasn't much water in Lunathal, and he wasn't the greatest swimmer, so it took all his strength to keep his head above water as he was spit out of the river's mouth and deposited in a still pool.

Light filtered in from the open ceiling of where he had landed. Lyra splashed in beside him, wet curls plastered to her face.

"What in the rottin' sap is this?" Lyra exclaimed.

Above them was a circular shape cut into the mountain ceiling that exposed blue skies and floating clouds. The light illuminated the cavern room. Long spirals of patterned stone dripped down from the ceiling like melted wax. Stone shelves lined the pool's walls where fuzzy creatures napped. All around them, the slippery critters swam and played. Some floated belly-up and others dove into the pool and came out with small fish, which they munched on happily.

Theryn hoisted himself out of the pool and took a seat upright on the edge of the water. Lyra did the same. She shook her head and fluffed her damp curls with her fingers.

"Are we seriously in a whole city of these things? They must rule the mountain or something. Maybe the whole surface is just full of different types of wood rats."

Theryn spotted the white creature he had connected with sliding forward on the side of the pool. It submerged itself into the crystalline water and emerged with a handful of translucent green stalks. Theryn was amazed by its skill in the water. These creatures swam with surprising efficiency and grace. It ducked its head under the water, and in a moment, his new pal was next to him. It extended its stubby hand in an effort to hand him the algae, all the while blinking inquisitively.

Theryn took the plant. It was translucent and sticky like jelly lichen, and he held it out in front of himself, albeit a touch confused. The creature stared at him.

Does it want me to eat it?

Theryn wasn't sure why he did it… Perhaps it was instincts, but he tore off a portion of the plant and popped it into his mouth. It had a strong salty taste unlike anything he had ever eaten. It wasn't particularly good, but he was so hungry he would eat about anything right now. He offered some to Lyra.

"You want me to eat some moldy plant that some aquatic chipmunk just handed you inside a giant water basin?" she asked. The slippery critter looked at Lyra and cocked its head. "Ok, fine," she resigned and grabbed the rest of the water plant, dropping it into her mouth and letting out a dissatisfied groan. "Ugh, it tastes like fermented jelly lichen. The texture is awful."

The creature scratched its nose and slid belly first into the pool again.

"I think you offended our slippery friend," Theryn said. Somehow, he kind of knew that she offended him. That was weird...

"Rats can't speak Folktalk, kid. And even so, I would rather go hungry than eat this stuff."

"Will you stop calling me *kid*. Moon Above, I just finished Academy. I'm probably older than you!"

Lyra rolled her eyes, "Ain't no way you are older than me, kid."

"Would you *stop*! I've lived practically twenty winter solstices!"

She let out a laugh that echoed in the cave. "Twenty! That's still a sproutling by my standards."

"Oh yeah?" Theryn began, "And how old are you, oh wise ancient crone of the Lower District?"

"Twenty-three."

Theryn threw up his hands in frustration, "That's pretty much the same as me!"

"Not really, kid." Lyra said, leaning back against the wet stone. "You learn a lot in those three solstices between twenty and twenty-three."

Theryn rolled his eyes. Bub had just had his one hundred and fifty-fifth solstice last summer. That was pretty old for a Winterborn. The blue-tinged Summerborn could live upwards of three hundred years, while Winterborn usually grew old and sickly by their one hundred and fortieth year. That seemed so long to Theryn. Three lunar cycles was a small span of time to the people of Lunathal.

There was a splash in the pool beside Theryn that surprised him. The slippery animal had returned, carrying something. The animal opened his mouth and deposited a thin, silvery fish right on Theryn's britches, completely soaking them.

Theryn picked it up. This thing was easily worth a full season of *fruit fly* wages back home. Fish were farmed in the pools of the Upper Districts and extremely expensive. It wriggled in his hand.

Lyra snatched it from him and stood up quickly. "I heard about these, they are like swimming rooks, you can cook 'em up and eat 'em!"

"We are not eating a living animal!"

"So, what, you Middle Districters eat eggs, don't ya? Those are practically living, I think? And in the Upper District they eat ducks and goats and all that other rich people stuff. My uncle told tales about how Moonfolk ate fish all the time when they lived on the surface. Plus, look around, everybody's doing it!"

The fish wriggled out of Lyra's hand and flopped back into the pool where it disappeared in the clear water. The slippery critter gave Theryn a look that he swore meant to say, *you were supposed to eat that, moss brains.*

Inside the eyes of the creature, Theryn knew things. He could feel that the little slipper-critter had seen people like Moonfolk before but mostly ignored them. He could sense the creature knew he was harmless now. The critter continued to stare at him. There was an intensity in its gaze...

A flash of blinding blue light snapped in Theryn's mind, and he felt himself tether mentally to the small creature. Its thoughts mixed with his own like stars dotting a night's sky. Each emotion was its own constellation in his head. The feeling was as if a small bridge linked them together, and in that moment, the bridge became whole, truly connecting them.

Strong emotions came to him in a rush like flooding waters. It loved swimming. It loved the feeling of the sun on its belly in the summer. It loved being around others of its kind, yet it strangely felt alienated from them. It had felt heartbreak, rejection... just like Theryn. The black eyes continued staring into his, unblinking.

He urged the creature forward mentally and another surge of light sparked inside him. The creature approached and reached out its tiny hand. Theryn met it with his fingers and...

Something strange happened.

Theryn's fingertips began to glow with a soft sapphire light.

After a moment of glowing, the light calmed, and he was left with the surprising urge to go swimming.

Lyra had shuffled back in shock.

"Theryn?" she asked. "Your hand is glowing! Do something!"

Theryn let his hand fall, and the glow completely faded. He felt different now. Not bad, or unpleasant, just different. The creature's thoughts remained in his mind, even when he broke eye contact with it. When the creature walked away, he felt like a sliver of himself walked away. It was as if the critter had taken a piece of himself with it.

It slid into the water and started swimming around excitedly, doing spiraling figures and jumping up from the water in streaming arcs. Theryn couldn't control himself. He jumped in and began to swim. The slippery critter danced around him in the water, weaving in and out between his legs and body.

For the first time in a long while, Theryn felt understood. His worries melted away. Now he just wanted to swim, and he was unbelievable at it. It felt so natural, like he had done it his whole life.

The two splashed in the pool together, all anxiety vanishing. For the first time in Theryn's whole life, he finally felt needed.

Chapter VII
The Robbery

"Oh great, he's lost it," Lyra said to herself from the side of the pool. "Can we not do this right now? We have to find a way back, Theryn."

Her companion had finally snapped. Theryn was strange, even by her standards, but this was a new level of bizarre. The guy was now flailing around in the water with the little fuzzy slipper-thingy and smiling widely. His poncho fell from his arms like webbed wings as he splashed around.

"You know," she called over the splashing, "out of all the people I could have gotten myself into this mess with, you are starting to seem like the worst. You are making me wish I fell down here with that stupid clerk!"

Theryn ignored her. He just continued to splash around, diving deep and reemerging with a gasp. The pool wasn't that deep, which was lucky because Lyra had no idea how to swim. Back home there wasn't enough water to swim in, especially in the Lower District. It made her wonder how Theryn knew how to do it at all.

Next to him, the little water rodent zipped around with expert skill. Lyra was about to make a bigger fuss about how ridiculous this was when the pair of strange splashers abruptly stopped. Theryn hoisted himself out from the water, panting with a wide smile.

Lyra crossed her arms, "Are you finished? What was that about?"

He shook the water from his dark hair and ringed out the sides of his poncho, "I dunno, just felt like swimming."

"Ok… while I'm glad you finally made your first friend, do you care to explain the glowing hand condition?"

Theryn bent over and took a long drink from one of the waterfalls trickling down from the cavern walls; he gulped audibly and sat back against the moist stone before answering, "All this time, I thought I didn't have arcana. I let everyone make me think my bond with animals was weird. But it's not weird."

He turned excitedly to look at her, his face beaming. "It's my weave… it's my arcana. I can connect with them!"

"So, you lied to me? This whole time you had arcana?"

"No, no. I had no idea. Back home it didn't work this strongly. It felt, I don't know? Suppressed, maybe? I could always sense animals' feelings, but I've never experienced anything like this." He gestured to the slipper-doodle rat thingy that was now wriggling around at his feet. It seemed to be scratching its back with the clasps of his sandals. Theryn leaned in closer to her, his eyes wide. "Lyra, I can like, read its thoughts and stuff."

This was too much. Of all the people she could have fallen with, she had to fall with the most insane person she had ever met.

"That's a load of droppings. Just because this thing hasn't decided it wants to eat us, doesn't mean you can go around claiming it's your new soul mate." Lyra rose and began searching for an exit to the cavern room as she talked. "I thought you said the Academy didn't sense any arcana. What, did they just forget to tell you about this?"

Theryn shrugged, "No clue, they did all the tests on me and everything. But Summerborn back home can only shape ice or wield sparks from the moonlight. This isn't like any of that."

It was the truth, but that response wasn't good enough for Lyra. She continued her arguing, a bit more indignantly. "Even if you do have a magical connection–whatever–with this thing, so what? Care to explain how that is going to help us in this situation?"

Lyra was in a truly rotten mood. Her muscles were feeling a bit better from the night's rest, but hunger wracked her brain. That combined with the fact they had plummeted a couple thousand meters didn't exactly leave her feeling all sunshine and rainbows.

Theryn didn't answer her for a long moment. Then to her disgust, he actually picked up the creature and held it to his face.

Gross!

It didn't even wriggle, it just let itself be handled. They stared at each other in the weirdest way possible for a while, both pairs of eyes completely glassy. Lyra couldn't hide her disgusted expression even if she tried.

"What in the rotten hells are you doing? This has got to be the weirdest romance story I've ever seen. Not sure how the magicians back home are gonna spin this one to be kid appropriate."

After a while, Theryn shook his head, and his little friend dropped to the floor and took off down the side of the pool.

"I think it can lead us to a town or something. I see houses made from wood and stone in its head. It's been there. Maybe we can ask for help."

He had to be kidding her now. He wanted to leave?

Lyra stomped her feet down and threw up her hands in dismay. "What? We can't go away from Lunathal, Theryn. We need to stay here and figure out a way up. What if we get lost out there?"

Theryn ignored her and began following his new friend. The critter flung itself forward on its belly down the damp exit.

"Look at him slip and slide, he's like a little water bug or something," Theryn called excitedly as he disappeared beyond the tunnel that led out of the cavern.

Lyra felt hopeless. She eyed the circle entrance overhead and tried her best to summon her arcana. Maybe she could figure out a way to float up there. If she could, she might be able to walk back to the Old Willow. Tight grip, eyes shut, she blocked out the sound of splashing in the cavern. She tried to make her mind the usual blank canvas, but she couldn't focus with the piercing sunlight. It seemed so bright, even with her eyes closed. Plus, those little water rats were chittering and splashing loudly all around her. As she gave up, Lyra let in a sharp inhale, completely unaware her breath had been held. Theryn was gone. All that remained were a group of brown versions of those big water rats.

They looked up at her with quizzical eyes while grooming themselves and snacking on fish.

"This way!"

The call echoed through the cavern.

With a feeling much like falling through the cloud sea, or flowing down a dark river, Lyra stepped forward into the unknown to follow *rat* boy once again.

In retrospect, Lyra shouldn't have been so harsh on the water plants. They had a decent crunch, and the flavor was briny but not overly salty. This rock they were eating on the other hand, was truly horrid.

The little fuzzy demon that Theryn had expertly named "Slip" was now foraging in the river outside the mountain for them. They had been descending the mountain, following a river for hours while Slip darted in and out of the water. Occasionally, he came back with some thin-ridged rocks, which he pried open and handed to Theryn with tiny hands. Lyra gagged as the inside revealed a white mucus-soaked glob, which the creature greedily sucked up.

Theryn held one up and sniffed it.

"Is it a plant?" Lyra asked.

"No clue, but at this point we either eat something or we drop." He scrunched his face in preparation and slurped down the contents of the split rock.

"How is it?" Lyra asked. The question was unnecessary, the young man's face said it all. She could tell he didn't like it. Theryn stuck his tongue out as if he had eaten a moldy omela.

"Salty," he finally answered.

Despite the less than stellar reaction, Slip kept bringing them, and they kept eating them. By the seventh one, Lyra thought maybe they weren't so bad.

After an hour of walking and snacking on rock snot, the ground finally leveled. The river emptied into a wide lake that stretched out before them. Slip emerged from the river, shook himself dry, and began fiddling with the round rocks that surrounded the shore. For the first time since they landed on the surface, Lyra actually felt the air was comfortable here. The further they got down the mountain, the warmer the weather became.

"I think Slip wants us to stop for the day. It might not be best to go into the forest at night. He's sending me flashes of danger, memories of predators or something coming out at night."

"Well, we can't stay out here in the open. What if that winged demon comes back? Being a Shade doesn't seem to want to work for me today," Lyra warned.

"Ahoy there!"

The pair turned quickly. Outside a tiny cabin of carved logs across the lake, stood the most peculiar-looking man Lyra had ever seen. He had a long gray beard and a bald head. His skin was tan like tree bark, and his clothes were woven with intricate patterns. He had a bucket in his hand, and he called out to them in a strange accent.

"Don't be scared now, come on over here!"

Theryn was looking at Slip for a long moment. He must have decided it was ok because the little creature ran over to the man and grabbed something from his bucket. The sun-kissed man laughed and offered Slip a few more of its contents. Theryn and Lyra approached him cautiously.

"Oh, you folks are Elves, I'm sorry. My accent must be a little strange, I know. Don't be scared now."

He gave them a smile producing a row of less than perfect teeth. He was strange looking, but Lyra thought the oddest part of him was his small, rounded ears. They came to no point, and they barely reached halfway up his head. His accent was hard to understand, but Lyra got the sense of what he was saying regardless of the fact every third or so word seemed to have some bizarre inflection or variation from the Moonfolk's older tongue.

"I'm a Crabber in these parts, see?" He held out his bucket, which was filled with things that looked like big reddish bugs. "I collect them from the lake and sell them to the folks in Oar's Rest. Lonely life, but I don't mind, sometimes these little guys come and visit me. Especially this one, he's the most unique-looking otter I've ever seen."

He scratched Theryn's pet water rat, which was apparently called an otter, behind the ears. The otter ignored him and worked at ripping apart the hard exterior of a waterbug and slurping down the contents of its limbs.

Gruesome, but no worse than eating rock snot.

"You guys are the most interesting looking Elves I've ever seen," the Crabber continued. "Never seen one with pink hair and skin so pale. No, you're definitely not Sun Elves… You guys aren't from Goldfyre, are you?"

Theryn stepped forward to reply. "No, we are Moonfolk from a city in that tree up there." He pointed to the Old Willow, and the wall of light blue clouds surrounding it. "It's a place called Lunathal. We need to get back there as quickly as possible. Do you know a way?"

Lyra wanted to stop Theryn from spilling so much information about them to this stranger. *Otter* boy, however, just seemed to inherently trust the round-eared man.

The man leaned back and raised a hand to his head to peer into the sky through the sunset. "Sorry, *erm*, I'm not quite sure I understand. Might be your accents or something. There were a couple words in there I didn't catch. You said you are from that tree? And you are some sort of sky-people?"

Before Lyra could interject, Theryn pointed at the moon which was becoming more visible in the afternoon sky. "Moonfolk. People who worship the moon, I guess? I don't know... I never really thought about it."

Theryn shrugged at Lyra. She shot him her best annoyed glance. Her patience was running thin, they needed answers, and they didn't have time to share history lessons. To her surprise, she could tell Theryn felt the same way as his tone became more stern.

"It doesn't matter what we are, we just need to get back to that tree as soon as possible."

This was the first time Theryn said something that didn't totally infuriate her. The old man considered the words whilst stroking the graying whiskers at his lip.

"A city in the trees. Wow... You learn something new on Tellis every day," the Crabber chuckled and picked up his bucket. "How did you survive your fall? You left that part out," the Crabber asked.

Theryn shot Lyra a concerned glance and lied quickly, "We got lucky. We slowed our fall with our ponchos and landed in some water."

Theryn was hiding the fact she was a Shade. In Lunathal, it was outlawed. She wasn't so sure if it was the same down here, but it was courteous of him to be safe. Either way, she appreciated it.

The Crabber looked unconvinced. His face glazed over in thought as if he was trying to discern if it was even possible to use their crudely woven clothing as parachutes.

"Interesting… Sometimes people visit that tree to pray, but I never heard of anyone living up there. It would be impossible to climb. As far as I know, it's been here for a long time."

"Yes, seven hundred years," Theryn replied. "Our ancestors climbed the tree as it grew to escape the floods. We've been living up there ever since." This clearly confused the old Crabber further because he looked to be deep in thought.

"The floods, eh? Very peculiar. I can't be doing all this thinking on an empty stomach though, come on in. We can talk over supper."

Lyra was astonished that supper turned out to be quite delightful. Of course, she had hesitated to try the hard water bugs filled with soggy meat, but once she did, she realized they actually tasted fairly good. Her favorite, though, was the root vegetable the Crabber had called yams. The soft orange pulp was mashed and mixed with fresh butter and served piping hot. It tasted amazing, and the fluffy, white bread the old man had served with it was far better than the mossbread back home in Lunathal. Lyra even enjoyed the way Slip ate. The otter had this funny way of grabbing things clumsily with his padded fingers and tossing his head back to eat with big chomping bites. She and Slip chowed down with ferocity while Theryn and the Crabber ate slowly, trying their best to communicate with one another despite having different accents.

"But there was this winged beast," Theryn continued, as he recounted most of their fall. "It attacked us on the way down. Like a big serpent, but with wings."

The old man leaned back in his chair. He raised a finger and wagged it. "Now, you mean to tell me that you got into a fight with the Wyvern of Evaria and lived to tell the tale? Was it blue? Heavens, you are the strangest dinner guests I have ever had!" He chuckled to himself and took a big bite of steaming yams.

"Have you seen anyone who looks like us? Pale or pale-blue skin, Moonfolk trying to get back up the Old Willow?" Lyra asked between mouthfuls of bread.

The Crabber shook his head. "Nope, seen a few fair skinned Elves in my day, but not like you two. You lot look as though you haven't seen a ray of sunlight in your entire lives. How can you live closer to the sun than me and look like that?"

"The tree has a contained atmosphere," Theryn explained. "When it grew from Seluna's Teardrop, it gave us everything we needed to survive. Food, water, shelter, and that included blocking that altitude's intense sun and wind."

"Most interesting," the Crabber said, thoughtfully. For a second there, Lyra thought Theryn actually sounded grateful for that rotten Old Willow. Sure, it had given them what they needed to survive, but barely. Most resources went to the rotting Summerborn in their high branches. Lyra and her mother had always been left with the scraps. She didn't know about that fancy Academy science stuff, but she did know that the Chief Astrologer and the council in Lunathal could be wrong. They had been wrong when they told everyone the surface was a burning hellscape, and they were wrong when they claimed their people couldn't leave Lunathal without dying. She was glad her mother had homeschooled her. It didn't take a fancy professor for her to know only the Hero of Lunathal had ever left the Old Willow and lived, and at this point, Lyra wasn't even sure he had ever existed in the first place.

Dinner concluded with a simple bowl of berries and spiced fruit juice the Crabber presented to them. The Crabber had suggested they go into the shoreside town tomorrow and ask around. After helping them put up their ponchos to dry, he gave them each a bedroll. The man had insisted they stay, claiming the forest road wasn't safe to travel at night. He climbed into his own lofted mattress and blew out the lantern that hung from the ceiling. Slip had decided to sleep outside, and Theryn had seemed alright with it. They unrolled their makeshift beds and laid down for the night.

Lyra stared up at the wooden ceiling in the dark. The only illumination came from the faint moonlight through the open window. This was the second night Lyra was away from her mother. She hoped her uncle had come to help her, otherwise, Lyra couldn't bear the thought of her mother all alone in their single room home. It was a longshot... her uncle was sick too.

Lyra held up her hands and focused. Her fingertips went cold, and she felt power surge inside her for a brief moment. She stopped short of expelling the power. The effort tired her, but she felt more at ease knowing she hadn't lost her arcana from the fall. She rolled over and thought about her mother's classes. They always ended in a story. Lyra loved those stories. As she remembered, sleep took her.

That night Lyra dreamt of a world devoid of color, inverted and muted, the vibrance of Lunathal swept away and replaced with smoking shadows. At the heart of the void was a matronly figure. It extended its arm towards her. Terrible inky tendrils shot in her direction.

Lyra awoke with a start.

"Time to rise, my little dough balls!" the Crabber shouted. The old man jumped down from the loft. He was surprisingly limber for his age. Normally, Lyra would be annoyed to be awoken so suddenly, but to be rid of that nightmare left her feeling more than a bit relieved. Lyra rose and fluffed out her hair. A lilac curl dropped in front of her eye, and she pushed it back behind her pointed ear. The lump next to her didn't stir, so she kicked it. "Up and at 'em, rat bo–" her leg hit the bedroll.

The *empty* bedroll.

Theryn was already gone. The little weirdo must have taken his giant rat and ditched her. Her heart sank, and the realization that she was alone left her feeling numb. The Crabber threw on his long boots, grabbed his bucket, and kicked open the door. Daylight streamed in.

What was she going to do?

Lyra put on her own sandals and followed.

The shimmering deep blue water of the lake spread out over the smooth stone shoreline. It was all nestled so perfectly into the valley that it looked like some sort of artist's outlandish painting. The Crabber handed her a bucket and began to pick up rocks. Occasionally, he would scoop up a handful of the crabs and drop them into his bucket.

"You want me to work?" Lyra asked.

"It's customary; I've given you shelter and food, the least you can do is help me with the crabbing until lunch… at least until your friend comes back."

"He's not coming back, he ditched me… and I don't have time for this. I have to head into town and find someone who can take me back to Lunathal." Lyra hesitated and looked at the man with sorrowful eyes. "You have been very kind to us, thank you."

She tried her best to show her appreciation to the man. It was difficult to restrain the loneliness and betrayal she felt by being left by Theryn.

Lyra placed the bucket on the stone shore and turned to leave down the forest path. At the same time, Slip came bounding in from the forest. He dove into the lake eagerly with a splash and reemerged, floating lazily on his back. There was rustling in the brush, and Theryn appeared. He had the same grin on his round face that he did when he was swimming around like a lunatic with his pet. She wanted to kick him for leaving without telling her.

Notwithstanding, Lyra could have hugged him. The fear of being alone in a strange land retreated. She hadn't ever thought she would feel so grateful to see the little weirdo. She wouldn't tell him that, of course.

"Where did you go? What's the big idea of leaving without telling me? I thought you left for good!" she snapped.

"I woke up in the middle of the night. I just couldn't shake the feeling that Slip wanted to show me something, and when I woke, he was waiting right there outside the cabin. He brought me into the forest and look," Theryn held out a handful of small red fruit with long green stems. Each fruit had varied colors ranging from a light scarlet to almost black. He popped off the stem and tossed one in his mouth. He chewed and smiled in a way that made Lyra want to push him over. They were trapped on the surface away from home, almost eaten by a winged beast, and this guy was collecting berries? His teeth were stained with red juice like he had been sucking someone's blood. He handed one to Lyra.

"Evarian Cherries, those are the best kind of cherries in all of Tellis," said the Crabber. The man had come up behind Theryn and plucked a cherry from his palm. "You should try the figs, we are known for our figs in this part of the country."

Lyra dropped the fruit and grabbed Theryn by his good shoulder. "Theryn, we've been gone too long. Won't your family be worried about you? We need to stop playing with animals and get a move on."

Theryn tightened his lips. His face warped with shame while he explained himself. "I know… but Lyra, I feel stronger down here. I can't explain it, but I do. It feels like I'm taking a deep breath of fresh air after being stuck under a blanket. My arm is totally fine now… How is that possible?" He waved it about in the air, demonstrating that he did indeed have a healed arm. "I tracked Slip without looking at him," he continued. "I can sense what he's feeling, and I can send him what I am feeling. I know where he is too, like all the time! He gives off these vibrations that pulse around him." Theryn closed his eyes and pointed in the direction Slip was floating in. He opened them and smiled. "I think what they teach us in Lunathal is flawed. The surface isn't a desolate wasteland, is it? It's just a normal place, with food and water, just like Lunathal. What if instead of the surface being a smoking ruin, it's magical? A place where everyone has arcana?"

"Ok, well I imagine in paradise there isn't a giant serpent that wants to eat people," Lyra argued, "and if everyone has arcana here, then congratulations because we aren't as special as you thought!"

"Not everyone, young Elf," the Crabber interrupted. The pair turned to face him. "Not everyone in Evaria has magic. Most of the Elf-folk, yes, but not all the Men and Half-Men. Seems it comes and goes in generations. Mostly rich folks have it. Wars have been fought over less here in Evaria."

"I'm not sure what Half-Men are, but for the most part, what you say is also true where we are from," Theryn replied. "Seems like anyone wealthy or successful in the upper parts of Lunathal has arcana. Like it's reserved for the important people."

"Ah," the old man nodded with understanding. Lyra could sense the wistfulness in his eyes. He was almost completely glazed over, as if recounting his own long history in a few moments. "That's what they want you to believe." He left his trance and gave the pair a wink before returning to crabbing.

"What do you mean?" Theryn pressed. The old man turned with a passionate look in his aged eyes.

"Listen, I don't know much about any city in the trees, but I do know rich folks, and they're the same in every city, no matter the race or country. They make it sound like they are the only ones who can do what they do and everyone else isn't as important. They make you feel like you don't deserve what they have. They probably have everyone tricked back where you are from, same as here. Kings, Nobles, Dukes, and Princes. It doesn't matter, they all don't care about us equally."

Well, that was something she could agree on. To Lyra, it sounded like the people who ruled the surface were no better than the Summerborn. "Seems like you are speaking from experience," Lyra commented.

The old man nodded in agreement. "I did my military time in some pointless Evarian crusades against the Imperium. Now I've retired from that life for something more simple. Simplicity is key in life, kids." The Crabber eyed Slip who was chowing down on a rather large lake fish by throwing his furry head back and guzzling it in large chunks. "I don't know much about magic, but from what I can tell, you and that otter seem to share something special. I can see there is a connection between you."

"Do you have arcana?" Theryn asked.

"You mean magic? Nope, but it doesn't take magic to tell when two creatures care for one another, and you two make quite the pair. Never seen a pale Elf with a pale otter before."

He extended the buckets towards them, "Now, how about we get to work, eh? Will you help an old man out with his crabbing?"

Lyra felt guilty… Perhaps they should help the man out for all his kindness. Theryn, however, bowed slowly with both hands on his forehead in the traditional Lunathal sign of appreciation. "Thank you for taking us in. We are grateful for the kindness and knowledge you have shared with us. One day we shall repay you."

Without so much as a glance back, Theryn turned around and began to walk briskly towards the forest. Slip shot out of the water and followed. Lyra stood there, facing the Crabber awkwardly. He gave her a hopeful smile, the bucket still extended in his hand.

She took off down the road.

"Thanks again!" she called over her shoulder.

"Wait, I thought you were going to help me with the day's harvest!" the old man called from behind them. Lyra felt a bit sorry for the kind old Crabber. Then she reminded herself she hadn't stolen anything from him. She considered that payment enough for his kindness.

They were a decent way down the road when Theryn slowed his pace and began to strategize out loud.

"We head into town, and we ask around carefully. We try to look for anyone who looks like us or anything resembling Moonfolk. We'll try not to mention too much or draw too much attention. Do you have any money?"

Lyra checked her pouch and pockets. She had dumped the omela pits she was holding, and now all that remained was her sharp pitting tool.

"Nothing."

"Me neither," Theryn replied. "It's okay, if anyone can bring us back to Lunathal, we can just tell them we'll pay them once we arrive. My Bub has some money stored away from my parents' savings."

Must be nice…

The chances of that working out seemed slim. Lyra wasn't so sure. "Theryn, there isn't going to be someone who can just snap their fingers and lift us thousands of meters in the air. I think our best bet is finding some sort of arcana wielder and seeing if they can open up an entryway to Lunathal."

"There is no entryway to Lunathal," Theryn gave her a quizzical look. "Didn't you learn anything at the Academy?"

Lyra knew there was no entryway… She had seen that firsthand on the surface yesterday. All that searching had yielded no evidence of any hidden stairway or lift. She was frustrated with how calm Theryn seemed down here. Shouldn't he be panicking and wanting to go home?

"Hello? I told you I didn't go to the Academy. I'm a Shade, remember? I would have had my arcana weaved away if I had gone!"

Theryn shrugged, "Not sure, maybe they would have missed it like they did mine."

A rustle in the bushes made the pair quiet their conversation. Even Slip, who had been a bit behind them, chasing a toad, stopped what he was doing and perked up. In front of them, the shrubbery parted, revealing a tall, lean figure in clay-colored leathers and a brown gambeson. A piece of dark fabric tied tight around his mouth obscured the lower half of his face. On top of his head sat a ridiculous-looking wide flat-brimmed hat. The stranger stood in front of them, blocking the road.

"Salutations, little Elves. Beautiful day for a stroll in Evaria, isn't it?"

His tone was eerily coarse, like he had a throat condition of some kind. His skin was a similar color to the Crabber's, and he had the same rounded ears. That was where the similarities ended. This figure was no kindly old man.

"What brings two little pointy-ears so far from Goldfyre?" he asked, taking a slow step forward.

"Just headed to town," Lyra replied nervously. There were few times in Lyra's life she had felt intimidated enough to appear apprehensive. The surface, however, was ripe with the unknown, and this newcomer cast a sinister aura.

Theryn had gone catatonic again, still and tense, eyes locked on the newcomer.

"I see."

Another step forward.

"Well, unfortunately, you are going to have to surrender your belongings to the law for search. Thems' the town rules of

Oar's Rest." He reached to his belt, slowly fingering the hilt of a blade at his side.

Theryn looked like he was going to vomit. Lyra wasn't so easily startled; she had dealt with thugs in the Lower District before.

"You're taking our things? What's our crime?" Lyra asked. The man's hat tilted back as he spoke, revealing an ugly gnarled face and thick, bushy eyebrows.

"Your crime…" another step forward, "is having stuff I want!"

With a flourish, the stranger pulled his blade from its sheath and pointed it forward, tip-first, in their direction. It was thin and deadly. Lyra's heart began to race. She had experienced her fair share of tavern scuffles in the Lower District, but never robbery. Never *armed* robbery.

"Weapons are outlawed where we come from, so technically, you're the one breaking the law," Lyra protested, grabbing Theryn and leading him away from the highwayman.

"Oh, weapons are *outlawed* where you come from? Well, this ain't no leaf-licking Elf kingdom, kid. This is Evaria, and I'm its deadliest highwayman. Now c'mere!"

He lunged.

The sword tip dove between the pair as they ducked in a scrambled panic. Slip let out a squeak and disappeared into the bushes.

"Your otter has got the right idea… *RUN!*" Lyra screamed.

They blew past the highwayman and bounded down the forest path. Behind, Lyra could hear the heavy footfalls of pursuit quickly gaining on them.

"I take it back," Theryn called, "the surface is the worst!"

Theryn yelped as his legs were swept out from under him, and he crashed to the forest floor. The highwayman was on him.

"Theryn!" Lyra screamed. She needed him, whether she wanted to believe it or not. Poor Theryn was being outmatched by the weight of his aggressor. Lyra tried with all her might to summon her arcana. She pointed her hands outward, praying for something to happen. Her fingers stayed warm without even the slightest tingle.

"Go," Theryn tried to croak through clenched teeth. He was working hard to break free from his attacker. The highwayman swatted away Theryn's arms and planted a fist across his face. The blow took him in the cheek and Theryn was out. His head lolled to the side.

"No!" Lyra cried as she jumped on the back of the highwayman.

She pounded and scratched and bit like a wild beast. She gripped her pitting tool and sank it into the man's shoulder. In the chaos, Slip reappeared and began gnawing at the aggressor's ankles. The robber kicked and flailed. He cried out in anguish as Lyra bit down on one of his stupid round ears. With a flourish, the highwayman flipped her over his shoulders. She sailed through the air before landing hard against a tree trunk. Lyra lay on the ground dazed. Dust and dirt rose into the air from her impact and blew away in the gentle breeze.

Everything felt so… wobbly.

Was that Slip licking her face?

"Gross. Stupid rat, cut it out," she mumbled. The tree line above her swam dizzyingly. Then a weight like a falling tree landed on her torso. The highwayman was on her. She saw the chalky blur of Slip darting away. A sack went over her head, and everything went dark.

Chapter VIII
Slip

Pointy Ears had named him Slip. He liked that. He liked Pointy Ears and he liked the name. It made sense, he was indeed slippery.

Slip had always been considered different. Throughout his life, the ivory-furred otter had tried to get used to that fact. No matter how hard Slip tried, he was always reminded of his differences. It didn't make sense to him, for he was one of the fastest swimmers in the romp. He was also one of the greatest fishers and crabbers. He could slide all the way down the cavern slope to the Otter's Grotto with only one jump. He had a great eye for the best clams and could always crack them open easily. All of these things should have made him fit in, but it only served to alienate him from the rest of his romp. Sometimes he loved being different, but most of the time, he hated it.

Once when Slip was a pup, he had tried rolling around in the mud to make himself brown like the other otters. The mud had washed off in the water, and the other otters had laughed at him. When he reached adulthood, his parents went to stay in another grotto and left him alone. The first couple of years they visited occasionally. Then a particularly cold winter came, and they stopped visiting all together.

One of the only good things in Slip's life had been growing up with a pretty brown otter who could swim as fast as he could. She rarely treated Slip like he was different and seemed to enjoy swimming with him. They used to race to the lake and back, and sometimes Slip would let her win. Sometimes she won when he was trying his hardest to beat her. Afterwards, they would gorge themselves on crayfish and freshwater mussels. He always gave her the best ones he found.

One day, when they were floating in the lake, sunbathing, Slip let her know how he felt. He wanted a romp of his own, with little unique pups just like them. She agreed and they went to tell the other otters the good news.

They were laughed at.

The others joked, saying their pups would be freaks. Many claimed white otters would be easy to spot by predators and give them and their hiding place away. The males said his family would have to leave Otter's Grotto.

Slip was devastated.

The Grotto had always been their home. He could sense his love's hesitation, and it hurt his heart. He didn't want to subject their future pups to a life of wandering without a romp. She talked to him less and less each day after that.

Slip couldn't take the slow decay of what they had together, so he departed the Grotto with a heavy heart. He went all the way to the northern rivers to find a new home. Part of him hoped to find his parents and their new romp; however, the north was treacherous and frigid. In those lands, the Half-Men hunted otters. It made his journey dangerous, and he was unable to find another romp. Eventually, he resigned and left the tundra, deciding to return to Evaria.

When Slip returned to the Grotto only a few days ago, he found his romp still there. Some had been worried about him, and that was a nice feeling. Others teased him like usual, but he had gotten used to that. Then he saw his love. The pretty otter who could swim as fast as he could. She had pups of her own, and her mate was a gray otter from the western sea.

She had looked at Slip with such sorrowful eyes.

Despite Slip's hard life at the Grotto, he had been on a great adventure, and he was used to pain and rejection. He decided to make a peace offering, a way for him to say that he still wanted to swim with her. If he did it right, maybe he could help teach her pups how to swim one day, if her mate let him. Slip had to choose the perfect gift.

When Slip was a pup, he loved shiny rocks and trinkets. So, he headed up to the caverns where the cave people used to live all those hundreds of years ago, and he tried to find something special for the pups.

Slip had found something special... Oh, that was for sure. It made him forget all about the pups and his broken heart.

It came in the shape of two pale-skinned and green-clad bodies with pointy ears. They were dirty and tired; Slip could tell that just by their scent. They smelled like they desperately needed a swim in the grotto, especially the tall one with curly hair. Then the male had looked at him.

When their eyes met, it felt like their minds had been sewn together. It was an overwhelming feeling, but not aggressive. It was gentle, like a slowly flowing river. It was as if the boy was asking if he could come inside. Even though he was shocked by the sensation, Slip let him in. In a moment, the otter felt he knew everything about the boy, and the boy knew him. They had been through similar traumas; similar emotions; similar pain and joy. Slip sensed Pointy Ears had a kind heart, and Slip also knew he was open-minded.

Slip felt like he could communicate with Pointy Ears. When Slip had wanted to swim, Pointy Ears had jumped in the grotto and splashed around with him. There was a strong sense of loyalty forged immediately between them. For the first time in Slip's life, he finally felt like he belonged. He finally felt like he had a romp of his own.

So, when the bad man with the stupid hat hit Pointy Ears and then put a bag over his angry lady friend, Slip was *not* happy. Slip had wanted to bite the man and open him up like a mussel, but the man was too big and strong and had kicked Slip in a way that didn't feel so good. In the heat of the scuffle, anger was overtaken with an impulse to run. Pointy Ears had urged him to run. He could feel it in his heart that he should listen.

So, he ran.

Slip scurried all the way back to Otter's Grotto.

"They've taken my friends, please, we must do something!" Slip begged and pleaded with the other otters to help him save his friend. He explained how Pointy Ears needed him and how the bad man had taken him for his valuables. The other otters scoffed at his request.

117

"We don't meddle in the affairs of Men, white one!" a male had said. "Why should we help Men and Elves, they hunt us more and more each year!" a female chimed in. Slip felt hopeless.

Even his love, the female that could swim as fast as he, remained silent. Her head was downcast to the damp stone floor and wouldn't even meet his eyes.

Slip grew angry. "You are all *cowards*!" he cried out. "You never appreciate things that are d-different! So, here's yet another way *I* am different from you. I am different from you b-b-because I am brave. I know when to help the helpless and when to float on my back and chew on algae. This time, I am going to s-s-save my friends!"

He stumbled over his speech a bit because he was so nervous, but that didn't hinder the speed at which he slid from the Otter's Grotto when it was finished.

Slip was at the lake in record time. In the distance, the smelly crab man was lifting rocks. There was no time for treats though. Rather, Slip tried to sense Theryn's mind.

There was nothing for a long while.

Slip scurried onto a tall rock on the shore and sat there, closing his eyes. As the afternoon sun began to fall, Slip could sense something: a faint pulse. Like a tiny rumble of thunder echoing from hundreds of meters away. So faint, yet so present. It was coming from the forest path.

Slip wasted no time. He grabbed a crayfish just in case he got hungry on the road. The sight of the crayfish made him immediately hungry and he ate it… then he bounded down the muddy trail, towards his friend.

Chapter IX
Black Eyes Barnett

Lyra was carried a long way, and during that time, she planned.

Theyrn and Lyra had been thrown on a rickshaw and rolled down the forest path for a majority of the evening. The bag was still over her head, and she could feel the slow unconscious breathing of Theryn next to her. Through bleary eyes and pinprick-size holes, she could see the illumination of the afternoon begin to dim. Even with the bag over her head, it was easy to tell that the sun had begun to set. She stilled her breathing and tried to shake Theryn awake. He inhaled raggedly through his nose and then went back to his slow breaths. Nothing... She would have to do this alone.

Lyra focused.

She concentrated first on making her fingertips grow cold. They began to tingle slightly. Next, her attention went on gripping the rope that bound her hands. The tingle turned into a numbness. She willed the power that rested deep inside her and slammed it into the rope. Her mind flashed with a spark of spiraling black energy, which shot down through her hands and into the rope. With a little pop, she felt the rope at her back disappear. Only the slight presence and weight of its forced shadow remained, an echo of its physical state. Her hands relaxed as the pressure of the rope against them released. She flung the bag off her head and dove at the highwayman.

Lyra pounced and began to strike with fist and fingernail. It was a blurry altercation, but Lyra tore into the highwayman's fuzzy backside.

Fuzzy?

Why is he so *hairy*?

There was a wail, and Lyra was tossed upward, landing on the compact dirt with a *thud*. The highwayman stood above her, his handkerchief off to reveal an ugly sallow face with a tight cropped beard. He was displaying an unsightly, gap-toothed grin as he pulled her up.

"Now, now, little Elf. Is that any way to treat my donkey?"

Lyra looked up at what she had been attacking and winced. This donkey creature was unlike anything she had ever seen. It looked like a woodrat had elongated its ears and snout and grown a dopey looking face. The poor beast seemed to be in servitude, carrying the cart along that held Theryn. Its back had a few red marks from where Lyra had attacked it. "I expect my guests to be a bit more courteous, especially you Elf-kind. Don't worry little lady, Black Eyes Barnett will set you straight."

Before Lyra could focus enough to summon her power, the bag was back over her head, and her arms were forced behind her—this time with two pieces of rope. He tied them tighter than before, and her wrists began to throb. He bent over and picked up the still knotted piece of rope sitting on the ground of the cart. "How were you able to get out of this and keep it perfectly intact?"

Lyra didn't answer him, and he must not have cared enough to press her. A long silence went by between them as he lifted her onto the cart next to Theryn. "Curious," he said as he gave the donkey a slap that made the cart lurch forward.

Lyra rolled along in the cart for a while, and in her head she began devising a new plan. This time it involved riding the fuzzy creature into the sunset and leaving the ugly highwayman in the dust. Before she could figure out how to distract him long enough to pull it off, a chorus of new sounds lifted around her.

The orchestra of lively sounds gradually surrounded them as the cart rolled into what sounded like a small city. Strange birds called, bells rang, and townsfolk chattered around them. Carts and animals passed by noisily. The sounds of a large body of water could be heard in the distance, rising and falling with the tide. She thought she could even hear the faint sounds of a fiddle playing down the block. The cart wheels began to roll on cobblestone and then on wood. People talked loudly around her and hushed hurriedly as the cart passed. They rolled through the town for a few minutes before the cart came to a stop, and Lyra was hoisted out.

"Help! I'm being taken by a crazed lunatic!"

Cry as she might, the words merely evaporated in the ambiance of the town.

As she tried to scream further, the highwayman lifted the bag off her head. Sudden light blinded her. She winced as clarity returned to her vision. She was standing on the deck of a large structure made from dark wood. It was bobbing in a vast sea at the edge of a town. Wooden buildings on docks lined the shore, almost like Lunathal except built on water instead of a tree. That water… she had seen bathhouses with small tubs of water in

Lunathal, but never anything like this. It was like something straight out of the history books about the great flood.

"I wouldn't be screaming too much, lass," a new voice croaked from behind her. "No shining Evarian knight is likely to help you now that you are in the charge of Captain Black Eyes Barnett."

Standing behind Lyra and her captor was the oddest looking man she had ever seen. At first glance he appeared rather seasoned and ragged. He was short in stature and had a thinly cropped brown beard with a long mustache that drooped on either end. The long mustache hairs were twisted in braids that fell almost to his chest. He wore a similar hat to the highwayman but fancier clothes. His velvet jacket was shorn in places, missing buttons and looked as though it hadn't been washed for a decent amount of time. His wardrobe and facial hair were secondary to what really drew her attention about the man. A mess of brown hair flecked with silver perfectly framed his eyes.

Those eyes.

They were fearsome. Like Slip's beady little eyes, these were black as night, as if his whole eye was a pupil. They were deep pits of an endless void. His face held a long red scar from right eyebrow to left ear that only served to draw further attention to his eyes. He stared at her, unblinking. "You've done the crew well today, Tate," the captain croaked. "We'll deliver our cargo north and sell these slaves in Hàva or Blastmounte. Those Men and half-breeds are always looking for some fancy Elf slaves. These ones are unique too… I bet we will get a pretty box of marks for them," he cackled a bit at the idea and rested his hands on the cart while the highwayman lifted Theryn off.

"I was thinking we could sell them to the king's mummer troop, Captain. This freak's got pinkish hair. Elves don't usually have pink or purple hair, right? A ringleader would pay good for this one, plus she did something fancy with her hands to get out of the rope. Must have some sort of magic or something."

The captain narrowed his creepy eyes at Lyra. It was as though he was trying to look right through her head.

She wanted to shout that almost all the Moonfolk back home have some sort of lilac or blue colored hair and that Theryn was the weird one, but she couldn't. Those eyes, they terrified her. They were like a night sky without stars.

"Please let us go, we need to get home."

It was all that came out, and it was pitiful.

The captain only chuckled, "Aye lass, you'll be going to a new home soon. For now, the Hyena is your home and her crew your new family!" He began to snicker, his voice rough like sawing lumber. "Tate, keep 'em below deck. We'll sell the girl to the mummers when we dock at Castle Evaria, and we'll bring the boy with the rest to Hàva."

Oh Seluna Above, what have we gotten ourselves into.

Theryn was starting to awake and began mumbling to himself. He sat up for a moment and began to look around frantically, bag still over his head and hands still bound.

"Put them in the cargo hold with the rest, Tate. The lads are out having a last minute of fun. We set off in a few hours."

The highwayman, Tate, obliged and hoisted Theryn to his feet. "Come on, walk on your own Elf-scum."

He grabbed Lyra roughly and led them to the lower levels of the ship and down rickety wooden stairs.

A woman was lounging in a hammock just below deck, and she called out as they walked by.

"Oh, looks like Tatey's gone and nabbed himself some new pets!" The woman had brown almond-shaped eyes and tan skin. Her long black hair was covered by a piece of cloth tied in the back. Lyra would have even considered her to be pretty if not for the line of scars around her mouth and the general filth of her velvet coat. "You almost managed to find creatures uglier than you, Tate. Nice work!"

"If you weren't the captain's favorite, I'd throw you overboard Aranna." The highwayman sneered and kept on pushing them below deck.

Lyra had heard the stories of ships when she was a kid. Her uncle had nicked a book from the Academy library and used to read to her after his shift. The books told stories of a rising tide that swept across Tellis. Moonfolk ancestors built houses of carved wood that floated on the water. It led them to the mountains of Evaria where they made their final settlements before becoming Lunathal. She had imagined them as magnificent structures, like finely polished branches extending with neat platforms. She envisioned a place for each person to sit with the sea breeze in his or her hair and high, tall limbs for everyone to have plenty of space.

The Hyena was not what she had in mind.

It was beat up and shaped like a curved willow branch. The lower decks were stuffy and rancid smelling. Its scent was reminiscent of woodrats, rotten omela fruit, and the drainage gutters of Lunathal. Lyra had to practically hold back from gagging as they descended. The cots and hammocks were stacked on top of each other and provided very little personal space for the crew. Tate continued to shove them forward.

"Not exactly the Upper District down here, eh?" Lyra said nervously to Theryn. He gave no response.

Bag is still over his head, a bit insensitive of me.

The prisoners were led down another few rickety stairs and soon found themselves in the lowest level of the ship. The air was stale and humid, and there was a thin layer of murky water sloshing back and forth on the bottom of the waterlogged floor. At the end, was a cell.

"In you go, little Elves. Enjoy your new home for the next fifty days. Takes a long time to get to Hàva. And not a peep out of you! The last slaves who woke up the crew ended up taking the rest of the trip tied to the bow of the Hyena."

Tate shoved them in and tossed the iron bar gate shut with a *clang*. The dark metal rattled for a moment and then stilled. The holding cell was large; the whole back of the ship had been sectioned off as a makeshift prison. The highwayman locked the padlock with a rusted key and slipped it into his back pocket. He brushed off his hands and departed only after giving them another malicious leer.

"Just like home," Lyra said nervously. Theryn didn't respond, his face still covered by the woven sack. Around them were empty sacks, barrels, crates, and... people? They were huddled in the corner, watching her, little muddy stained blobs. She had briefly mistaken them for piles of worn out cloth.

Lyra went to work removing Theryn's bag. "Lean over and hold still, let me get that bag off of your head. We might have company down here." She lifted her arms the best she could behind her back and flicked the bag off of the young man's head.

His mouth was bound with a cloth, and he let out a series of muffled grunts.

"Ok ok, don't make me regret this otter boy, don't start screaming. Just hold still." Theryn leaned over again, and Lyra set herself to work undoing the thick knot behind his head with her own clasped hands. He spit frantically, and the gag fell away.

"Oh, *Seluna Above*, the smell. Put the bag back on!" he pleaded.

She nudged him and pointed with her chin subtly to the people hiding in the corner of the cell. Theryn stopped and observed with suspicious eyes.

The edge of the brig was the only elevated area, and therefore the only part that wasn't covered in a thin layer of sloshing water. Lyra could now make out three figures, one of which was a child, and all of them filthy and ragged. A low, sing-songy voice came from the corner.

"Looks like old Black Eyes Barnett has got himself another curious lot to exchange for marks. Surely, I must be worth more than them, ain't that right, Stringbean?"

To Lyra's surprise, the voice belonged to the figure she had mistaken for a child. He stepped forward revealing a wrinkled face and graying skin. He had long pointed ears like the Moonfolk, but they went straight back instead of slightly curving. A thin line of black stubble lined his face, and one of his eyes was bruised shut, a greenish-purplish mark with swelling. His nose was enormous, and it wiggled when he talked.

"Welcome to the Hyena, the best luxury ship line in all of Oar's Rest."

"What are you?" Theryn asked, keeping his distance. The man raised his hands as if offended. Lyra noticed his wrists were bound, but loosely and had been tied in a way as if to presume he was still restrained.

"Whoa, that's not a very nice question to ask, kid. You are so pale *I* should be the one asking if you're some sort of blood sucker or something." He smiled, revealing a mouthful of sharp teeth, some discolored from decay, others gold and silver. "You folk never seen a Quarter-Elf before?"

Lyra and Theryn shook their heads simultaneously.

"Huh, I guess we aren't very common 'round these parts. Must be why old Black Eyes wants to sell me to some mummer's troop. And here I thought it was because I was so handsome!" he chortled. "They probably figure I might make a good ball to juggle or somethin', ain't that right, Stringbean?"

To Lyra's surprise, there was actually a chuckle in response. A low dumb sounding giggle from another lump of cloth in the corner. It rose, revealing the tallest person Lyra had ever seen. This one looked more like her and Theryn, but his skin was faintly amber, almost copper in color. His face was expressionless and had a slight straw-colored beard on a blocky jaw. His ears curved to a point like hers, but were mostly obscured by the round mop of golden hair that sat on his big head. It was streaked with mud and grime, much like his clothes.

"Never seen an Elf with purple hair before," the big man said, slowly, as if each word took a bit of concentration to form in his mouth.

"Well, I've never seen one with yellow hair," Lyra snapped back defensively.

"Really?" responded the small man in front of them. "They're pretty common, lady. In fact, I've never seen an Elf without gold hair."

"Some Sunfolk gots red hair," Stringbean noted. The scrappy looking one only shook his head.

"Yeah, but they ain't so common, Stringbean. Plus, you are one of the only Elves I've seen around these parts anyway. The big oaf's pretty unique, ain't that right, Stringbean?" The stubby man pointed to the tall Elf who smiled at them widely.

"I'm Pimbo, by the way, and you are?"

Lyra was questioning whether or not to respond to these strange people when Theryn spoke up on their behalf.

"Theryn, and this is Lyra. Can you cut our bonds?"

Lyra shot Theryn a warning glance, but the otter boy didn't seem to care. She didn't really trust anyone on the surface after their run-in with the self-proclaimed law enforcement. The little man, however, set himself to work, sawing at their bindings with a sharp fingernail.

"Well, Theryn and Lyra… you lot are just in time for Pimbo's great escape, and lucky for you, it's a three man job, but four is even better. You came just in time because I think poor Matty over there is dead."

In the corner of the cell, a wispy-haired man was limply strewn over a mat. At first glance, Lyra had assumed he was a discarded sack of moldy vegetables. "That, or he sleeps a lot without breathing. Not sure; he was here when we got here, and he loves that mat so much we named him Matty."

Lyra let out a disgusted groan. The expired looking man on the mat was a stomach-wrenching sight of sinew and protruding bones. The living contents of the cell didn't exactly look or smell much better. She had to get out of there. It made the dark cavern and the city of water rats look like a paradise.

"I was just going to have Stringbean call down that crew member, and I was planning to swindle him into getting the dead guy out of here. I was gonna claim he's got gold in his pants or something. Next, we pounce, tie him up here using Stringbean's expert fighting skills and my expert knot-tying abilities. Then we make for the top deck and jump overboard. Afterwards, we can head to my safe house in the corner of town. It's owned by my Ma, and the old lady makes some pretty good fish-eye stew." Pimbo smiled and patted his stomach while Stringbean let out a hungry hum.

"If you ever need help in Oar's Rest, you can just ask around town for Ma's famous fish-eye stew, and you'll end up at my hideout's doorstep. I'm kind of a big deal here in Oar's Rest."

Pimbo nudged Stringbean to agree, and the big Elf nodded blankly. The funny little man finished gnawing through their restraints with his sharp teeth. After much vigorous chewing, the rope fell away to the damp floor. Lyra rubbed at her wrists, relieved to have feeling in her hands again. Theryn wore a mask of uncertainty as he regarded their cellmates. "I don't really understand what all that means, but I believe you. Is this your first attempt at escape? How long have you been in here?" he asked.

Pimbo scratched his head, "I think we've only been in here a day or so, ain't that right, Stringbean? Got us heading out of town on our way to sell trinkets in Goldfyre. Trinkets... we may or may not have acquired very legally."

The fact they had been in there for only a day did not bode well for their hygiene habits. Lyra thought they had been imprisoned for at least a week. It was enough evidence for her to decide to no longer waste time with them.

"I don't exactly need your help," Lyra said, dismissively. She lifted her hands against the metal bars and began to concentrate.

"Wait!" Theryn said in a hushed tone. "Lyra, don't do it." His eyes darted nervously between her and Pimbo. "We can't play all our cards at once, and these guys may be useful. Plus, I can sense Slip, he's coming for us. Just save your *strength* in case we really need it." He rested a reassuring hand on her shoulder, which she promptly shrugged off.

"I don't need your stupid rat to escape, and I definitely don't need the Hero of Lunathal and his trusty donkey here," she said, pointing to Pimbo and Stringbean.

"Whoa there, some fire under this one!" Pimbo said, as if impressed. "They make the Elves angry where you guys come from, eh? Where is that again?"

"Lunathal," Theryn answered.

"Lunathal?"

Lyra went back to focusing on the bars, trying to block out the sound of the pointless conversation.

"It's a city nestled atop that huge willow tree surrounded by clouds to the east. Our ancestors lived in it for hundreds of years after the floods," Theryn explained.

"I see… A creative solution to the *'oh no, we are all gonna drown'* problem. Ya know, most folks just sailed to the deserts in the west or the mountains in the north and were fine. No big trees needed. The flooding just eventually stopped, and the waters died down," Pimbo said, in his almost comical accent.

Lyra felt her concentration on the bars subside as the reality of the conversation soaked in. Other people on the surface? Other places like Lunathal? Theryn must have been feeling the same because his words were ripe with the realization that the surface was inhabited by many kinds of folk.

"We had no idea there were other people on the surface, let alone towns and cities. After the floods stopped, we thought it was all just desolation, fires, and volcanic ash."

Lyra couldn't focus with all this talking. Her hands stayed warm, and the blank canvas she had been told to try and find by her mother was being rather elusive. She felt like the conversation might be worth paying attention to at this point anyway.

"Well, some places are like that down here, yeah, but mostly life just carried on after the flood waters dropped. Must not be a lot of sun up there in Lunathal, you guys are pale as can be."

"It's a protected atmosphere in Lunathal. The clouds are enchanted and block out pretty much anything that can harm us.

Seluna provided it just for our people," Theryn explained, again…

Lyra rolled her eyes. How many times did she have to listen to how great Seluna was? She was sick of it. Why wasn't Seluna here to save them now?

Pimbo didn't look so convinced. "Yeah yeah, and my boilin' Goddess made it so that I can sneak under dinner tables and eat the scraps. Come on, kid, if our Goddesses believed in us, we wouldn't be rotting in this cell right now."

"Now that's something I can finally agree with," Lyra said as she surrendered with a sigh, giving up on altering the bars.

The group sat thoughtfully for a while. Through the leaky upper deck, the afternoon light grew dim. Stringbean had made himself busy stretching, preparing for what he obviously thought was an upcoming brawl.

"Now, when I yell, you guys make it look like you have come to terms with your enslavement. Curl up in the corner and—"

Pimbo was cut off by the muffled shrill of an ear-piercing shriek that sounded outside of the ship. It could be heard clearly, in spite of the creaking of the boat and the sloshing of water inside the brig. Lyra shot Theryn a worried glance. He was holding his temple with one hand, the other tight on the bars. His expression was blank, as if he was somewhere else at the current moment.

"The beast," Theryn began, behind haunted eyes. "I can sense it; the person who rides it is controlling it. It's hunting."

Somewhere in the town, bells began to ring… followed by the sounds of screams.

Chapter X
The Winged Blizzard

The Wyvern had flown for almost a full day in search of the Moonfolk boy. The pulsing had continued in the distance, guiding the way. It had stopped only to have a meal of some roaming livestock and to ransack an old tower in search of gold or silver.

It had found none.

The Wyvern had flown so far south-west, the sea was visible on the horizon. Just on the last stretch of the peninsula, almost completely surrounded by water and forest, was the town of Oar's Rest.

The Elf-boy was here. The faint pulsing around the shipyard proved it. The beast could sense him. Could feel the pulses of his mind. The vibrations were like rhythmic heartbeats that echoed in the depths of one's psyche. The pulses were much the same as when it had tried to catch the young Elf in his fall to the surface. Although, now something had slightly changed. A piece of the boy's spirit, just the smallest sliver, no longer remained with him.

He has bridged the soul of another.

This was no matter. The Winged Blizzard would find the creature the boy Soulbridged as well. The Rider would greatly reward the Wyvern for this additional bounty. Perhaps, they could destroy that ancient relic... The one that had caused so much pain to its kin.

The beast soared over the town, casting a long serpentine shadow over the raised buildings and dockways. Bells chimed below, and shouts rang out in the man-tongue of the south. Townsfolk, looking like small insubstantial specks, ran to seek shelter from danger within the wharf town. There was whistling in the air around the Wyvern as it hovered. A thin object bounced from its scales. Another pierced in between them. The Wyvern spread its massive wings and let out a tremendous shriek.

Few had wounded the beast and lived, and it would take a lot more than a flimsy arrow to fell an ancient Wyrm.

The Winter Wyvern lowered its head and inhaled deeply. With each exhalation, a violent blizzard expelled from its mouth in strong bursts. A tower holding a man with a bow was soon covered in frost. The man cried out as a spray of sharp icicles pierced his body. The beast continued to spray frozen terror in large arcs over the town. Some of the buildings were flimsy and couldn't withstand the blasts. Splintered wood flung into the evening sky as bells and wails continued to sound on the coast.

Stop wasting time. Find the one who was able to bridge your mind. He is near the docks.

The beast flapped its slender wings and dove forward. Hovering over the docks, it began to rain down upon the dozens of ships that had made port. They teetered and crashed into one another as the winds of concentrated blizzards crashed into them.

Memories in the beast's head flashed of a time many hundreds of years ago. There had been more of the Wyvern's kind back then. They had needed to use their connection to the winter to stop themselves from going extinct. Men, Elves, Half-Men. They all coveted Wyvern scales or teeth, and they had hunted the Wyrms. Centuries of fear had turned this ancient predator into prey, and it resented them for it. Then the floods had come, and the Wyverns of all different kinds had mostly drowned, all because of that ball of evil light. Now the beast was totally alone... except for the Rider.

The beast landed on a large trading ship, unsure if it contained the Rider's target. It began to rip at the deck with talons and claws. Crew members tossed themselves overboard frantically. One lunged forward as if to strike, curved sword drawn. The Wyvern flicked him into the sea with a swipe of its armored tail. The screaming and crashing of ships continued all around, threatening to drown out any recognition of where the target may be.

The pulse sent waves of vibration from another direction. It was faint, but there was no mistaking its presence. The beast ripped apart the ship it stood on with a satisfying tear from its sharp talons. The boat crunched and began to sink into the briny waters.

The Wyvern would happily destroy every boat it could. It hated boats or ships or even rafts. They had saved Men from the floods and brought them to their safe havens from the waters. The Men and Elves had rebuilt their world from their ships and hiding places, while the Wyvern's brothers and sisters sank to watery graves.

Another volley of ice covered a nearby ship in a coating of thick frost. The Wyvern watched the wooden mast split and begin to tip over. It felt good to destroy sometimes. The Wyvern felt satisfaction at revenge against the Humans. It didn't necessarily enjoy causing suffering, but revenge was needed for those fallen kin. The Rider let the Wyvern have that revenge on occasion.

Even though it was controlled revenge, it was still revenge, nonetheless.

The pulse sounded... it was so faint. Stuck somewhere, possibly hiding.

Memories flashed in the Wyvern's mind again as it rained down winter flurries. Visions of past events. The Wyvern, retreating from the Half-Men who had invaded the northern mountain perch. Searching frantically for a place of refuge. Racing through an endless sea of clouds. Perching frantically onto the limb of a great tree. The terrifying sensation of having its mind bridged for the first time.

Then there was the Rider, promising to be equals, to fulfill any wishes. The Rider helped it defeat the Half-Men who conquered its winter home. The Rider had aided it in reclaiming the Wyvern's hoard.

But it had come at a price... for this life of servitude was unheard of for a beast so ancient and dominant. Fortunately, the grim recollections faded away, and all that was left was the will to finish the task the Rider had commanded.

The Wyvern flooded its own mind with despair in an attempt to have it reach the one who linked their Soulbridge. The boy would enter its mind, but this time the beast would be in control. In the past, when the Wyvern did this, it was able to resist the

Rider's will. The trap had been laid. The boy would become lethargic and unmotivated… and the Wyvern would strike.

There it was again, the faint pulse. It was on the move, frantic and terrified. The Wyvern let out another tremendous shriek and dove towards the docks.

Chapter XI
The Hunt

Theryn was usually pretty honest with himself about his ability to do things.

It was lackluster.

He was never the best, never the worst, rarely good enough. When that shriek sounded, however, Theryn was sure of one thing—he was probably the best at being terrified.

Pimbo and Stringbean looked confused; Lyra looked as though she had almost expected the inconvenience of their pursuer to show up; and Matty... Theryn was pretty sure he really was just a dead guy. The man remained slumped in the corner on his soggy mat.

"What do you mean it's hunting? Like that thing is after us?" Lyra pressed, sounding more anxious than usual.

The smashing of a building collapsing above deck reached their ears. There was a faint pulsing in Theryn's head, similar to the one he felt when he first spotted the Wyvern over Lunathal. Theryn was totally immersed in the sensation of the pulse that the following events almost made him relieve himself in his britches.

The man in the corner woke up with a sudden gasp. The jarring sound caused everyone in the cell to cry out. Stringbean jumped behind Pimbo, who was not even half his height. The filthy man in the corner leapt upright from his mat, shirtless and gasping for air.

"Matty! You're alive!" Pimbo exclaimed. The man ignored him, instead, panting and clutching his chest.

"What's happening out there?" Stringbean asked, emerging from behind Pimbo. The large blonde Elf pressed his ears to the cell wall in an attempt to listen.

"It's a winged monster. An ancient Wyvern!" It was the unhygienic man in the corner. He wrapped himself in a ball and began rocking back and forth.

"I've seen one before. Sacked the Duke's stronghold in the north. Turned buildings into rubble and men into popsicles. He's come back to finish me off!"

"Finish you off? What's so special about you?" Lyra asked.

"I was there delivering wine to the Duke when the beast last attacked." The man snapped back, wiping a streak of grime from his forehead. "I only survived by hiding in a toilet in the castle privy. I figured it would mask my scent. The southern wall collapsed, and the privy went with it. I fell right through to the courtyard where I crawled my way through the battle. The Duke's soldiers were being eaten by all sorts of beastly animals. I covered myself in mud and ran my way to Oar's Rest. That's when I got picked up by Black Eyes Barnett, and now, the beast has come back to track me down. No one survives its dreaded hunt! We're doomed!"

"Why did you cover yourself in mud?" Pimbo asked, giving a look of amusement to Stringbean.

"*That's* what you got out of his story?" Theryn replied before scratching his head in thought. "Wait... why *did* you cover yourself in mud?"

They were interrupted by the Wyvern's shrieking, which continued growing louder outside. Theryn could tell it was hovering over the docks now. The urgency of the situation just now set in for him.

Lyra began focusing on the bars again while Pimbo and Stringbean set themselves to screaming for someone in the crew to come down.

It was sensory overload. What could he do? Theryn was helpless, nothing he could do would help them out of this situation. If the monster landed on the ship, it would surely sink, and they would drown in their prison.

Theryn felt his anxiety wash away. His mind flooded with… determination? Vibrating waves of pearly light rippled in his mind. This pulse was different, more determined, matched equally by the energy of something that meant a great deal to him for some reason. An unexplained bond.

Slip poked his head through the lower deck staircase.

"Slip!" Theryn called. "Down here!"

The white otter scurried down the steps and slipped inside the cage. Theryn couldn't explain it, but he felt an urge to grab the creature in an embrace. Slip hopped into Theryn's grasp and stuck out his tongue. Laying across it was an old metal key. Slip gave him a look, and Theryn felt he could understand what it meant.

Take it, you do not want to know what I had to do to get this thing.

Theryn plucked the wet key from the otter's mouth and waved it in the air. Lyra had stopped focusing on the bars and instead stood slack-jawed, facing them.

"Things are happening faster than I can comprehend. I'm just going to ignore the fact that the giant rat we met a day ago is now so loyal to you that it will break us out of prison." Lyra grabbed the key and jammed it into the padlock. It clicked, and the metal doors swung open.

"Right on, kid. Remind me we gotta get ourselves a pet with hands one day, Stringbean, could be useful." Pimbo put his hands in his pocket and began to stroll out of the cell.

"No use running!" Matty called from the corner. "The beast will gobble you up as soon as you go above deck. It's safer down here."

That was a risk Theryn had to take. He was not about to sit in this cell and drown. Plus, he had Slip now, and because of that, Theryn even felt a bit brave. There was a creaking of stairs, and the highwayman appeared at the entryway step. His hawkish face was covered in scratches, and he had a bite mark on his neck. He did not look pleased. The bandit seethed, drawing his blade and proffering it at Theryn and Slip.

"Where is that weasel? I'll have your pet's head for a trophy, Elf-scum!"

Slip gave Theryn a guilty glance.

Tate the highwayman lunged forward, blade outstretched. A crate launched through the air and slammed into Tate. Pimbo was on him in a moment, biting and clawing with his pointed teeth and sharp nails. Stringbean sent another crate hurtling through the air, this time striking Pimbo as well and sending them sprawling back aside the stairway.

"Careful, you big oaf! Aim for the ugly one, not me!" Pimbo called as he readied himself to continue grappling with the highwayman. "We can handle this one. Get out of here, meet at the safe house! Remember, Ma's famous fish-eye stew!" The slightly gray skinned Quarter-Elf dove forward. Theryn didn't have time to see what happened next, instead, Lyra grabbed him, and they rushed up the stairs.

The scene above deck was pure chaos. The beast was on the other end of the dock, and he was covering a ship in jagged shards of frost. Theryn froze up, terrified and unable to move. Slip beat at his shoulder where he clung, as if to urge him to keep moving. A rhythmic pulse like a low heartbeat vibrated off the beast... It was coming for him.

"Theryn, the bridge, we have to get off this boat!" Lyra yelled with desperation.

The winged monster turned in their direction. An idea popped into Theryn's mind. He was unsure of where it originated from, but it was his only option.

Theryn wasted no more time.

He ran and dove overboard, splashing into the briny sea. The cold water knocked the breath from him. His eyes burned as he tried to open them to see where he was going. All around him splinters of wood and metal fell slowly into the deep waters. A blur like a graceful white arrow appeared in the water next to him. Slip circled him and shot off towards the shoreline.

Theryn followed.

Lyra hadn't.

He didn't see her anywhere, so he came up for air to look for her. Above him, the flapping wings of the Wyvern hovered in place. Those wicked silver eyes stared down at him, unblinking. Emotions slammed into Theryn's mind.

Terror, hopelessness, subservience.

Theryn tried to concentrate. He tried to tell the beast he wished it no harm, that it was an accident that he had connected with it in the first place. At first, he imagined he saw the creature's eyes flinch for a moment. There was a fleeting glimpse of conscience on the serpent's expression.

Then it was gone like sand blowing in the wind. It was like the ideas he was trying to show the beast hit a barrier and bounced off into a bottomless chasm. The Wyvern's mind was working hard to be shut off from him. The monster was in control.

Theryn called out to Slip as the horrible talons of the Wyvern wrapped around him and lifted him out of the water. The otter tried frantically to climb up to him, but the beast was too quick. He was raised higher into the air. Theryn was trapped in a cage of three massive cobalt talons.

"Theryn!" Lyra screamed from above deck. "Theryn! No!"

The wind took away the rest of the noise. Theryn could only watch in horror through tear-streaked eyes as he was lifted from the dock and the ice-covered town. His heart felt like it was going to beat out of his chest and fall to the sea below.

Theryn opened his mind, trying to reconnect with the beast and will it to let him down. An emotion slammed into his mind—despair. Despair that was so tiresome, he just wanted to curl into a ball and sleep. Exhaustion dulled his thoughts to the point where he felt he could barely keep his eyes open. His muscles relaxed and went limp. His eyes became blurry, and his vision went black as sleep took him.

Chapter XII
The Rider

Theryn awoke in a cold sweat. His clothes, still damp, clung to his body. He was in a dimly lit stone room with animal skin rugs littering the ground. A gentle fire blazed in the corner hearth. He was nestled on a wooden frame bed topped with furs. Around him, large banners hung on each of the dark stone walls. Theryn rubbed at his eyes, and as he did, his vision refocused.

The purple crescent moon of Seluna. A blue serpent on a clay-hue mountain. A silver tree topped with clouds.

Theryn sat upright, and to his surprise, seemed to be completely unharmed. Even his previously injured shoulder and ankle barely held any memory of pain or aches. He had fully expected to be ripped to shreds by the beast. It was a nice surprise that he still had his life, let alone all his limbs, fingers, and toes.

Theryn began searching his mind for any sign of Slip or the winged serpent. Breath held, brow furrowed, and fists clenched… When he did this, it seemed to help him tap into his connection with the animals.

Somewhere in the distance, a faint ping impacted and rebounded on an imaginary surface. It was a calming rhythm and felt like home to him. Theryn could tell it was Slip… and it was far. The furthest it had ever been since they bonded. The rhythm was so faint, Theryn thought his mind might have been dreaming it up just to give him hope. A smooth, low voice rocked him from his trance.

"Do not despair, Theryn. You are home. Slip will not be the last creature you bridge your soul to."

Theryn stood up with a start.

Sitting by the fire in an ornate armchair was the hooded figure.

The Rider. How had he not noticed? The dark hood blended perfectly with the purple velvet of his seat. Theryn couldn't explain how he knew this was the Rider… he just sort of felt it from somewhere deep in his mind.

"I apologize for bringing you here in such an uncivilized way. It was distasteful… but I thought it would be the quickest way to get you here to me. To get you where you belong."

The hooded figure rose and removed his cloak. As the man lowered his hood, it revealed a handsome face. Pure silver-streaked alabaster hair. One strand, braided in an ornamental ring, fell to his shoulders. His skin was pale white but had the slight pinkish tint of sun exposure. His black jacket, lined with silver furs, was open, the white shift under revealing a bit of a muscled chest. The Rider had intricate black tattoos up his chest and neck that stopped at his chiseled jawline. His ears were curved to a point. Just like Lyra and Theryn.

"You're… from Lunathal?" Theryn asked carefully.

The Rider smiled and nodded. He pointed at Theryn. His fingers were long and slender, and they were adorned with many gem covered rings. "Winterborn just like you. Born and raised in the Lower District."

Theryn's shock subsided with the realization that this man had attacked him. He hadn't stopped clenching his fists, and now he tensed them further, and his fingernails bit into his palm. To Theryn's surprise, he actually felt angry.

"You attacked us when we fell from Lunathal. You almost killed us!"

The man frowned and cast his gaze back towards the crackling hearth. "Ah yes, again, I apologize. It was dreadful business, and I was trying my best to control the Wyvern. Sometimes the beast's primal instincts overpower even our strong connection."

The Rider was older, but he had an air of youth to him. When the man talked, he spoke with sincerity as far as Theryn could tell. Either that, or he was a better liar than Pimbo when the little man looked at himself in the mirror and came away thinking he was handsome.

"How did you know my name?"

The Rider smiled, and as he did so, Theryn noticed his eyes for the first time. They were the purest icy blue. So frigidly blue, Theryn actually felt a slight chill looking at them. "It was left in the Wyvern's mind when you bridged it. You leave much in another's mind when you link with them. I merely had to unlock it to find out all about you. That is the price we pay when we Soulbridge, we leave imprints of ourselves in others."

"Who are you, and why am I here?"

The man walked over slowly and sat at the edge of the bed.

"I am known by many names, and I understand you have many questions. Unfortunately, there is not enough time for me to answer all of them right now. For the time being, you may simply call me by my given name. Azir. As for why you are here…"

He patted Theryn's blanketed leg, "It will be explained in time."

The Rider, Azir, rose and approached a dining table in the middle of the room. He picked up a piece of green-skinned fruit sitting on a plate. He held out his right hand, and the air around it began to dance. Snowflakes and crystalline ice shards spun together like a tiny contained blizzard in his palm. After only about two blinks of Theryn's eyes, the flakes had formed a small sharp blade of translucent ice. He cut the fruit in half with a quick sideways chop and handed one half to Theryn. He took a bite of his own and tossed the frozen tool to the floor. It shattered and evaporated, as if it never existed in the first place.

A Winterborn who could shape ice?

Theryn shakily set down the fruit… He didn't have much of an appetite right now. This man was clearly very powerful. Theryn became panicked, feeling as if he needed to explain himself to this intimidating man.

"I-I didn't mean to bridge the mind of the Wyvern! I just noticed it hovering over the Astral Palace while I was picking fruit. This is all just a big misunderstanding."

Azir only shook his head at the distraught explanation.

"This is no misunderstanding, Theryn. Being able to bridge the mind of a beast so great... It takes extraordinary skill. It's something only I have been able to do in the past, and we have dozens of students here able to Soulbridge." He took another bite of the fruit and continued, "You have an incredible empathy for other creatures, and I think this fuels your arcana." Azir pointed at himself as he chewed. "You remind me greatly of myself. A young man who knows not his own potential... I want you to come with me, let me show you something."

Azir strode forward out the chamber doors. His words sounded like more of a command than a suggestion, so Theryn followed, all the while searching for any faint sign of Slip in the distance.

They made their way across the corridor towards the courtyard. There were other men and women here. Some stood guard with their warbeasts, while others did menial tasks. One Winterborn woman with no animal was sweeping the corridor lethargically. She had sunken, cloudy eyes that stared blankly into the distance. She swept the same spot on the ground... seemingly without noticing her surroundings. Theryn tried not to stare, but something about her made him feel strange. There was no lucidity in her eyes, and Theryn found it odd that Azir strode by her without even a second glance.

They trudged up a spiraling staircase that led to a moss-covered slate stone parapet. Eventually, they were on the wall of a circular stronghold. Armored animals trained in the courtyard square below, seemingly running through aggressive agility exercises. A cat, easily three times the size of a Lunathal housecat, was jumping through rings and tearing at hay-filled targets. Theryn broke his attention from the strange beasts and combat stances to what Azir had led him to. They stood above the parapet overlooking the vast valley the fortress was nestled on. From here, Theryn could get a scope of his surroundings.

The fortress they stood on was probably double the size of the Academy in Lunathal, and it had high walls and a gate on either side. Azir nudged him with a ringed finger and pointed out into the distant landscape.

"You see that?"

Theryn squinted in the rising sun. He saw groves of fruit-bearing trees growing in lines, small streams coming down from hills. The colors of the vista were extraordinary greens and blues. He could even make out the Old Willow to the east. The landscape was all truly beautiful. All except for one section. In the far northeastern corner, a seeping mass of discoloration had spread into the valley. It looked like a stain of spilled ashy paint on a beautiful landscape canvas. Dead trees lay in its wake, and the plant life in that area had all but shriveled away.

"That salted earth there... That is the Blight that has seeped here from another realm. Nothing can grow on it, and those who go too close fall ill. It is the antithesis of life, Theryn, and it must be dealt with."

Azir turned around and pointed to the south. It was all forest with the occasional bog and swampland.

"The Kings and Lords and Dukes of Evaria caused this issue in their greed for control. You have had almost a week on the surface, tell me… What do you know about the Humans?" Azir asked.

Theryn shrugged, still trying to draw his attention away from the eerily colorless valley. "They didn't talk about them much at the Academy, only that we used to war with them… Oh, and didn't they cause the flooding of the world?"

Azir tensed, rather visibly. He spoke in a cool, almost strangely calm voice, "I see the council continues their propaganda… Well, they are right about one thing, Theryn. Our ancestors did war with them. They are lustful, dangerous people. They would rather squabble for money and power than deal with this imminent threat. I'm sure you have noticed some folk falling sick in Lunathal?"

Theryn nodded.

"This is because the roots of the Old Willow run deep, and the Blight has begun to spread up the tree like an infection."

The Rider stepped away from the wall and clasped his hands behind his back. "The situation is dire. It is why I've had to take matters into my own hands. I've saved Lunathal before, and now I will save the surface."

It all came together in a moment for Theryn. How had he not seen it before? How had he been so blind? He turned, facing Azir, hands pressed against his chest in sudden realization.

"You… you're the Hero? The one who saved Lunathal from countless monsters. Stopped an army of ogres from climbing the tree. Brought back the poor folks gifts from the surface."

Theryn had to stop for a moment and think before blurting out, "But the Hero of Lunathal is always said to have been Summerborn. He would be almost ancient by now."

Azir sighed with a smirk, "The council and Chief Astrologer would like for you to think that, wouldn't they? The truth is, they are intimidated by our kind, Theryn. Their arcana may be powerful in that tree, but us, the Winterborn… we have the whole rest of the world to use our power. As for being ancient, our arcana is stronger down here, and it preserves me, just as it will do for you. I am sure you already noticed how much healthier you feel down here."

Theryn flexed the arm of his injured shoulder. There was almost no pain at this point.

"In Lunathal, Winterborn lives are almost twice as long as a common man of Evaria. Here on the surface, I've already lived two of those Winterborn lifetimes and look… still youthful."

Theryn felt his concentration become submerged in his own racing mind. He gripped the parapet with tense fingers. Everything he had come to believe seemed false… like all the truths of the world were flimsy lies stored in a jug that had now been riddled with holes.

Next to him, Azir continued to survey the colorless land in the horizon.

"I know this is overwhelming, and the answers to your questions will come. But for now just know this…" He placed a strong hand on Theryn's shoulder. "You have been lied to by the council for so long that it will take time for you to come to terms with the real world. The truth is that supplies are limited in Lunathal. The Old Willow cannot support so many Moonfolk. Haven't you ever wondered why the Summerborn live longer? Their arcana preserves them in the safety of the cloud wall. The Winterborn are merely excess to the council. They let us do their labor, and then have us rot in the lowest districts. Here, however, we are all equal." Azir tried to speak with serenity, but Theryn could hear the resentment in the man's voice.

Theryn took a slow deep breath; as if it was going to help with the absorption of the fact that his entire upbringing had been a deception. When the breaths didn't help, he asked the only question that spun wildest in his whirlwind of thoughts.

"Why do you need me?"

Azir turned to face Theryn with those round ice chunks for eyes.

"For one, Theryn, you were able to change yourself and your friend into shadows during your fall. This means you have access to multiple weaves of arcana, much like me. Although, I am not a Shade. It is a very rare trait and will be quite useful in stopping the Blight."

Theryn shook his head, "That wasn't me. That was Lyra. She's the Shade, not me."

"Oh... I see."

Azir was trying to hide his disappointment in hearing this, but Theryn had always been rather empathetic. He heard it instantly, a small seed of doubt that popped out of the ground more noticeable than it had meant to be. Had Theryn once again become completely useless? Theryn searched for the words to say before the seed grew further, but it was Azir who cut in first.

"It is no matter. Your ability to Soulbridge is still instinctually powerful, and you may develop multiple weaves yet. You will stay and become one of my personal Acolytes. I will train you here in the Stronghold in the art of Soulbridging."

Flashes of anxiety hit Theryn like a bent branch to the stomach. He wanted to learn more about his arcana, but he couldn't just abandon Lyra and Slip, and then there was Bub. The poor old man had lost his only family left in Lunathal. It broke Theryn's heart to think about his grandfather up there all alone. He knew the guilt would consume him if he stayed. "I'm sorry Azir, but I need to get back to Lunathal."

The Rider looked at him sternly. The slight silver stubble on his tense jaw relaxed into a frown.

"Theryn, there won't be a Lunathal left to go back to if you do not help me. We need to train you so we can retrieve what we need to close the Rift. The other Acolytes cannot bridge the mind of the Wyvern, and I need you there to control it while I get what we need. I can't keep the Wyvern from going on a killing spree if I am being attacked at every side by my enemies. I need you Theryn."

He wants me to control the mind of a soulless man-eater?

Theryn had to get out of this, but the inflection in Azir's voice was weighted with finality. Azir had already made up his mind, Theryn knew he was simply along for the ride. The sunrise concluded, and warm rays began to wash over them. Below, more Acolytes began to emerge and join in on the training routines.

Azir regarded him again. "Eventually, we need to find your friend as well. She may have the ability to interact with the

Blight. If so, it is possible she could help close the Rift that lets it escape." Azir shook his head as he spoke, as if considering unspoken options only to reject them. "No, no… You must remain here and train. I will send the Wyvern to fetch your friend, unharmed of course."

Theryn gave him an uneasy look. There it was again. That feeling of being trapped. This feeling kept reemerging for Theryn lately, and he was getting rather sick of it.

There was a part of him that relished in the idea of helping. To assist the legendary Hero of Lunathal? To be trained by him? It was something Theryn wouldn't have considered possible in his wildest dreams. To be honest, the Hero was different than he had imagined.

"Why do they weave away our arcana… back home?" Theryn asked. Azir set his lips tight against one another, as if deep in thought, before answering.

"To subjugate us. The ability to weave away another's arcana only comes from possessing a powerful awareness of your own magic. I believe it is their attempt to understand us and keep us weak."

"To understand us?" Theryn asked. He had never considered the Summerborn might be interested in anything the Winterborn could do, other than their ability to perform hard labor.

Azir nodded, "When they weave the arcana from a Winterborn, they are proving they are frightened of what we are capable of. It is a painful and brutal process, as if they are tearing the very soul of a person apart. That is why most don't live through it, and those that do, come back broken shells of their former selves."

The woman sweeping in the hall...

Theryn had seen this a couple times in Lunathal. Beggars in the Lower District who had gone insane and lay in heaps all day. The clarity of their pupils was covered in dullness.

When Azir spoke, he had a seriousness to him, an intensity that made Theryn's stomach feel like it was jelly. The fact that basically everything he had been taught in Lunathal had been a lie didn't aid the situation either. Theryn was almost jealous that Lyra had been homeschooled instead of wasting her time with a formal education.

At the conclusion of their discussion, Azir led him to the once great hall of the Duke that now functioned as the Acolyte's common area. It was already filled with a dozen or so people when they made their entrance. The Acolytes, most of them Moonfolk and some resembling Stringbean, paced about in purple robes and tunics. Stringbean, however, had skin golden and vibrant. These Elves were clearly his kin, yet their skin's luster seemed dull. It was as if their skin was going pale, like the

Winterborn. A few were armored and carried spears and short swords. Two of the unarmed Acolytes approached. They bowed to Azir who smiled at them.

"Please, see that Theryn is given whatever he requires this morning and is brought to my training study later this afternoon." Azir turned to face Theryn. "My lad, put on the robes and get some breakfast. It will be a challenging day. The first always is."

Theryn was led to a corridor by one of the Acolytes. The pale man patted him on the back and smiled. Theryn recognized this man instantly. He was a tailor from the Middle District who had been missing from Lunathal for years. Theryn had seen him on his way to the Academy almost every day of his first three years. Many claimed the tailor had jumped to his death.

"Congratulations," he whispered as they descended the stairs. "Azir has chosen you to be his personal squire. That's a great honor. He rarely trains anyone individually."

Theryn glanced at him, "Weren't you a tailor in Lunathal? I think I remember you. Your name is Orlo."

The balding, bespectacled man nodded, "Yes, that was my former life. Now I am something much greater than a tailor." He held out his hand and his fingertips began to glow a faint sapphire blue. An enormous creature bounded in from the opposite end of the hall. Theryn cowered at the appearance of the predatory animal, his cautious instincts getting the better of him. He relaxed as it began to purr and slink through the tailor's legs. The creature looked like the house cats they had in Lunathal, but this one was huge and adorned with speckled brown fur. The cat's long pointed ears were topped with dark whiskers and it had a shaggy face.

It looked as though it could rip Theryn in half.

The large cat continued to purr softly as the tailor stroked its head. "Now I can summon powerful beasts with a flick of my wrist. Azir saved me. He saved all the Winterborn here. In Lunathal, we would still be rotting away, but here we are free."

The cat set itself down, lifting its leg and licking. "Don't do that in front of guests! I'm sorry, I'm still working on her social awareness."

They reached a storage room where the other Acolyte, a blonde Elf with tan skin, found Theryn his own set of purple and ebony trimmed robes. The Acolytes waited outside while Theryn changed, and when he emerged, they led him back down the way they had come. Orlo leaned in close as they walked, "What did it feel like," the tailor asked in a whisper, "to glimpse the Wyvern's soul?"

Theryn shrugged, trying to figure out a way to spin it without making him sound like a lost child. "I don't really know. It felt unnatural. It felt forced. To be honest, it was an accident."

The man nodded, "Sometimes the bonds feel that way. Other times they feel like they were meant to be. Each animal has a different personality, much like people. For example, myself and my lynx are quite similar. We match in mindset, and so, she is easier for me to command." Orlo adjusted his spectacles, "My wolf, however, has a mind of its own. He barely listens to me, and I have trouble relating my emotions to him. Azir senses this, and he's stopped training me all together, he just puts me in the group exercises now. He's a busy man, so you should be honored you get a private session with him." The tailor looked sad, and Theryn detected the slightest hint of jealousy in his nasally voice.

They took a different way across the lower part of the fortress, this time leading out through the courtyard. Eventually, they reached the common area again on the opposite end of the walled stronghold. The wide double doors were kept open, and inside was a symphony of controlled mayhem. Dozens of Acolytes, all dressed in the same tunics and robes, sat around with their variety of Soulbridge animals. Some read, some played cards, some talked while others prepared food. A few brushed their animals, and others snoozed alongside their furry partners in their bunks.

The tailor began to identify the assortment of creatures that littered the hall. Theryn was grateful, for he had never seen almost any of these animals before.

One woman lay outstretched on top of an animal called a bear in the center of the room. One of the golden-haired Sun Elves next to the doorway was fitting crudely shaped metal armor onto a creature called a boar. Opposite the doorway, a man was chopping vegetables for a stew. He worked his knife with deftness while he ordered a nearby monkey to stir. The small brown primate added a pinch of spice with a smile and looked at the cook who nodded in approval. Most of them were Moonfolk. The rest were the same kind of golden-skinned folk that Stringbean had been. The Moonfolk here were all Winterborn, with pallid skin and light blue or silvery lilac hair. Theryn even recognized some. There was a beggar who he had given amber chips to on occasion, there was even a mossweaving girl who he had gone to Academy with. All had been thought to have fallen to their deaths, yet here they were.

"Theryn?"

That voice.

He hadn't heard that voice since he was a small child.

Theryn whirled around.

A dark-haired man stood outside the common room threshold just behind them. On his shoulder perched a large white-headed bird. The man had pale skin and gentle brown eyes. He was missing his right arm at the elbow. His cheekbones were high, and he had a round face with faint wrinkles around his cheeks. His nose was small and pointed, like Bub's, and his hair was a lustrous onyx. Like… like his.

"*Seluna Above…* Theryn, is that you?"

After thirteen years, Theryn was standing face to face with someone he thought he would never see again in his whole life. He was staring into the eyes of his father.

Chapter XIII
Ma's Famous Fish-eye stew

Lyra stood on the bow of the Hyena frozen in shock. She hadn't wanted to jump in, they would be sitting ducks in the water, but Theryn and Slip had slid overboard like yams rolling down a hill.

Lyra watched helplessly as Theryn was lifted into the sky by the monstrous talons of the winged serpent. Lyra screamed after him, but her words were swallowed by the vacuum of sound that surrounded her.

"And where do you think you're going, miss Elf?" Black Eyes Barnett stood behind her, curved cutlass brandished in his hand. Next to him stood the woman with almond-shaped eyes. She had jewelry in her ears and golden loops pierced through her eyebrows and nose.

"Maybe she called in the Wyvern to save her friend?" The brigand woman said, brandishing her own curved sword.

"Not a chance," the old captain snapped. "That creature attacks at random, she's just trying to escape with the rest of them. I won't be having all of my bounty slip from my fingers!" Black Eyes charged in an attempt to grapple her. Lyra braced herself and caught his outstretched hands in her own. He wrestled her for a moment, trying to throw her down. The black-eyed captain was old, but he was strong, and she would surely be forced into submission if she didn't do something quickly. Lyra tried to steady herself against Barnett, but the man was sent toppling to the ground as a flying figure hurtled into him. The figure was Tate, the highwayman, who had been thrown across the deck. Tate slammed into his captain, and the pair groaned on the ground in front of Lyra. Behind them, Stringbean brushed off his hands and smiled, Pimbo at his side. The brigand woman scowled and dove at Pimbo. The small man picked up a discarded barrel cap and began to deflect her blows. "Jump, kid!" Pimbo yelled. "Remember, the safe house and the code words!"

Tate and his captain had roused and readied themselves to strike at Lyra. They lifted their swords over their heads and charged. Lyra turned to face the sea. She wasn't about to stick around to find out what happened next. She was running out of options, which were to either receive the pointy end of a sword or get a bit wet. She puffed up her cheeks, plugged her nose, and plunged into the churning sea.

It was frigid cold, like a *'sitting under the little waterfall that fell from the Middle District when it rained'* kind of cold. All around her, debris from other ships floated and sank to the depths. She swam with all her might towards the light of shore, but she was unpracticed. To make matters worse, something tugged at her leg. Bubbles surrounded her face as she screamed. The bruised and battered face of the ugly highwayman was behind her, and he had a strong grip on her leg. She tried to kick, but he just held tighter, trying his best to get his arm around her waist.

They were sinking fast. Lyra was running out of breath. Her heart began to pound, and she kicked harder. The man only held on tighter. They were both going to drown because Tate was making a better anchor than he probably had meant to.

Lyra turned towards the sunlit surface. It was getting further and further away. She was being dragged down, and if breath didn't come soon, she would surely suffocate. In a last frantic effort, she extended her hands towards the surface. Lyra concentrated and tensed her muscles. She felt her fingers go… warm? The water seemed to rip in front of her as a thin line of dark purple energy emerged from her fingers.

The overwhelming sensation of becoming vapor engulfed her. Lyra's shadowing form was being sucked through a thin line and out another. There was a moment of dizziness, and then a return of the sea's water pressure. She was swimming in line with where she had been a moment ago but was about two meters closer to the surface now. Somewhere below her in the depths, the dark outline of Tate searched frantically for her.

Lyra crashed through the top of the sea and gasped for air. She was a bit away from the Hyena under an extended dock, and she quickly paddled away, trying her best to stay hidden.

What did I just do?

One moment she was being held by Tate, dragged to the sea floor, the next her whole body had become a malleable mist. She hadn't even had to hold or tense. The next thing she knew, she had been above the water.

Lyra waded past a narrow sea wall that separated a small beach and the docks. She crawled ashore, clinging to the seawall so as not to be seen.

The town around her did not sound like it was the most tranquil of communities at the current moment. Yelling and crying was only overpowered by the groaning and creaking of ships as they battered into each other around the docks. Ahead of her in an alleyway, two men ran carrying their house cats in their arms. Lyra set to quickly wringing out her hair and clothes while she waited for the coast to clear. When it was, she walked briskly from the rocky beach and towards the narrow pathways of the town.

What am I going to do now?

She had been on her own in life before, but never like this. Lyra was in a new place, being hunted by smelly pirates, and her fruit picking partner, who she didn't even really like that much, had just been abducted by an evil serpent thingy. This was a new low, even for her. She looked back at the beach from the side of a building to see if Tate was in pursuit. The ugly highwayman was nowhere to be seen.

Just when she figured things couldn't get any worse, a small white creature washed to shore at her feet. Theryn's water rat scurried over and looked up at her with beady eyes. It rolled over flat on its back and let out a surprisingly human-like sigh. The creature looked tired and defeated but was rolling around as if scratching its back.

"Oh wonderful. In my greatest moment of need the giant albino rat has come to save me. Praise be to Seluna above! She is a wise and powerful Goddess, for my prayers have been answered."

Lyra clasped her hands on her forehead and bowed low in the traditional Lunathal sign of appreciation. When she bent down, she was face to face with Slip. The slender otter narrowed his eyes at her as if to suggest annoyance.

Lyra got up and surveyed her surroundings. The town was a mess and no one seemed to be paying much attention to her. The Wyvern had left, but people ran around screaming like it was still attacking. Possibly because of the noise, and also possibly because her only companion was snotrock-eating vermin, she had a tremendous amount of trouble centering her thoughts. Her head was in a flurry of the past day's events. She had never had so much excitement happen at once, and now, she found herself unable to decide her next steps.

Lyra knew she should look for Theryn, but she didn't know where to begin. The idea of him already being digested by the beast made her stomach turn.

Could she go back to the Crabber and ask for help? Should she head back to the Old Willow trunk and see if she can climb back to Lunathal?

No, those wouldn't work, they were stupid ideas. She had been full of those ever since she had forged her name on that workforce list. How could she have done that? That single idiotic decision had completely ruined her life. Lyra was wallowing in her own despair, pressed against the side of a building and ignoring the prods of the rat at her ankles when it hit her. One idea stuck out in her mind. Oh, it wasn't a good idea. Far from it... It was simply the only idea.

Four words danced in her head.

Ma's... fish... eye... stew.

The mayhem of the Wyvern attack had transformed one section of the town into splinters and the other half into a barren winter-covered disaster. Favorably for Lyra, most folks had abandoned what they were doing and ran for their lives. The streets near the docks were almost totally empty. She found a piece of cloth on the ground to tie around her head like the female brigand had done. It covered her hair and ears except for a few loose curls that popped out in the back. A wooden rack of clothing had spilled onto the floor outside a shop, and she sighted a white linen undershirt, a dark blue sleeveless button-down vest, and long, black cloth leggings, which she traded for her wet Lunathal clothes. Lyra even found a black scarf to cover her neck and some gloves to cover her hands. All in all, it was a pretty good disguise. The sunkissed people of the surface might look at her and only think, o*h there goes that girl that never leaves her house*, which she decided was much better than, *oh there goes that girl who lives in a tree and uses outlawed arcana.*

It dawned on Lyra that only one glaringly obvious oddity remained.

Slip padded along behind her, still dripping wet.

I can't exactly go incognito with a big white noodle following me around.

Lyra found herself a nicely spun satchel outside a crumbled merchant's bazaar and slung it around her shoulder so the pack rested on her hip. "Ok, climb in, can't have you out here clear as day. You're a dead giveaway for pirates, slavers, and flying monsters."

The otter looked at her and actually had the audacity to shake his head. Of course Theryn had picked the one animal on the surface that had the nerve to argue with her right now!

Lyra stomped her foot on the alley street, "We don't have time for this, Slip. Do you want to find Theryn or not?"

The otter narrowed his eyes again before reluctantly crawling up her leg and into the satchel. Slip curled himself in a ball becoming mostly concealed inside, only to pop his head out from the top of the bag a moment later.

"When we talk to people, hide," she warned sternly.

The citizens of Oar's Rest began to emerge from their homes as Lyra made her way toward the center of town. Most of the Humans had tanned, dark skin and rounded ears. They were dressed in interesting ways, and they talked with the same accent as the Crabber. One older woman was sweeping some rubble from her doorstep when Lyra approached her. The woman wore a folded cloth over her head concealing her hair and had long wooden earrings. Her clothes were a wrap of dark green, pinned at the shoulder. "Dreadful, just dreadful."

"Excuse me?" Lyra approached trying her best to be timid and unassuming.

"Yes? No no, I won't be needing a ship to get out of here. Oar's Rest is my home, and by the Gods I'll die here. Go try and peddle your ferry service somewhere else," the woman dismissed her and went back to sweeping with an unconcerned wave.

Did she say, "Gods"? Multiple Gods? That's strange…

Lyra scratched her head, "I'm sorry, I am not trying to sell passage or anything like that. I'm actually rather hungry."

The woman looked up.

Lyra continued, "You wouldn't happen to know where I could get some… *fish… eye… stew?*"

Lyra winked with each of the final three words. The woman's expression warped into one of utter confusion.

"I'm sorry love, but I've got no time for youngin' slang, and I can't cook to save my life. You will have to find lunch somewhere else."

Lyra kept walking, scratching her head in confusion. Hadn't Pimbo said his Ma's fish-eye stew was famous? Lyra thought saying the name was all she had to do, and anyone in Oar's Rest would parade her right to the safehouse. Perhaps she pronounced it wrong? Pimbo had been strange, that was for sure, but he had insisted he could offer her help, and right now, it was the only lead she had.

Lyra tried asking a few more people, but it yielded the same results. She rounded a corner, thinking to try the outskirts of town when there was a tap on her shoulder. Lyra whirled around, fists ready to strike at Tate's jaw. There was no ugly man; instead, in front of her stood a little girl. Her height came up to just a bit past Lyra's belly button. She had faintly purple tinted skin with a dewy complexion. The girl had a long nose and a long chin that looked a bit familiar. Her dyed hair was braided in alternating colors of gold and blue, which she had to admit, looked pretty cool. Her own hair wasn't long enough to pull something like that off. The small girl wore clothes similar to the ones Lyra had found.

"You say you're looking for some fish-eye stew?" the girl said with a voice that was surprisingly mature in tonality. She leaned in close. Now that they were close, Lyra could see clearly from the faint crow's feet around her eyes that this was not a girl, but in fact a grown woman. "Perhaps you want to try my Ma's famous… *fish… eye… stew?"*

With the last words, she winked three times. Lyra expelled air loudly from her mouth in a huff of relief.

"Do you know Pimbo?" Lyra started, but the woman held a finger to her mouth.

"Shhh! Are you trying to give away the operation, kid? Right this way, but don't follow too closely."

The woman began to walk hurriedly down the cobblestone streets. Slip poked his head out, his little black eyes blinking rapidly. "Get back in there," Lyra scolded as she stuffed his fuzzy head back in the satchel. She took off down the street after the short woman.

Eventually, they descended some wooden steps to the lower sewers under the shoreside town. They reached a narrow alleyway that, judging by the smell, seemed to connect the sewers under the town to the sea. At the end of the alley, there was a stone door with a small mail slot inlaid in the building's wall. The short woman tapped on it three times. She looked all around them in the alley before speaking into the mail slot, "We need some… *fish-eye stew*."

There was a momentary pause and the door grinded open. Behind it stood Stringbean, the pointy-eared oaf with the bowl cut hair. He was soaking wet, and his face boasted a ripe black eye.

"You came!" he said, smiling stupidly and ushering them inside.

Lyra had found mostly everything so far on the surface to be quite unusual. Being confined to a city in a tree your whole life did something to your expectations. She found herself to be surprised and shocked by most of her encounters on the surface, and because of that, she just expected everything to be mind-shattering to her by now. With the amazing landscapes, forests, rivers, and seas she had encountered thus far, she expected to be dazzled by pretty much everything she saw. The hideout, however, was sorely underwhelming. She tried to hide her visible disgust as Stringbean led them into the more than humble abode.

They were in what looked to be a cellar, surrounded by dimly lit lanterns and old wooden furniture. The humid air smelled of sea water and rancid fish. It was dark, with the only window being on the opposite end next to some straw bunks. The fattest woman Lyra had ever seen was furiously stirring a cauldron half the size of her. The fat woman was short, like a lumpy ball, and had a similar skin tone to Pimbo; however, the obese woman quite obviously had been around for much longer. She was completely bald and had applied an offensively bright red lipstick on her mouth.

"Helfi, you are back so late, you scared me half to death! I heard some shouting through the pipes, what's going on up there?" The fat woman regarded Lyra, her eyes shone wide like two large chunks of polished amber. "Oh dear… look at how skinny this one is. Don't worry, I'll fatten you right up with some homemade stew… Pimbo! Your sister is home!" she called out in a gravelly voice.

"I'm coming, Ma, I'm coming!" Pimbo appeared around the corner. He was still dripping and was toweling himself off. Pimbo was wearing Black Eye Barnett's wide brimmed hat, and his pouch clanged with coins as he entered. He tossed the damp towel to Stringbean and held up his hands as if to greet Lyra. "Whoa, you actually came! Pretty narrow escape, eh? I see you met my sister, Helfi. Count your coins carefully around that one, she's got slippery fingers!"

Helfi, who was now leaning back in a chair picking dirt out of her fingernails with a dagger, gave her a smirk.

Lyra shrugged, "Haven't got any money on me to count anyway. Thanks for taking me in." She cast her gaze down at her satchel where Slip was cradled. "I didn't know what else to do. The winged beast took Theryn."

Pimbo set down his hat revealing his shiny bald head."I know, kid. I'm sorry to have seen it with my own eyes. I've heard tales of that flying beast tearing up a few towns and turning some folks into its lunch, but I ain't ever heard of it carrying off a fella. It's probably long gone by now, but who's to say he's being digested right now? Maybe the lad pulled through!"

Lyra's stomach turned, nauseated. She was glad it was empty, or she may have wretched just at the thought of Theryn being mashed by those fangs. She hadn't particularly gotten along with Theryn, but that didn't mean she wanted anything bad to happen to him. He was overly optimistic, and although it had been annoying at first, he was starting to grow on her. Just in time for him to be swept away by a giant flying hellbeast.

Helfi pulled over a chair and offered it to Lyra before sitting down across from her. "How did you escape old Black Eyes Barnett?"

She had directed the inquiry at her brother. He took a seat, kicked up his feet, and crossed his arms smugly.

"Oh, just the usual tactic. Utilizing my incredible charm and Stringbean's unusual strength. Plus, Stringbean tossed a couple of well aimed crates. We were able to subdue the pirates and make our escape." He pointed to the hat on the table. "As an added bonus, I got a new hat. Barnett's own, and he won't be happy about that. He'll be out there looking for the Gnome who took it!"

"Gnome?" Lyra questioned. "What's a Gnome?"

"It's us, skinny!" Helfi said, "It's what happens when Half-Men and Half-Elves have kids. They make this handsome group." She smiled and waved to herself and Pimbo. Their extremely rotund mother began to spoon out ladles of stew into bowls and pass them around. She hobbled over to Lyra and set down her own steaming bowl. "Eat up, child. Any skinnier and you'll blow away in the wind!"

Slip emerged from the satchel and began to pick at Lyra's bowl. He spooned out a tiny fish with his hands and began to crunch on it loudly.

"Nice pet," Helfi remarked, giving Lyra a strange look before diving into her own stew. "What are you supposed to be anyway? I've never seen an Elf so pale."

Lyra pushed Slip out of the way and took her own sip of stew. She had to admit, despite the stench, it was good. Like, really good.

The bowl was salty… but not too salty. Steamy… but not too steamy. Fishy… but not too fishy. It was good, fresh fishy not old, dead fishy. It was the best bowl of fish stew Lyra ever had. It was also the only bowl of fish stew Lyra had ever had, but that was beside the point.

Slip tried to reach into her bowl again, but Lyra shoved his head back into the satchel and went to work herself on the pieces of fish that bobbed in the stew. "I guess I don't really know what I am. We just call ourselves Moonfolk. I didn't even know I was one of these Elves you keep talking about until everyone down here started calling me one."

Helfi gulped and let out a thoughtful hum. "Usually, Elves look like Stringbean here… and they worship the sun. Like weirdos."

Stringbean probably didn't hear her because he was busy tilting his head backwards with the bowl in his hands and drinking the broth greedily.

"Thanks, Ma," Pimbo said as his mother served him last. He picked up a fish head and popped it into his mouth. After a few more, he continued speaking through mouthfuls of stew. "Well, you may be odd looking, but I'm grateful I met you. If it wasn't for your friend and his pet, me and Stringbean might still be locked up in that crusty ship. For that, we feel indebted to him. Gnomes always pay back what we owe! Ain't that right, Stringbean?"

The tall straw-haired Elf shrugged, "I dunno. I ain't a Gnome, Pimbo."

"Yeah, but you are an honorary one, and being the upstanding, morally righteous citizens that we are, we feel helping your friend is the right thing to do."

"Plus," Helfi added, "that Wyvern is said to have ransacked the Duke's keep and the King's storehouses. He's probably sitting on a pile of coins and jewels so big we'd be able to pave the streets of Oar's Rest with gold!"

"That's right!" Pimbo slammed the table with a fist, causing Stringbean to yelp. "The dirty mat man talked about the Wyvern attacking the Duke's Stronghold. I remember some chatter in the town about the King gathering his men, probably to seize the Stronghold back." He paused as his eyes went wide. "Probably… because that's where the treasure hoard is!"

Helfi pounded her fist against her open palms, biting down on her bottom lip as she smiled. Pimbo shook his head with a wide, mischievous grin. "So as you can see, kid, it's in our best interests to help you out. You got a smart little creature here that would make thieving easy. He can slip and slide in and out and tell us if the coast is clear. Stringbean can handle any lone guards we encounter, Helfi can pick the locks, and you can get us out of there, especially if you can do that little shadow thing you did when you puffed through the water." Lyra gave him an innocent look. Pimbo only smiled, his teeth like an uneven row of daggers in varying colors. "Yeah, don't act so surprised, skinny. I know magic when I see it."

Lyra winced, she had blown her cover. They had seen her escape the highwayman in the water, and now they would surely want to use her. The only problem was, she wasn't sure if she could do any of that again.

"I heard of people like that, they can be in one place and then *blink, blam, bloomy*, they are in another place," Helfi added.

They wanted her to do it again. Lyra wanted to shrink away from sight. Suddenly, she was envious of Slip who got to hide in the satchel and avoid everyone's gaze.

"Pimbo, you promised you would fix the dinghy for your father. The holes are getting worse, and he can barely go fishing in it anymore!" Pimbo's mother called from the kitchenette.

"Don't interrupt company meetings, Ma! When we are done with this job, I'll be able to buy Father a whole stinkin' yacht!"

The stubby Gnome slurped down the last drops of his stew, retreated down the hall, and then returned with a pointed piece of charcoal and a blank piece of thin parchment. "Let's outline the plan."

Helfi chimed in right away, as if this was the usual routine for their ludicrous aspirations. "I've been hearing talk from the sailors at the docks that no one will sail past the Stronghold. They say it's too dangerous and this has to be why. The beast probably took it over and ate all the King's men and the Duke himself. If he's got treasure, that's where it will be."

"Ok," Pimbo began to write. "Infiltrate the Stronghold, locate the treasure."

"And Theryn?" Lyra added annoyedly.

"Right, right, and Theryn, but that goes without saying. The hoard is just a little extra bonus. We will need a cart or something and disguises. Also a reason a motley group like us would be heading to a place even sailors are avoiding." His fingers tapped the table rhythmically as he bit the edge of the charcoal in thought.

"We could be wine merchants, delivering wine to the Duke? Fancy folks love to drink," Stringbean offered.

"No, that's too suspicious and would attract attention. Plus, we don't have any cart or wine to complete the disguise." Pimbo tapped the charcoal against his forehead, leaving black powder residue on his lavender-gray skin. "What about wandering musicians? No one will think twice to search us, and it may be easy to find some instruments and musician's garb."

"I can play the wooden flute," Lyra added.

"That's great! If anyone asks for a song, we will just clap along to you. Stringbean hasn't got rhythm to save his life, and the last time Helfi sang, all our glassware shattered."

Helfi shot him an irritated look.

Pimbo seemed satisfied with the idea because he began scribbling lists of things they would need. Fatigue hit Lyra as they planned. It must have been late into the night by now. She let out a yawn hoping they would get the hint. The group only continued on, Pimbo was like a rambling songbird who couldn't get enough of his own chirps.

"So, we pretend to be musicians, we camp out in the forest outside the Stronghold, and send in the otter to do some scouting."

He wrote on the parchment.

Otter scouts. Locates treasure… and Theryn. Lyra infiltrates.

"Once we've found what we're looking for, Helfi will lead us in, and Stringbean and I will deal with any guards we run into." Stringbean cracked his knuckles with his usual dopey smile. Pimbo continued to scribble away at the parchment. "Once we are inside, Helfi can pick the locks to Theryn's cell or any chests we find. Then Lyra can use her magic to get us out of there with Theryn and the gold in tow. If anything goes wrong, we just say we are wandering minstrels, there to perform music for the lords and ladies of the fortress. It's a foolproof plan!"

"And what about the giant flying man-eater?" Helfi asked.

"Oh, Lyra will get us out of there with her smoky hands. Wyverns can't eat what they can't see!" Pimbo finished his scribbling and sat back looking satisfied.

Lyra wasn't convinced by this group or the plan. Something inside her suggested that if they had been quality thieves and tricksters, they wouldn't still be living with their mother in some sewer.

Lyra swallowed her last spoon of stew and shook her head at the parchment. "I'm not sure I can do that again. It was a one time thing, and I can't control my arcana so well."

The words didn't seem to discourage Pimbo, he just smiled and waved at her dismissively. "You'll be fine, kid, and you will have plenty of practice before then if we get found out by old Black Eyes. We will have to deal with that when it comes. Not sure we can take the old rapscallion in a fight, especially if he's got that brigand, Aranna with him. She's supposed to be one of the best sword fighters in the south of Tellis. Yup, if he has his crew with him, we'll just have to do what we're best at, which is… run."

The group placed their bowls in the ceramic sink basin and readied themselves for bed. Pimbo offered to lead her to the bunks. "Not much we can do tonight, Lyra. If Theryn is still out there, he will have to wait for morning."

"Fix that dinghy before you leave tomorrow, Pimbo!" his portly mother called.

"Ma! I don't have time. We have an important business trip to go on tomorrow."

"You promised your Father, young man! Helfi needs to run to the store for me before you go anyway."

Helfi let out a groan.

"We don't have time for any of that, Ma!" Pimbo argued.

"You will make time for your dear old mother! I'll pack you all lunch for tomorrow. How's fried fish wraps?"

Stringbean rubbed his belly and nodded happily.

"Fried fish wraps it is, then. I'm off to bed, you kids be careful tomorrow, and Pimbo, be a good boy and make sure the dinghy is fully patched up!"

"I'm forty-three years old, Ma," Pimbo grumbled under his breath. "Come on Lyra, I'll show you to the guest bunk."

Lyra took the bunk below Stringbean's, who, despite his size, had insisted on getting the top bunk. The faint smell of sewer was masked by the aroma of fish and spices that wafted in the air. Slip curled up in a ball beside her and was snoring softly. Lyra pulled the cotton covers over her and held her hand out in front of her face in the darkness.

She searched for that blank canvas in her mind, eager to make sure she could still find it.

Lyra felt it. Calm, cool serenity washed over her before the canvas began to flood with visions of her mother.

Beautiful and gentle, but also wickedly funny. Her infectious laugh… then her skin going that sickly green… her cough worsening… her breathing becoming more labored… their stock of the crushed up herbal medicine running out.

Lyra was biting her lip, eyes closed tight and tense. She tried to push the thoughts away.

The canvas needs to be blank. Why wasn't it going blank?

A flash of her cousin. One moment a strong and lean man, the next reduced to a sickly heap in a bed… his last gasping breaths as the sickness finally took him.

She bit down further, she could taste the blood in her mouth.

A flash of her father. Just a faint memory of him through her crib… his eyes red with fatigue… he had long black veins that wove through his skin like a spider's webbing. He tried to smile at her, but he was too weak, the life slowly draining from him before her very eyes.

Anger and sadness overwhelmed her mind, and with it, her fingers began to burn white hot. She furrowed her brow and bit down even harder. She let out a muffled scream through clenched teeth. Lyra could feel the power course through her veins. Her hands began to vibrate with a warm purple glow. She felt a hot tear roll down her cheek.

The world around her faded into that endless dark void and suddenly she was no longer in her bunk. She was standing on the edge of an abyss. A solitary pit with only a thin layer of obsidian sea below her. There was no color, or sound, or even smell. A thought entered her mind, placed there by someone else. A voice she had never heard before.

Are you enjoying my gift?

Like the snuffing of a candle, Lyra felt herself turn to vapor. In a moment, she rematerialized in the air. She was back in the bedroom and as her form reshaped, so did its sense of gravity. She fell uncomfortably onto something.

"Ow... Uh, occupied?" Lyra grasped her aching head and scooted her body over. She was on top of a confused looking Stringbean. "How did you get up here?"

Lyra looked around, feeling just as startled as he was. Hadn't she just been on the bottom bunk a moment ago?

"Sorry Stringbean, I was looking for my pouch and thought I left it up here."

Lyra scooted over and climbed down the ladder to the bottom bunk.

"Yeah, yeah, I know what you were doing. But I already called the top bunk," the big Elf grumbled and rolled over on his side.

Lyra settled back into her bed, her temples still pounding from the strain of focusing so hard. She wiped away the blood from her lip and drew the covers over herself once again. This time, she tried not to think about her mother. Instead, her mind seemed to wander to Theryn. That look on his face as he was lifted away was familiar to her. He had looked much like she had when she had found out her mother was sick. It was the look of someone who had something terrible happening to them but understanding that the worst was yet to come.

Lyra wished she could help him right now, if he was even still alive.

He had to be, she needed to hold out hope. She had to help him so that maybe, just maybe, there was a chance he could convince some giant bird or something to fly them back to Lunathal. Then Lyra would bring her mom to the surface and search all of Tellis for a cure.

It was a long-shot plan, but she didn't have any other choices and that last shred of hope filled her with determination. It was enough to keep going, she wouldn't give up yet.

Chapter XIV
The Acolyte

T heryn had so many questions. He was slack-jawed and stuttering. Eventually he was able to stammer out a single word.

"Dad?"

"Seluna Above, it *is* you. It's like looking in a mirror at myself forty years ago. Come here!"

His father embraced him, holding him tight. Theryn couldn't control himself, his face turned hot, and his eyes began to water. He was hugging a person he never thought he would see again for the rest of his life. This person was virtually a stranger to him, someone who had been ripped from his life when he was only seven years old. Yet, Theryn held on, clung for dear life in that hug; afraid if he let go, the man would vanish like some arcane illusion. "I tried every day to get back to you, I swear I did," his father whispered into his ear, voice tight. They released one another, and the stranger held Theryn at arm's length, one hand on each shoulder and looking him up and down. "Bub made good on his promise to keep you safe from the council, bless that man. Seems he did well with you, you are a grown man now. How is he? He must be ancient for a Winterborn."

"He's fine," was all Theryn could sputter, still unbelieving that one of his parents stood in front of him.

His father looked relieved, followed by a wave of sadness. "I'm glad… If only your mother was here to see you. She tried every day to get back to you in Lunathal, Theryn. The whole reason we have been here with Azir is so we could find a way to get back to you."

Theryn's head was swimming. After a few more moments of shock, he was finally able to form an understandable question.

"Where is she?"

He longed to see her face… needed to see it.

Theryn's father gave him a regretful look. "Oh Theryn, I'm sorry, lad." He cast his eyes downward. "When we helped Azir take this fortress, the Duke's men trapped us in the courtyard. She didn't make it. I tried to save her. I tried to be the one who was taken, but I paid my own price, albeit, a smaller price." He held up his stub arm, which still held some faint scabbing at the mark of the cut.

This should have shocked Theryn, but until two moments ago, he had thought it was impossible to see either of his parents again. His face remained blank as he stared at his father's dark eyes. It was like his mind couldn't decide what emotion to feel. Theryn finally settled on a sharp sting of sadness that was soon overpowered with a feverish bitterness.

"How could you do this? You jumped from Lunathal and left me alone! You mean to tell me you've been down here fighting wars and playing with animals?" Theryn pulled out of his father's grip. The man's face was dark with guilt, the harsh words had found their mark.

The bitterness swirled away, replaced by remorse. Theryn felt volatile, dizzy, and more than a little betrayed. One moment he was seething, the next incredibly sad. Tears began to streak down his eyes. "I needed you! You abandoned me, and I needed you both."

His father held him again. This time gently. His voice was choked as he spoke. "Theryn, we tried new ways every day to get to you. The council doesn't want contact with the surface. Lunathal is an impenetrable fortress. Azir is the only one who promised us we could change things. He promised us if we helped him, he would lead us back home. Back to you."

His father held him out again, this time, locking his brown eyes on Theryn. The eagle on his shoulder had taken off as they embraced, now re-landing with a squawk. "We were watching over you in ways you didn't know, Theryn. The Evarians had a power relic that threatened Lunathal, and we reclaimed it. When Azir is able to breach the cloud wall of Lunathal fully, and we are able to bring down the enchantment that protects it, everyone in that place will be free. It's why your mother was willing to die for him. He was going to lead us to you!" A crowd had gathered around them now. Acolytes, most of them Moonfolk, looked at him solemnly. Their Soulbridge animals of different varieties sat or perched around them.

Theryn tried to speak softly for the sake of privacy. "You jumped. Everyone told me you had gone crazy."

Theryn's father shook his head. "It's not true, Theryn. Sit, I can explain everything." He led Theryn to a finely carved wooden chair with a comfortable cushion at the back. The other Acolytes made space and dispersed as his father shooed them away. The man took a seat next to him and grabbed Theryn's hand as he recounted his past.

"Strange things started happening in the Rookery around the time we left. Your mother's arcana was beginning to emerge, and she had forged a simple Soulbridge with one of the rooks. The bird sent her visions of things it had seen… a man riding a beast in the clouds, watching, searching for Winterborn with arcana. We sent messages with the rook. Each evening, we tucked you into bed and stole out in the night to find answers to the mystery of what was happening to your mother."

He squeezed Theryn's hand tighter as he continued.

"The rook told us that the man wanted us to follow him. He could offer us a better life on the surface. We agreed to go back and get you and Bub."

What was his father talking about? Their life in Lunathal hadn't been glamorous, but they certainly had it better than most. Sure, the Winterborn were treated poorly, but Theryn had access to food and an education there.

The man's face dropped slightly as he recalled the next part of his story. "We had it all planned, and the day came when we were going to leave. Bub wouldn't go… he said it was too dangerous, but we convinced him to let us take you after the day's work. That's when we got word that a group of council members were headed towards the Middle District. They had seen us, Theryn, in the night. They knew about the beast in the clouds, and they knew it was trying to convince people to leave. We ran back from the Rookery, but they were on us. They were going to weave away her arcana, son. We would have let them do it, if it meant we could stay with you... The only problem was most people do not live after the weaving process. Azir says they are afraid of folk who can Soulbridge. Like being a Shade, it's viewed as too dangerous to keep in Lunathal."

"And do you know why that is?"

A stern voice sounded in the double door threshold of the common area. The crowd of eavesdropping Acolytes held their heads down as Azir entered the room, his long black coat swaying behind him. Theryn thought at that moment he looked like a figure from folklore. Regal, yet brutal. Delicate hands glistened with jewels, while his muscled chest was laden with tribal looking brands.

"It is because the Summerborn love to keep the lower class of Lunathal subjugated. They weave away Winterborn magics, and they take with them the potential of any resistance."

Azir's slow footfalls clicked through the crowd as he drew near to Theryn and his father. "The idea of a shifting power frightens them. They keep the Winterborn weak, letting them do the hard labor so that the Summerborn may live privileged lives of luxury. They take away our arcana because they are truly afraid of us, Tarvin has seen this firsthand."

Theryn's father nodded in agreement, his watery eyes still locked onto Theryn.

"It's true. We were cornered by them. We had no choice, so we jumped. The rook had promised us we would be saved, and it was right. Azir rescued us. We wanted to go back home and get you, but we didn't want to lead the council back to you and Bub. We knew they wouldn't harm an old man and a young boy. Summerborn killing innocents would cause an uprising, and the council hates instability… so we just left. When we crossed the cloud sea, we had no idea we wouldn't be able to get back to you. I'm so sorry, Theryn… for everything."

His father, still squeezing his hand, broke down. Having only one arm, he released Theryn's grip to wipe away the tears that streamed down his pale cheeks. Theryn felt sympathetic but also a bit uncomfortable. He still felt like he barely knew this man who had bore his soul to him. Theryn looked to Azir who gave them a pitying smile.

"I hate to interrupt this reunion, Tarvin, but I need your son. His first lesson must begin now. It is most urgent."

Theryn's father nodded, continuing to dab at his cheeks. "Do as he says, Theryn, he will teach you things you didn't think would be possible." Tarvin gave his son a final pat on the back. "I'll see you for dinner tonight, lad. We will catch up on everything."

Theryn was so swallowed by numbness at the exchange that he just let his body lead him. It was as if he was watching himself move from a distance, not totally in control of what he was doing. Azir led him down a long, stone hall. He was too stunned to speak, he simply let himself be led because it seemed the only thing to do. He had been given his father back and had his mother taken away from him again all in the short span of a few heartbeats. Currently, he was a visitor in his own body merely watching things happen. He thought about how simple it would be to just slide into a river and splash around. The small sliver of Slip inside him comforted him. Life was simpler when he thought like Slip.

They entered a wide room that resembled a study. Bookshelves lined the walls, and tables holding maps, globes, scrolls, and figurines were scattered around in cluttered heaps. The center of the room had been cleared out with only a single metal platform. On the platform sat a solitary gem of swirling whites and purples. It was perfectly round in shape and fist-sized. Azir led him up to the gem. It had a glow orbiting its spherical shape like the rings around some distant planet. Looking at it felt like looking through one of the Academy telescopes back in Lunathal.

Azir picked it up and held it close to his eyes.

"This, Theryn, is why we took this fortress."

He offered the crystal to Theryn. Theryn took it and noticed it was surprisingly light, almost as if it was made of air. It vibrated slightly in his hand, which made it a bit uncomfortable to hold. The aura of light danced around the gem in his hand. Looking into it was like looking into an animal's eyes, one that was completely accepting of a Soulbridge. Theryn found he didn't want to let it go and gripped it tight.

"This is a meteorite of concentrated arcana, Theryn. It fell from the heavens here much like Seluna's Tear, only long before. It was discovered by our people who tried to use it in their struggles against the Humans. When that proved catastrophic, it was found by the Evarian Royal family who kept it hidden for decades. They studied it, hoping to unlock its power and use it against their enemies."

Theryn tried to listen, but he couldn't shake his gaze from the radiance of the orb. It seemed to beg him to use it, pleading to enter his mind. A chill ran down his hand where he held it and extended all the way to his toes. Theryn visibly shivered as he clutched the strange beacon of light. Azir spoke calmly as if he was blissfully unaware of the temptation Theryn was undergoing.

"The Evarian fools finally did it. The King's magician was tempted by its power. They opened the Rift years ago. A hairline fracture, barely noticeable, now tenses like a cork in a pressurized bottle. It slowly sucks the vibrance from our world, waiting for its chance to pop."

Theryn tried to relax his palm, desperately attempting to give himself a shred of relief from the strain of holding the orb. The luminous sphere seemed to be begging him to explore its full potential.

Just when Theryn could hold back no longer Azir plucked the meteorite from his palm. Instant relief washed over Theryn. Azir placed the orb on its dark metal pedestal and stepped back. Theryn continued to eye the meteorite cautiously. A single question lingered inside him.

"Can it be used to close the Rift?"

Azir shook his head solemnly, those frigid blue eyes unblinking on Theryn. "A great question, Theryn. Unfortunately, the meteorite seems to be more of a one-way path. A key to unlock gateways to other planes of existence seemingly at random."

Hope slipped from Theryn. Why was this thing so important to Azir? Also, if it couldn't stop the Blight, why did his mother have to die for it?

As Theryn turned over the thoughts in his head, he concluded that perhaps this thing was better off in here rather than in the hands of someone who would use it to do more damage.

"However…" Azir began, his voice taking a more motivated tone, "The Summerborn have something in the Astral Palace. Something I believe will be the key to stopping the Blight and closing the Rift. Something that stopped the great floods long ago. If we don't retrieve it, the world could be consumed within the solstice."

Theryn drew his eyes away from the pedestal and shoved his hands in his pockets to try and bring some warmth back to them.

"Why do you need me? What can I possibly do?"

Azir pointed out a long window at the far corner of the study. Outside it, the Wyvern was landing on the parapet with flaps of its slender wings. He hadn't even noticed it draw near, the pulses had been overshadowed by the humming meteorite.

"The rest of the Acolytes here have had to train many solstices to Soulbridge effectively. Your mother was by far the most naturally talented. Perhaps it explains why you were able to pierce the mind of the Wyvern after seemingly no training. In truth Theryn, I believe you have been training your whole life for this. Your connection with animals fuels your arcana."

An Acolyte, the tailor Theryn had recognized, entered the room. Behind him padded the nimble footfalls of a medium sized feral dog. It had a chain harness on its back, which linked to a leash and muzzle around its mouth. Its long, narrow face held wide yellow eyes. It was snarling, completely wild looking, and it was obviously quite scared.

Orlo handed the leash to Azir, bowed low and exited the study.

"Try to create a Soulbridge with this coyote. Your first fully formed Soulbridge is always the strongest, so do not worry if this one does not feel as natural."

Theryn glanced at Azir with unease.

"You now understand how dire our situation is, Theryn. You need to do this."

Azir pointed assertively at the animal. The coyote's fur was a matted gray with streaks of brown and black; it growled behind its muzzle as he approached.

Theryn held out his hand, and the mangy canine readied itself to strike despite its restraints. Theryn locked eyes with the coyote and exhaled slowly. Its large, golden eyes fixed on him. There was a tingling in his hands, a twitching in his mind. Theryn's peripheral vision faded to darkness. Before long, all that stood in front of him was the coyote standing in an endless void.

The creature thrashed for a moment, letting out more muted growls. Theryn could see something above them, the foggy tethers that held their minds together. Spindly tendrils of sapphire mist. They were thin, unstable, and aimlessly floating above them. The feral dog was still resisting him. Theryn tensed and held his hands in front of himself, palms upturned. They glowed faintly with the same blue sparkle as the tendrils. He willed the coyote to trust him, showing the beast he too was afraid. The spindles of light extended out and recoiled against an invisible barrier. The coyote resisted further, and the shock of his thoughts being rejected snapped Theryn back to reality. It felt like someone had hit him in the forehead with a rock. He winced as lantern light flooded the void and returned him to the study.

Theryn fell to his knees and gripped his throbbing head.

"I can't, it's too different. It's not like the rooks and Slip. This creature doesn't want me."

Azir looked at him with a hint of disappointment. Theryn rose, trying to shake off his migraine.

"What the creature wants matters little, Theryn. Sometimes we need to create a Soulbridge for our own survival, and when that time comes, we cannot always rely on their desires."

Azir held up his hands and a blast of sapphire light erupted from them. The coyote let out a whimper and fell to the ground. It strained and thrashed on the stone floor like it was being pushed down by invisible hands.

"Stop! You're hurting it!" Theryn screamed.

Azir continued to focus. The irises and pupils of his eyes had gone completely foggy. The coyote began to calm, its thrashing turned into twitching. There was a sudden sound of escaping air and the coyote lay still. Its chest raised and lowered with calm, deep breaths.

The coyote was asleep.

Azir turned to face him, his eyes returning to their normal lucidity.

"You must remember, Theryn, these are beasts we deal with, some of them mindless killers. Many of them only know their own instinctual hunger. Therefore, for our own safety, we must make it clear that we are the masters and they are the servants. It is a partnership, yes, but there needs to be a clear hierarchy in dominance. Much like the animal kingdom itself, you must show you are the top predator, or you will become the prey of your own partner. Only then will your Soulbridge achieve its true potential."

He handed Theryn the leash. "I want you to continue to practice tonight. It is important that you are able to create a Soulbridge with any animal quickly in case you need one to defend you in battle, or–"

There was an echoing cry from the hall. Shouts and wild shrills of anguish carried through the narrow stone corridors to their ears in the study. Azir's frozen gaze flashed to the doorway.

"Stay here," he commanded. Without hesitation, he sprung down the hall with surprising agility. His fur coat billowed behind him as he exited the room. The chaos of whatever was happening continued to echo throughout the fortress. Theryn eyed the sleeping coyote. The feral canine's ears twitched in its sleep.

Theryn dropped the leash and took off after Azir.

A crowd was formed in the center of the common area. There was shouting and growling. Acolytes clung to their Soulbridge charges, trying to keep them back from the fray. Theryn, being rather short, jumped onto a table for a better vantage point.

In the center was the cook's monkey in the jaws of a wolf. The monkey reached desperately for the cook, who was trying to pull it free. The wolf let go and turned on the cook. It sunk its teeth into his forearm, and the man let out a howl of pain. Orlo was behind the wolf trying desperately to halt its aggression. A flickering glimmer surrounded his hands, but the wolf seemed to ignore it. Instead, the creature turned on the monkey again and bit down on the primate's leg. Theryn watched in horror as the wolf snarled and shook its head, tossing the screaming monkey about like a ragdoll. Theryn's father was there, gripping his eagle's talons. The bird was flapping, trying to pull away from him as if to join the fray.

Orlo let out a pleading cry, "Stop it! Stop it!"

The crowd parted for Azir, who had seemingly been watching from the corner of the room.

He lifted his hands, "Enough!"

Spindles of light appeared from his fingertips. The wolf tossed the wounded monkey away and let out a howl. The wolf was sent flying backward, crashing into the stone wall. It tried to rise. From across the room, Azir forced his hand downward in a jerking motion, fists clenched. The wolf let out a muffled whimper before crunching down to the floor and lying still.

A silence fell over the crowd.

The only noise Theryn could hear was the heavy breathing of the cook, who was grasping his forearm, and the exhausted cries of the monkey.

Azir turned his eyes on the crowd. His face was hardset like iron and his jaw was clenched. Despite this, he spoke with surprising coolness.

"Do you know why you all fail? Do you know why this continues to happen?" Azir paced, meeting the eyes of each terrified Acolyte in the crowd. "It is because you insist on being equals when you create a Soulbridge. This is what happens when you are equals with these beasts." He pointed at the cook, who was lying on the stone floor, his forearm still welling with dark red blood.

"We must be in control," Azir continued. "We must treat these animals like animals, and lead them. If you all stopped feeding into their primal desires and focused on what *you* want from them, things like this would never happen. Imagine the control you could have if you were truly their master. Imagine how many of our brothers and sisters' lives we could have saved when we took this Stronghold."

Azir's eyes fell on Theryn's father. Tarvin was standing there, eyes now downcast, but he raised them to meet the icy stare of Azir. To Theryn's surprise, there was resentment on his father's face.

"Orlo," Azir snapped, turning to face the tailor. "Come to me tonight after you have cleaned up your mess so we may discuss this further."

The tailor's already pale face went even whiter. Theryn could see through the man's spectacles that he was terrified. "Bind his arm, and see to it the wolf is disposed of outside the gates."

Azir departed from the room. As he passed Theryn, he spoke to him in a low commanding tone. "Don't give the coyote a choice, Theryn. You are its master. You have to act like it or others will get hurt."

That night, Theryn's mind swirled with dreams. The coyote's golden eyes watched him, taunted him. The feral canine jumped about in the endless void around him. He tried to control it, but it only continued to mock him. In its jaws was a fuzzy creature, white and lifeless. The black beads of Slip's eyes stared out absently. The coyote bit down harder.

"Slip!" Theryn called out.

A pulse rocked Theryn, like an earthquake in the endless void. The thin layer of black water around him rippled. It piled up, forming a shape. From the dark pooling liquid, the silvery eyes of the Wyvern lit up.

Theryn was jerked awake, dripping with sweat. His Acolyte robes clung to his body, damp and hot. In the hearth alongside him, a gentle fire crackled, offering up its meager light.

Theryn steadied his breath as another pulse shook his mind. This one was not like Slip's. It was not light or rhythmic, it was instead a deep boom.

Theryn drew away the fur blankets and rose from his bed. The boom sounded again, and it echoed in his mind. It was coming from the hallway. He followed the sound with bare feet, walking lightly and carefully. The stone floor was smooth and cold, and it sent a chill up his damp body.

The boom sounded again, this time closer.

Theryn followed the light of the sconces to the courtyard. The vibrating pulses began to quicken with deep echoing thuds, like a heartbeat. Theryn snuck quietly through the courtyard, past an Acolyte and his badger companion who were keeping watch on the wall. The booms were coming from the parapet.

Theryn climbed on his hands and feet up the shrouded stairs. His ears continued to pound as he drew closer. Just when he felt like his head was going to explode, he crested the top step and...

Theryn was face-to-face with the Wyvern. Its silver eyes stared at him. He felt himself thrown into the blank chasm of its mind. Soon, he was alone with this creature, its large form slowly wriggling in front of him. The beast's tail pointed in the abyss. To Theryn's surprise, it did not seem to want to eat him. Instead, it looked at him, expectantly.

Don't you wish to see the true nature of our Master?

The voice was low and otherworldly. It created no actual sound, it only carried that character as the thoughts flashed in Theryn's mind.

The creature released him and he fell back to the stone parapet, dropping to one knee. The Wyvern's eyes closed, and it slithered away, resting on the opposite end of the turret wall.

Theryn could hear voices now, through the window of the study. He shook off his interaction with the murderous monster that had just stared into his soul and walked along to the opposite end of the wall. The Wyvern let him pass, eyes still closed in its coiled position.

Theryn hugged the smooth wall to the outside of the study tower and peered through the window. His breath caught as he observed the contents of the study.

Azir stood over the kneeling tailor. The man's arms were blocks of ice at his side, and his knees and legs had been frozen to the ground.

"I do this for your own safety, Orlo. Do not fight it, and you are more likely to survive!"

Around them, a dark purple energy mixed with sapphire blue tendrils swirled and leaked from Orlo. The man's expression was pure pain, his teeth biting down against each other, spectacled eyes glued shut. Azir's icy eyes glazed over white as the swirling energy intensified. A cracking sound, like the snapping of a tree branch struck with lightning, sounded out in the study. The aura surrounding Orlo rushed towards Azir and enveloped him. The man's hands absorbed the wisps of energy. Theryn felt his heart palpitate. The frozen shackles around Orlo melted away and he slumped to the ground.

Orlo lay there… limp.

Theryn backed his head out of the window, sickened by what he had seen. Azir had just weaved arcana from someone… and it had been deadly. Theryn poked his head in for a final glance.

Azir had walked over to Orlo and checked his pulse. Then he leaned over and picked up the lifeless man and began to walk towards the doorway.

Alarm sounded off in a frenzy inside of Theryn. It was as if Slip was splashing around in his stomach.

He had to hide.

Azir appeared in the courtyard below him, Orlo still on his shoulder. Theryn panicked.

You now see the truth. Hide now… over the turret wall.

The thoughts flooded his mind. Theryn, not knowing what else to do, sat up on the wall. There was a ridge of square stone that lined the top of the parapet like some sort of ornamental trimming. He heard the booted footfalls of Azir ascending the steps.

Theryn carefully dangled himself over the other side of the wall and balanced on the small squares. One foot stood on each of the decorative squares that jutted from the opposite end of the wall. He gripped the top of the parapet and pressed himself against the cold stone.

Theryn could tell Azir was on top of the wall now and close to the parapet. There was a sound like the dropping of a body on stone. Theryn tried to silence his breathing. There was no need; the Wyvern let out a shriek as Azir approached.

"Eat… then find the girl, the one we saw fall. Bring her here as you did with the boy, and you will be rewarded. But know this… you will be punished if it is not done quickly."

Theryn poked his head over the wall. The Wyvern actually snapped at Azir. The man only laughed. "Do not test the strength of our bond, beast. I control you, remember? Now eat. Do this for me, and the relic you seek revenge upon will be destroyed."

The Wyvern exhaled a long plume of ice at the promise. Theryn could feel its ravenous hunger, its lust for revenge. The beast turned to the corpse.

Theryn ducked back below the crest of the parapet. He couldn't watch.

Instead, he quietly climbed from square to square, tracing the outline of the fortress wall.

Eventually, Theryn reached the opposite tower and tossed himself through an open window. The room was luckily abandoned, and he hastily snuck down the hall back to his own bunk room. Theryn ripped the door open and shut it behind him, panting against its wooden frame.

The Hero of Lunathal was no hero at all. He was a monster.

Chapter XV
The Minstrels

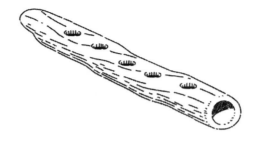

Lyra tugged at her long ornate collar. It itched like crazy.

The baggy purple and red-striped shirt was loose around the arms and tight fitting on her torso. She adjusted her bulbous, floppy hat so that the three giant plumes on the top fell towards the side and out of her face. Her insistence to continue to wear the clothes she had found had fallen on deaf ears. Apparently, surface musicians had a bit more... pizazz. She hated wearing this sort of attire, but it covered her hair and that seemed to be a benefit while she was on the surface. The only good news was Pimbo hadn't found a mirror, so, luckily, she didn't have to see what she looked like. Judging by how the others were dressed, she knew it wouldn't have been a pretty sight anyway.

Pimbo approached from the bushes, zipping up the fly of his baggy striped britches. "Ah, few things bring a man joy like relieving himself in the woods. It just feels so natural, like I am back in sync with my primitive roots." His own musician's clothing was intricately designed. The purple stripes that lined his doublet were ornamented with gold fabric trim. His long burgundy stockings ran up to his knees where his britches ended. The Gnome still wore the old pirate hat, but he had sewn a giant white feather onto the top.

Stringbean hoisted his pack over his shoulder with a grunt. Out of all of their outfits the large Elf's was by far the least convincing. He was so tall, it proved difficult to find authentic performer's outfits in his size, so they had resorted to some simple jester clothing that was roughly stitched together. Stringbean wore a goofy pointed hat with a bell on the top that made an infuriating noise with each of his steps. The poor Sun Elf had been designated the *muscle* of the group, and unfortunately for him, that meant carrying their supplies.

"Can I throw away this tambourine? The bloody thing keeps jingling with every step. Between this thing and Stringbean's hat, we make so much noise that we look and sound like Evaria's most depressing parade!" Helfi gripped the wooden instrument and shook it furiously. The tiny discs of metal rattled in her hand. A few birds in the tree line of the forest road took off at the noise. Pimbo shook his head and adjusted the old lute strapped to his back.

"No, it was expensive! I had to trade Father's dinghy for these instruments, so no wasting them!"

They filed down the packed earth road, Pimbo at the lead. Lyra was grateful they had gotten such an early start. By the time she had woken up, the Gnome siblings had already been returning with everything they needed. At the moment, her acquaintances chatted nonchalantly as they trudged ahead, seemingly unconcerned with being spotted or heard.

"I liked the garlic job better, less things to carry," Stringbean called as he lumbered behind them with most of the bags.

Helfi snorted, "No way are we going back to that job ever again. We smelled for weeks, and I'm pretty sure they will throw us in jail if we go back to the capitol after that one."

"Garlic job?" Lyra asked, quickening her pace so that she was walking alongside Helfi.

"Oh, the garlic job was one of my best! It was a little sales opportunity I concocted," Pimbo sniggered. "First, we buy some dead animals from a hunter and have him drain them of their juices and scatter them around the castle town. Then we put ash root powder all over Stringbean and Helfi and have them start talking in all the inns and taverns about strange bloodsucking monsters. Next thing you know everyone outside the castle walls starts burning sage and spreading holy water around. They think they gots a real bloodsucker invasion on their hands. Then comes their savior!" Pimbo jumped in front of them in the road and adjusted his collar, trying to look dignified.

"Pimbo, the holy garlic farmer. Selling a special brand of blessed garlic guaranteed to keep bloodsuckers away from your home! We sold cloves of garlic so fast we couldn't keep up. We had to have crates from Figsville farms brought in just to stay in stock."

"People really fell for that?" Lyra questioned.

"Sure did!" the Gnome replied. "Sure, there were folks who thought it was a hoax enough to not buy from us. In those cases, we made sure to convince them, personally. Stringbean left them a little surprise on their doorstep!"

"Dead squirrel."

Stringbean and Pimbo broke out laughing.

The conversation had decided something for Lyra. She had known it before, but this only served to confirm her suspicions. She was truly traveling with a bunch of greedy imbeciles. Helfi, however, did not join in on the laughing.

"Yeah, well, these jobs don't usually work out for us so great. This *genius* plan only lasted a bit. They caught on when the hunter showed up and started talking about the strange people who kept buying his dead animals without having them butchered properly. They chased us out of town while Pimbo was using the bath in the double suite room of the Whistling Lizard Inn. He didn't even have time to put on his pants. Just ran the whole way back to Oar's Rest with only a towel wrapped around him."

Pimbo gave his sister an annoyed look as she snickered to herself. "You don't have to tell every detail. We made enough money from that job to buy Mom a new cauldron and pay for Stringbean's wisdom tooth removal."

Stringbean opened his mouth wide exposing more than a few missing teeth in the back. Pimbo gave the tall Elf a pat on his shoulder. "Those donkeys kick hard, and they don't kick for free."

As the motley crew of uncomfortably dressed scam artists made their way through the dense forest, Lyra considered two very probable things. First, she was surrounded by idiots; and second, she was probably going to die that way. It was afternoon and the sun was at its highest point in the mostly clear sky. Spring on the surface turned out to be rather pleasant when there was a breeze. At other times, when they had to mount a ridge or hill where there was little tree cover from the sun, they began to bead with sweat. Lunathal had always been a controlled climate, in the summers it was a bit warm, but the wind that would break through the cloud wall cooled them down nicely, and there was always plenty of shade below the boughs of the Old Willow. It was a bit odd to Lyra how she didn't miss those things at the moment. Sure, she missed her mom, but she felt she would still live if she didn't see another willow branch again for a while.

While they walked, Lyra held out the wooden flute that Pimbo had bought for her. It was different from the kind the carpenters shaped in Lunathal. The flute was made from a lighter, softer wood. It had a few extra holes, and the mouthpiece was a bit curved at the top. She had tried it out earlier, and although she hadn't sounded particularly good, the instrument had proved to be in working condition. Lyra observed it carefully. Faintly grained knots in the wood, smoothed out and polished, giving it an elegant look. There was a faint shadow on her hand where the instrument sat.

Lyra tried to summon that blank canvas in her mind.

Breathing in deep, calm, measured breaths.

Her fingers felt a slight tingle. Not enough to go numb, just enough to feel the presence of something within her. Lyra tried her hardest to make the flute disappear, to have it puff into another place, replaced only by its shadow. When she closed her eyes, her vision seemed bright. The sunlight beams through the trees proffered a piercing, distracting light. The light of day seemed to bore into her, making her feel as if her power was just out of reach. This always seemed to happen when she tried to use her arcana during the day. When the sun was shining, her power felt similar to when she tried to use it in Lunathal, distant and hard to conjure. As if it was in a different world, far from her grasp.

Night, however, was a different story.

Lyra's mother hadn't taught her much of their arcana, but she had taught her two basic rules. The first was, don't use your arcana to steal. The second was, when you undoubtedly did use your arcana to steal, make sure no one sees... especially the Summerborn.

That second was the most important rule. Anyone showing even the closest signs of being a Shade in Lunathal was taken away by the council, and their arcana was weaved forcibly from their bodies. Her mother had told her most times folk didn't live through it, and those that did, came back with broken minds and feeble bodies.

The narrow road led to a wide river surrounded by swamplands. The breeze died away and was replaced with a wall of rather uncomfortable and sticky humidity. It was already late in the afternoon when they saw smoke rise in the distance. It streamed lazily in the air from the opposite end of a bridge that intersected the marshland with the forest road. Lyra could barely make out a handful of figures sitting around the stone arch.

Pimbo pushed past them to the front and shaded his eyes from the sun to get a better look. "What's this about? An Evarian flag and some soldiers, huh? Must be a checkpoint or something. No worries, they'll be letting a bunch of minstrels through now, won't they?"

As they approached, Helfi delivered Lyra a worried glance. On either side of the wide stone bridge stood almost a dozen soldiers and guards. Pimbo had told her during their planning to be wary of any armored Humans wearing blue and gray. These soldiers wore the characteristic dark-colored tabards of his descriptions, under which clinked dark-metal plate. They each carried a long spear, a bow on their back, and some of the more heavily armored ones had long blades strapped to their sides.

Pimbo took the lead, walking with a swagger of confidence. "Act naturally, they have no reason to stop us, we're just wandering performers. Let me do the talking."

Lyra tried to interject, hoping to discuss their options. Unfortunately, Pimbo was already on the move. As he approached one of the guards, a woman with wavy brown hair and no helmet, crossed between them and the bridge.

"Hold on now! This bridge has been decreed off limits by King Radeus Evaria the Second." The soldier produced a scroll and unfolded it. Golden letters Lyra couldn't recognize were scribbled all over it. The symbol of an ash-colored fist on a blue castle was stamped onto the bottom.

"That is most unfortunate ma'am," Pimbo began in his most aristocratic voice, "for this humble band of talented young maestros hungers to spread our artistry around the countryside. We sing tales featuring the great deeds of Evarian soldiers and royalty. Their heroism is our inspiration for we are humble servants to history, and we must tell this history through song."

Lyra was actually impressed for a moment. She could tell this wasn't Pimbo's first time duping someone. Pimbo fingered at the roughly carved lute strapped to his shoulder, as if threatening to play for the guard. "Might we please be granted permission to cross this bridge so that we may impress the four corners of Tellis with the beautiful ballads and jigs of Evaria?"

Pimbo bowed courteously after his plea. To Lyra's surprise, the woman looked amused. Another guard approached, this one large and male with a long red beard.

"Funny little bugger, aren't you, eh? You sing songs about Evarian heroism? Yet there isn't an Evarian among you. I see two Gnomes, a pale Elf, and a giant for a Sun Elf." The guard took a step up to Stringbean so that the two were almost eye level. "Isn't your fancy little Imperium an enemy of the crown, Elf?"

Stringbean looked around nervously. Pimbo briskly stepped between his friend and the guard. "Now, now, my good man. We have lived in Evaria our whole lives! Right here in Oar's Rest, and we can assure you we are patriotic and bear no love for the Imperium. My friend here is a bit different and was cast away at a young age, this is why he's joined up with me! He's an honorary Gnome." Pimbo accompanied this explanation with a hasty nervous laugh but stopped quickly when no one else joined in. He cleared his throat, "Now please, if you would be so kind, we request passage across this river so we may continue on."

The guard looked at them for another few heartbeats and took a step back. The female put her scroll back in her belt and spoke. "If you are from Oar's Rest then you should know why the north is off limits. That Wyvern's been nesting there. The Duke's been killed and his Stronghold has been captured by enemies of the crown. They have an army of beasts and man-eaters. We've been ordered to make sure they receive no trade in goods or services."

The male guard stepped forward again, "And that means no music either."

Helfi offered Lyra another anxious glance.

Lyra wasn't familiar with the politics and social norms of the surface, yet even so, she could tell that this deception was not going well for them. Pimbo didn't seem to know when to stop, and Lyra feared they would end up right back in a jail cell, this time dressed like idiots.

"We might be convinced, though," another guard said, approaching and taking a seat on the stone handrail at the front of the bridge. "How about a song? Let us hear some of these tales of Evarian bravery."

"Oh yes, um… of course. How about an instrumental?" Pimbo gave them a nervous smile and unshouldered his lute.

Lyra sighed and held the flute to her lips. She didn't wait for a count off or a tempo, instead, she pursed her lips and began to trill away. The flute had a nice hollow wooden sound and she held a long note before ripping into sweeping eighth notes. She picked a fast tempo that was impressive enough to have her fingers move quickly but not so fast someone couldn't tap along. Helfi took her cue and began tapping on her tambourine. A long shake and a tap to release, long shake and a tap.

Stringbean began to dance in front of them, he was goofy, so his uncoordinated motions produced a few smiles from the guards. Pimbo's eyes lit up, as if he couldn't believe it was actually working. He held his lute close and strummed an out of tune chord.

"Oooooh!"

The Gnome called out as if to begin the verse of a song. Lyra shot him an angry glance. She tried her best to say with only her eyes, *Don't you dare. Don't you dare start singing and mess this up.*

It was too late, he started singing. It took all of Lyra's self control not to grab her flute and shove it down his throat to stop him. The Gnome sang of how an Evarian hero fought a bear and came away with a new coat. He sang of how the king once wrestled an ogre and came away with a new best friend. He sang of how Stringbean once tried to fight a wolf and came away with a few less toes. After the longest minute of Lyra's life, Pimbo ran out of verses and she was able to bring the music to a gradual halt. Stringbean fell down into a split pose and removed one of his pointed shoes, revealing a foot with less toes than normal. Slip emerged from Lyra's pouch and began walking around with a hat in his mouth. Pimbo had instructed the creature to collect tips in the off chance they actually had to perform. There was silence… but the guards were smiling widely and one of them was wiping away tears of laughter.

After a moment, the red bearded guard finally spoke up. "That, lads and ladies, was truly terrible. As much as it pains me to deny whoever killed the Duke the torture of that performance, I'm sorry to say we still can't let you cross. Decent flute playing though." He opened his jingling coin pouch and flicked a single disc of copper into Slip's hat.

"All that and a measly copper mark," Pimbo grumbled, letting his accent drop for a moment. "Can you tell us where the nearest town is at least?"

"Anchor Point, follow the river down to the western shore for about three hours," the female guard responded. "But be careful, Wyvern's been spotted out and about. Wouldn't want you to be his next meal."

"Those two would just be light snacks, and the tall one would be the full entree. Maybe the pale one's made of cream—she could be dessert!"

The red bearded guard laughed with the others. Lyra heard the tambourine hit the floor with a jingle, only after it was slammed into the temple of the guard. The bearded Human's helmet vibrated and let out a ring as Helfi dashed up and cut his coin pouch free from his hip with a quick flourish.

"Thanks for the tip, good luck catching me wearing all that armor." She took off down the river shore. Pimbo hooted and followed after her. Slip dove into the river, letting the rushing current do most of the work, and Stringbean threw his shoes at the guard before he ran after. Lyra had no choice but to follow. She took off beside Stringbean who was laughing wildly, "Classic Helfi!" he called.

The guards' shouts behind them grew more and more distant. The musicians hadn't escaped particularly fast; Lyra thought perhaps the heavily armored guards just couldn't keep up with the lightly clad musicians. Alongside them, Slip dove in and out of the river water in graceful arcs. For the first time since Lyra left Lunathal, she found herself smiling. She hadn't smiled too often in Lunathal either, especially since her mother fell ill.

As Lyra ran along the river shore, white sand squished under her boots. The sun beat down on the glimmering water, and Helfi and Pimbo were cheering and hollering, staggering along, almost falling over from laughter.

Eventually, they stopped next to a large rock and collectively huffed and puffed against it. Helfi let out a cackle as she undid the pouch. Coppers, silvers, and some small gold coins fell to the ground. They laughed and scooped up the coins, and for a single moment, Lyra forgot all her other worries; instead, she just watched them and laughed.

Another two or so hours of walking put them on the outskirts of the town, Anchor Point. The town was smaller than Oar's Rest, but other than that, it was rather similar. It was built out over the swamplands and river that connected to the sea with messily stacked wooden buildings and walkways. A half dozen ships floated idly in the docks outside the seaside drink hall Pimbo led them to. It was a smaller building, and most of its occupants seemed to be sailors or traders from distant lands. Many of them looked like Humans, who Lyra figured out were round-eared people, but most in the drink hall were half their size. They were sturdy with intricate facial hair that had been delicately trimmed into funny shapes. They had skin color similar to Pimbo and wore mostly clothes you might expect to see ancient warriors dress in.

"Half-Men, probably from the north," Pimbo whispered as they entered the drink hall.

The group took a seat at a corner table.

"There has got to be a ship headed north to Moonglow or something. I'll find us passage—you lot just sit here and order some food. We have to get out of here quickly before those guards come looking for us."

Pimbo set down one of the square silver coins with a hole carved into it, which he had grabbed from the guard's pouch. Stringbean held it up and called for some of the serving staff. Meanwhile, Pimbo set himself to work, talking with the sailing men at the next table.

An hour passed slowly. The air was stale in the drink hall, and Lyra didn't particularly enjoy the food. The serving staff brought them a bitter-tasting brown drink and small breaded cakes with bits of fish in them. She was so hungry she ate them all and ordered more despite not being too keen on the flavor. At last, Pimbo returned to their table.

"Seems like no one is heading north... we may be out of luck, kid." Lyra's heart sank. She couldn't give up. This was her way back to Theryn... if he was still alive. The only way back to Lunathal. Back to her mother.

"Looking for passage, you little rapscallion?"

A female's voice called out from across the swinging doorway of the drink hall.

In the corner, a woman emerged from the shadows. She had a wrap around her dark hair, and her eyes were almond-shaped. She had tan skin, and she approached with slow booted steps.

The drink hall went silent as Aranna, Black Eyes Barnett's best fighter and crew member of the Hyena, stepped forward. Behind her, Tate, the highwayman, followed. He was still looking beat up, covered in bruises and scratches Lyra had partly been responsible for. She readied herself for a scuffle, her chair scraping against the floor as she left it quickly.

"Perhaps the Hyena can take you. I'm sure old Black Eyes would love to have a word with you."

Lyra froze, waiting for her companions' response.

Pimbo and Stringbean rose as well while Helfi produced her small knife and held it forward. They seemed to think a fight was coming; Lyra's instincts had been correct.

Lyra readied herself, trying to focus in case she needed her arcana. "Come now," Tate said with his ugly grin. "We lost our crew in that Wyvern attack, and we could surely use some extra hands on deck. Wouldn't you like to join up?"

"How can we trust you?" Pimbo asked cautiously.

Aranna drew her sword and placed it on the table. "Truth is, we are the only ones crazy enough to head that way. Wyvern is said to be sitting on a wide stack of the Duke's old gold. We need money to hire more crew, and Black Eyes has no respect for the beast... he wants its head. Barnett does, however, respect cunning, and you lot have proved you have plenty of that; especially, the girl who has the ability to disappear."

Lyra felt butterflies in her stomach. Slip poked his head out from the bag on her lap and locked eyes with Tate. Tate drew his own sword. "Oh, drop it, Aranna, this is a waste of time. Let's just kill them, take their money, and get back to the Hyena. I want that otter fur as a scarf anyway."

He smiled wickedly. Pimbo and Stringbean stepped in front of Lyra in a protective stance. Tate's eyes were wide with bloodlust.

This was going to get ugly.

They were unarmed other than Helfi's tiny knife, and *that* seemed like it would even have trouble cutting a piece of fruit.

Tate held up his sword to strike at Pimbo first.

"GAHH!!" The highwayman let out a wicked cry as his hand holding the sword hit the wooden floor. He turned from them with wide eyes. Aranna met his bewildered gaze and drove her sword through his belly. Tate let out a gasp and fell backwards onto the table.

They stood there stunned as Aranna wiped her curved blade on Tate's clothes and sheathed it. Slip let out a concerned noise and submerged himself back into Lyra's bag.

The brigand woman gave them a shrug, "Tate has always been a bit too ruthless to trust. Either I did that to him, or he would have done it to me in my sleep eventually. He was dead weight anyway. Now he's just dead."

She extended a hand to Pimbo, two gold coins sparkling in her palm. "A down payment. The Hyena needs more crew and no one is crazy enough to head towards the Wyvern. Black Eyes is more forgiving than you think. So—do you want that treasure hoard or not?"

Lyra couldn't believe she was willing to walk onto the vessel that served as her place of captivity only a day prior. Before she could reason with herself, Lyra was already headed out the door and onto the bridge of the Hyena. The ship had been badly damaged by the Wyvern. The mainmast had been partially splintered, and the sails were riddled with holes. At its helm stood Old Black Eyes Barnett, surrounded by still-defrosting ice that littered the ship. His obsidian pits for eyes fell on them. Lyra saw an immediate change. The man looked partially defeated, no longer holding the lust and vigor she had seen during her capture. The pirate captain carried an expression like a folklore hero who suddenly realized he is just an old frail man.

"I see you brought us new crew members, Aranna. No hard feelings right, mateys? Where is Tate?"

Aranna gave him a shrug. "I traded him for these four. Seemed a fair trade."

Black Eyes stroked his beard thoughtfully, not even a hint of regret on his weathered face.

"Hmm, a fair trade indeed. Though they smell a fair bit worse." He wandered over with labored steps to Lyra. "This one will be key for getting the Wyvern's treasure."

Pimbo stepped between Lyra and the old pirate. "Whoa whoa—wait a moment now. We had eyes on that treasure first, and she's with us. Don't think we are going to be so quick to share it with the folks who were about to make us slaves and carnies for the rest of our lives!"

The old captain's focused gaze found Pimbo, and he cowered a bit. "You don't seem to have much of a choice, my Gnome friend. The roads are all blocked, and the Hyena's the only ship heading north. You will need a ship to haul all that gold anyway. We only ask for a third of the treasure," he smiled, producing an uneven mouthful of yellow teeth with the occasional shiny metal one.

"A fourth, and we get all the jewels… and you have to promise to sail us back to Oar's Rest when the job is done."

Black Eyes' face twitched in annoyance before Aranna stepped in. "You have yourself a deal, Gnome!"

The brigand woman shook Pimbo's hand.

The old pirate looked to Lyra. He seemed not to care much about the rest of them. Instead, he mostly remained focused on Lyra. "You are rather special, girl. Do you know what you are? Do you know why you can do the things you can?"

Lyra shrugged, "I only know that where I come from, folks like me aren't supposed to be able to do what I can do."

His eyes glinted, like a single star appearing on a blank night sky. "That's because they are afraid of other realms… and anyone who can access them. Show me how you summon it."

Other realms?

This old pirate was talking like his sanity had suddenly gone overboard. Barnett waited, obviously expecting Lyra to show him. Maybe it was curiosity that made her do it, but Lyra held up her hand and tried to bring out her arcana.

Her fingers tingled, and although the sun was just now setting, she felt the power closer than normal. The blank canvas first, then the numbness; it was becoming easier now. Lyra urged the power forward, and her hand erupted into purple light; crackling energy began smoking from the palm of her hand. Aranna and the rest of the crew took a step backward. "Now hold it to your face and peer through, tell me what you see," Black Eyes instructed.

Lyra shot him a worried glance and hesitated. The old pirate urged her on, nodding for her to do as he asked.

Lyra raised her hand slowly.

The energy vibrated in her palm, and her ears began to ring as she drew it closer to her face. When it was right at her eye line, she took a deep breath and plunged her head forward.

The sound was pulled from the world around her, just like the experience she had when she jumped into the sea to escape the pirates, with it all the color of the world seeped away. Instead of being on a ship, her head now appeared in an endless sea of black, a thin line of onyx liquid lining the ground. In the sky, thousands of multi-colored stars twinkled. She gasped for air, but she found she didn't need it. Her eyes darted around for any signs of interest.

Despite the lack of substantial light when she stared into the liquid ground, she saw a reflection of the surface.

A valley, surrounded by leveled mountains and dead trees.

A humming rip hovering in thin air, slowly sucked up the color from the world. It left plants and trees dead in its wake. It made rivers dry and mountains crumble. It made people sick, green with fever. She could feel its hunger and its desire to consume Tellis. She saw a flash of her mother, sick and coughing somewhere far away. Lyra saw the power to save her mother. It rippled in front of her, a swirling negative energy, begging her forward to seize it. If she could only harness it, maybe she could control this power that seeped into the world. It beckoned her forward, willing her to step fully into the darkness.

It was over in a flash as she was ripped from the energy in her hands. Black Eyes stood there holding her by the shoulders. The rest of the crew wore pale expressions. Slip had jumped from her satchel and was now sitting on Helfi's shoulder, looking about as concerned as a water rat could.

"Careful, lass," the old captain warned. "It's a good thing you only put your head in, or else I might not have been able to pull you back."

"Your head was a shadow!" Pimbo shouted, looking as though he had just seen an ogre in his living room.

"Tell me what you saw," the captain demanded, hands still gripped tightly on Lyra's shoulders.

"I saw an endless sea of black, it was spilling into our world, consuming everything," Lyra said with a haunted expression, remembering the desolate feeling of hopelessness she felt as she watched the world being consumed.

"And the monster? The hunger's origin, did you see it, lass?"

"I d-don't know," Lyra stuttered, still trying to gather her thoughts as she pulled lightly away from Barnett's grip.

"Aye, it's as I feared. She's seen the void that leaks from the Rift. An all-consuming realm. A realm whose only goal is to make its endless space even more endless."

"What do you mean all-consuming… and how do you know this?" Lyra asked, shaking her hands in an effort to have them regain feeling. "I've had this power my whole life, so has my mother."

The old captain looked over his crew as he paced forward. "I've heard tales of magical folks having tried to open Rifts to other realms. They seek power or lands of bounty and wealth. It's how the world flooded all those years ago, and it's why a plague spreads in the north now. I know because I was approached by a tattooed man to find the key to opening those realms–a meteorite."

"A meteorite?" Pimbo asked

"Aye, but he merely told me he would pay well if I happened upon it. I had heard a tale that it was in the royal family's custody, but the Hyena doesn't seek out that kind of heat. It was too risky, so we let the job go. Turns out that man was the Wyvern Rider, the same one who senselessly attacked Oar's Rest."

What did the Rider want with Theryn?

"We think that Rift is connected to the Wyvern," Aranna cut in. "Ever since it came back and started terrorizing us, that Rift opened and started making people sick. I was just a kid when it opened."

"Aye," Barnett agreed. "But Evarian magicians did it, I heard."

"Why? Why would they open a gateway to an endless plague?" Lyra asked incredulously.

Black Eyes only shrugged, "Probably to find the wealth or treasure inside. The Evarians have tried to stop it. A trading vessel we boarded was coming back from dropping off supplies to the King's magicians. The cargo ship was still fat with bounty... Sailors said when they arrived, the camp was empty. Rift had swallowed the magicians whole."

Lyra's face went cold with goosebumps. She wanted to go home, to forget about all this and hug her mom before it was too late. She was reminded of the image of her sick mother from the void and realized something. Even if Lyra could get home, the

Blight wouldn't stop. She had to do something to help save the surface.

"Where is the Rift?" Lyra asked finally.

"It's just north of the Wyvern's nesting place. The direction we are sailing towards."

"Good," Lyra said with determination. "Because if you want this world to still have things to buy and people to buy from, you are bringing me there… after we rescue my friend."

The seasoned captain gave her a daring look and started barking commands to the crew. "You heard the lass! Weigh anchor! Hoist the Mizzen!"

The new crew stood around looking confused before Aranna sighed loudly. "Don't worry, Captain. I'll show them what to do."

Chapter XVI
The Astral Palace

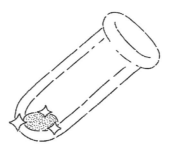

Theryn tried his best to go through the daily exercises with the other Acolytes. They had given him a small pigeon to create a Soulbridge and perform simple tasks with. The bird had opened its mind to him almost immediately and with little resistance. The Soulbridge between them was a bit stronger than the coyote, perhaps, because the pigeon didn't want to eat him. Within Theryn, the bond felt empty. The bird was simply uninterested in Theryn, or seemingly, anyone at all. Its mind revealed the pigeon had been Soulbridged many times, and because of that, small stamps of other personalities clouded the true intentions of the creature.

The pigeon was simple-minded, completely food-motivated, and stubborn. It listened to him begrudgingly as if Theryn was its cruel master, and that relationship felt uncomfortable to him. It lacked the understanding and mutual respect he felt with Slip. Theryn's heart longed to see his otter friend again.

The Acolytes performed sweeping motions with their hands, and the birds darted about the great hall, fetching seeds and flying back to deposit them in jars placed at the edge of the doorway. Normally, this would have been amazing, something Theryn could only dream of doing; however, given the events of last night and his tossing and turning in bed afterward, Theryn had lost his appetite for learning more about his arcana.

Truth be told, other than the fact Theryn had barely slept after witnessing Orlo's death, he had felt mostly dissuaded by his father.

Tarvin had come to wake him and accompany him to the morning training. The few moments they had shared alone had been unbelievable for Theryn. He hadn't seen his father in years, yet it felt so natural to talk to him. When he looked in his father's eyes he felt like the man truly understood him, much like Slip had.

However, Tarvin displayed such unyielding loyalty to Azir that it made Theryn uneasy. Attempts to mention that something seemed strange about Azir and his plans had merely warranted a dismissive wave. His father only told him to trust in the Hero of Lunathal. Theryn knew Tarvin meant well, and he made his best effort to trust in his father's words. Although he tried to forget what he had seen, the horrifying vision of Orlo's arcana being pulled from his dying body resurfaced. Theryn couldn't shake the image of the poor tailor's lifeless form on the cold stone floor of the study. Azir had picked him up so nonchalantly… and then the Wyvern had eaten Orlo.

It was difficult to stay focused during training. Theryn's mind would wander to thoughts of his mother who he would never get to spend more time with—then to Bub who thought he was dead—then to Slip who still carried a piece of his soul with him somewhere, out there on the surface—then to Lyra. She was here because of him, and that guilt gnawed at him from the inside. The idea of her all alone, still trapped inside the cell of that rotten ship, made his skin crawl.

Theryn decided he could no longer stay at the Stronghold. If the Wyvern brought Lyra to this place, he would figure out a way to get them home. He had to get her out of the circumstance he had wrapped her up in.

"These animals, they are like imprints of ourselves," Theryn's father explained over the next day's breakfast. "When myself and my eagle bonded, it felt like a part of me was taken and placed into him. I can still feel that piece, and it is still present, it's just in another body." He ruffled the bird's feathers as it sat regally on his shoulder, watching with diligent eyes.

"What did Mom Soulbridge?" Theryn found himself asking. He wasn't even sure where the question came from, it just felt like the right thing to ask.

"She had an eagle also, those two were pretty close." His words were laden with melancholy as he stroked his own eagle's feathered head. "Poor beast was struck from the sky with an arrow in the battle. Your mother shared its pain, and I couldn't react quickly enough. I tried to get her away from the Duke's trained swords."

A sick feeling in Theryn's stomach bubbled. Theryn felt bad for asking; he had brought down the mood, and it hadn't been his intention to learn about his mother's death either. Sometimes these things were just better left unanswered.

Theryn had been in the Stronghold now for almost two days. While he was grateful for the time with his father, he longed to reconnect with Slip and Lyra. The Wyvern had been gone for a while, and he could sense it still exploring the countryside far away.

"You have probably been surprised by the level of intellect your Soulbridge partner shows, right Theryn?" His father asked. They sat at a table alone in the common room, eating the soaked oats that the cook and his wounded monkey had prepared. His father spooned the soggy meal up with his good hand. "Sometimes I can't believe some of the things my eagle understands and does. It's truly amazing. It's like we give them a little piece of humanity when we bridge their souls. Kind of like copying yourself and stamping a piece of each other's minds."

Theryn liked when his father talked about Soulbridging. Tarvin's ideology of the bond was wholesome and fulfilling.

A peaceful bridge between partners.

A way for the best of two beings to combine into one. It reminded Theryn of how natural it felt to be with Slip. How he hadn't truly known how to swim well until a fragment of the otter's soul merged with his own. Truth be told, even though Theryn had found his long lost parent, something still felt incomplete without Slip around. He imagined it must feel the same for parents because their children were like copies of themselves. When your children walked out the door on their own, it was like a piece of the parents' own heart was walking away from them.

Breakfast concluded, and they were halfway through an afternoon training exercise when Azir summoned Theryn. They were working on getting their animals to jump through hoops, and Theryn was actually making progress with the coyote. Since

Theryn was against commanding the creature as if he was its master, he sought other methods to obtain obedience. He found that if he could bribe the animal with snacks from the kitchens, it was more inclined to listen to him. Theryn was just giving the coyote a spare fishtail from the kitchen when the training room fell silent. Azir swept into the training room with intention and held up a hand for them to pause.

"I have need of my apprentice today."

The other Acolytes looked at Theryn with jealousy. Tarvin just patted him on the back with a proud look and nudged him forward. Azir wore his usual long black jacket trimmed with fur. He had goggles hanging around his neck, and his silvery hair was tied back behind his head.

"Tarvin, I require your son for an expedition. I apologize that it has to be so soon for his first mission, but you understand how dire the situation is. The Wyvern has returned... and reported the Rift is growing. The Blight that leaks from it will consume the Stronghold within days. It is time to act."

"Of course, Master Azir. What shall we do here while you are away?" Tarvin asked.

"If our mission is successful in Lunathal, we will have the power to close the Rift. We need to ensure that the local governments do not jeopardize this. They must fall into line. Muster our forces and prepare to seize the capitol. You are headed towards Castle Evaria, immediately. This fortress is no longer needed."

A mission in Lunathal? Am I really going home?

The Acolytes shifted uncomfortably. The room was quiet save for the panting of winded animals.

"But, sir," Tarvin began, looking disappointed, "we sacrificed so much to take control of this place. It's the perfect defensive position. Shouldn't we hold out here until you return from your mission?"

Azir gave him an icy stare. Theryn could tell the Rider was not thrilled at having his orders questioned. To Theryn's surprise, Azir's eyes softened slightly on Tarvin. "We have all sacrificed much, Tarvin. But this is the only way to save Tellis from the Blight that threatens to consume it."

"But Master Azir, we don't have enough strength to take the capitol. The King has legions of trained men. We are so few and many here can barely control their animals," Tarvin argued. Theryn could tell his father was making sure to be as delicate as possible. Theryn had done the same thing when he argued with Bub in the past.

Azir patted Tarvin on the shoulder before regarding the group. "I will take care of that. When you reach Castle Evaria, the gates will practically be wide open."

This seemed good enough for the group. Their animals perked up as the mood in the room shifted. The anticipation of events long awaited. Tarvin bowed low. "We will follow you, Azir, you saved us and showed us a new world."

So, it was true—Theryn really was going back to Lunathal with Azir. He wanted to plead to wait until they found Lyra but stopped himself. Azir was in a determined mood, and Theryn's thoughts were interrupted by a strong hug from his father. The man held him close and spoke into his ear low, "Be safe, Theryn. Listen to Azir, and you will be safe."

"Like Mom was?" Theryn whispered back, his tone laden with uncertainty. The man didn't respond; instead, he squeezed a bit tighter before releasing Theryn from the hug. Tarvin's nut-brown eyes were damp. He seemed so familiar at that moment, like Theryn had known him all this time instead of losing him at a young age. Theryn's heart softened for the man. It was like looking at Bub a hundred years in the past. Tarvin brushed tears away with his sleeve before turning. "We have all sacrificed much, Theryn."

They walked at an alarmingly quick pace to the courtyard. "Your friend is proving difficult to find. Unfortunately, we can wait no longer," Azir began. "The Wyvern has returned, and it has shown me visions of the north. The Blight has almost reached the trunk of the Old Willow. Its plague has crawled up the roots. The protective enchantment over Lunathal is weaker than ever. We have to act now."

"We are going to Lunathal?" Theryn asked, trying not to display too much excitement at the prospect of seeing Bub again.

Azir only kept walking briskly, "This is not the homecoming you've imagined, Theryn. There is something in the Astral Palace we need. You are to stay focused and control the Wyvern while I deal with the council."

Dread hit Theryn and his heart skipped a beat.

I have to do what?

"Control the Wyvern?" was all Theryn could manage to stammer out. His face had gone hot despite the cool afternoon breeze of the courtyard.

"You have done it once before, and you will need to do it again today. Come now, get on."

In front of them, the Wyvern perched on the outer parapet wall. The serpentine head was bowed in subservience, yet those silver eyes still glistened with intensity. At first, Theryn was afraid to approach it. However, an inclination told him the great serpent would not eat him. It was not hungry… for now.

Azir flung himself over the neck of the Wyvern and settled against one of the spikes that lined the beast's neck. He held out his hand to help hoist Theryn up. "It's been almost two hundred years since the council cast me out to protect their own treachery. Their enchantment has kept me at bay. Since then, I could only hover beyond the cloud wall… today that changes." Azir put on his goggles and pressed his hand against the Wyvern. It thrashed about and Theryn held on for dear life. It shrieked loudly and lifted off into the air with incredible velocity.

Theryn rode the Wyvern.

It was an incredible, terrifying experience. The wind whistled through his hair and swept it back. The scales weren't exactly comfortable, but there were at least plenty of places to grip on to the ancient creature.

It sailed through the air with surprising speed and grace, much like how Slip swam in the rivers. The landscape below them was beautiful. Towns and towers dotted the countryside. There were assortments of greens for the tall narrow trees. Blues and swirling cyans for the lakes and sea. Clay colors for the jagged mountains and hills. It was magnificent.

Then Theryn saw the Blight.

Like a gray splotch of paint had been smudged onto the land, it seeped and slowly crept forward. Miles and miles of the surface had already been consumed, leaving a colorless graveyard in its wake.

They had flown for about an hour, and Theryn was freezing. His hands had gone numb, and his hair was so windswept, he was unsure if he would still have any by the end of the ride. The Wyvern leveled in altitude, and they were soon gliding peacefully. They hardly needed to hold on. Theryn used this opportunity to practice his Soulbridging; to prod at the Wyvern's mind.

Do I even stand a chance at controlling this thing?

Theryn's surroundings faded to black as he focused. Soon, it was just Theryn and the Wyvern. He could sense Azir as well, but the man's concern was on other matters, and he paid no attention to the current emotions of the Wyvern. The beast's soul was occupied, strongly connected to Azir and unyielding in its determination to fulfill their mission. Theryn dug deeper into the creature's mind. There were memories and desires, dreams and nightmares. Theryn pushed past all those. As he continued to search, he began to sense something different, a part of its mind left untouched by Azir's influence. The beast's true emotions, hidden deep down and suppressed. Theryn pressed forward, searching through its instinctual spirit. He could feel the Wyvern let him in, as if it wanted him to see.

The Wyvern was unhappy, that much was obvious, but this was no normal unhappiness. This was like a blanket of depression smothering its every thought. Theryn felt an enormous loneliness inside the Wyvern's spirit. It reminded him of his own when he found out his parents had jumped. Strangely enough, the Wyvern's loneliness had an even deeper intensity. The feeling was one of such pure isolation that it could only be understood by being the last of your own kind.

"Point me in the area where you fell through the clouds. That will be where the enchantment is weakest."

Azir's command brought Theryn back to lucidity. The wind picked up, and he held on tighter. In front of them, the cloud wall of Lunathal gently orbited the Old Willow. The clouds were less dense, and the usual slight blue shine of an enchantment they held was even fainter than normal. Theryn pointed at a lower section on the bottom of the trunk.

Azir urged the Wyvern forward in a dip.

"How come I was able to fall out so easily if there was an enchantment on the clouds?" Theryn called over the whipping wind.

"The enchantment isn't powerful enough to protect both sides of the cloud wall, Theryn. Summerborn who fall have all sorts of arcana tricks to save themselves. Winterborn are just supposed to die."

Soon, they hovered mere inches from the shimmering clouds. Azir held out his right hand, palm outstretched, fingers tightly against one another.

Straining, he let out a cry as sharp sheets of ice began to shoot from his hands. They seemed to be gathering just at the point of flesh from the middle of his palm as if the air was gathering and freezing right in front of his skin. The Wyvern shrieked and joined in. Theryn had to hold on tightly as the plumes of frigid winter ice evacuated the beast's open jaws towards the clouds.

It was as if they intended to freeze all of Lunathal. They sent deluge after deluge of unrelenting ice careening towards the enchantment. To Theryn's surprise, the clouds seemed to absorb the cold energy with ease. Azir and the Wyvern continued to pummel it. The Wyvern roared again, and let out a blast of ice, this time stronger.

"Break it, do it!" Azir screamed as he continued to throw volleys of hardened frost at the arcane boundary.

The Wyvern's continued blasts hit the cloud wall, and there was a shattering sound. Theryn had to grip his ears—It was so loud. Like a thousand wine glasses and ice sculptures all split at the same time. The clouds lost their faint blue tint and began to dissipate. There was a hole.

"It's time! Forward!" Azir demanded.

It seemed every Moonfolk in Lunathal had emerged from their hanging homes to catch a glimpse of what was happening. It was a bizarre experience seeing his birthplace from this vantage point. The city actually seemed small now that he had experienced the sprawling expanse of the surface.

From the sky, Theryn could see the Winterborn in the lower branches. The platforms held smaller homes, less carvings and shops. In the upper branches, there were large homes with faintly sky-blue skinned Summerborn pointing to the sky. They called out, and screamed, and raced around to find shelter from the Wyvern. Theryn tried to find the Middle District. He searched desperately to catch even a glimpse of his home and Bub. Azir, however, ignored the lower branches and urged them upwards towards the highest limb.

Theryn held on tight trying to ease the feeling of vertigo as they shot upward. He was grateful when they finally leveled over the platform that held the Astral District. The only building in Lunathal not made of wood and bark sat before them. The wide Astral Palace was made from a white marble that was streaked with hints of blue quartz. Statues, most of them of Seluna, lined the palace.

Azir urged the Wyvern down onto the platform with a lowering of his outstretched hand. The beast dropped and looked around defensively as Azir leapt from its neck.

They had landed next to a statue of the Hero of Lunathal, carved from wood, in the center of the platform.

"They got the nose wrong," Azir said before turning to face Theryn.

"Remember your task. Control the Wyvern, keep it subdued until I—"

Azir was cut off as a half dozen robed men emerged from the Astral Palace steps. They had blue-tinged skin and graying hair. Theryn recognized them as the council of sorcerers that governed the treetop city. At their head was the Chief Astrologer, a man Theryn had only seen a handful of times. The man was, of course, Summerborn. He appeared to be middle-aged, with faintly mossy-colored hair flecked with silver. He wore ornate pearl-colored robes and carried a wooden scepter with a large amethyst gem inlaid at the top. Azir turned to face him.

"Fyladreus, so nice to see you are still the warden who is suppressing the Winterborn and keeping Lunathal the perfect prison. What has it been? Two hundred years?"

The council of sorcerers fanned out on the marble steps in a defensive position, eyeing Azir and the Wyvern warily. The Chief Astrologer stepped forward and tapped his scepter on the ground. Around him formed a shimmering shield of orange and golden sparks. They orbited him as he called out from the steps.

"It has been one hundred and ninety-three years since your banishment, Azir. I see the surface continues to preserve you."

"The surface is where we belong, Fyladreus. People may live their full lives there. On the surface, there is water and food aplenty… and there are no Summerborn to rule over us."

The Chief Astrologer scoffed, "The tree wouldn't provide enough for everyone to live their full lives here in Lunathal anyway, Azir. We do what we must to survive here. I have no control over the fact the Summerborn live longer."

"You cheat the Winterborn of their true potential, you keep them lower class because you are afraid of them." Azir dropped his long jacket to the ground, revealing a warrior's sleek armor made from tough animal hide. It was lined with rings of chain-link metal, and it clinked as he stepped forward. He pointed to the Astrologer with a jeweled finger, "Well, I will give you a reason to truly fear them."

Theryn gripped the Wyvern. It was as if the creature could sense his nervousness because it lowered its great body in a defensive stance. The walkways surrounding the Astral District began to fill with curious onlookers. Theryn saw the Astrologer narrow his gaze at Azir, but it was Azir who spoke again, this time with a tone of proclamation.

"The Old Willow is dying, as I'm sure you know. Your home and its people are becoming more and more sick every day. Yet, you do nothing because it is the Winterborn who suffer more—"

"We will use Seluna's gift to heal the Old Willow when the time is right, Azir. There is no need for bloodshed. Be reasonable!" The Astrologer interrupted, which had more than clearly annoyed Azir. Theryn thought this exchange was a bit odd, they seemed to talk to one another with a hint of… nostalgia. As if they had known each other for a long time.

Azir paced in front of the staircase. His jeweled fingers interlocked behind his back as he continued his proclamation. "This is why I have come. I will take the gift and use it to prevent anything like this from happening again… I have come to free these people from this cursed tree."

"Blasphemous!" Fyladreus's voice had gone from its regal self-importance to one filled with scorn. "Seluna has provided all we need here in Lunathal. The Blight will consume the surface. We cannot stop that, but we shall live here protected as we have for many centuries. She intended for us to stay here. The gift will preserve us through the darkest of nights. You were once happy here, Azir. Everyone is given a life of purpose in Lunathal. There is order here, unlike the chaos of the surface."

Theryn could see this was not the response Azir had hoped for. This was going to turn ugly, quickly. But what could he do? He was a pawn in this fight.

Azir began to fume. He held his hand out to his side, a jagged blade of ice forming from the palm. "For years I believed you.

Then I learned the truth of what you did. The first Summerborn opened the Rift that flooded the world. Your ancestors were greedy for power just like the Humans we protected Lunathal from all those years ago. The Summerborn are responsible for all this. They left the meteorite on the surface where the Humans could open a Rift and release the Blight. I'm here to take the gift and stop it!"

Fyladreus stepped forward, "You know there were no Summerborn or Winterborn back then, Azir. We were one in the same. The Men of Evaria threatened our extinction, and our ancestors tried to find the power to fight back. Your hatred blinds you from the truth…"

The aura of dancing sparks around Fyladreus intensified. Theryn averted his gaze and even the Wyvern shuffled back a bit. The man raised his jewel topped scepter in an offensive position.

"And we will die before we let a heretic like you have the last Teardrop of Seluna."

Azir held his translucent blade aloft, a serrated sword of ice almost half the size of Theryn. The man's blue eyes were burning with hatred. "So be it, old friend."

Golden sparks shot out in all directions around the Chief Astrologer. Theryn hid behind a scale just narrowly dodging one of the projectiles. Like a miniature shooting comet, it whistled by, leaving a streak of flaring energy. Theryn peaked over the

Wyvern's scales. The figures on the stairs were locked in a vicious duel.

Azir swung at a spark, reflecting it and sending it hurling towards a council member. The man immediately burst into radiant yellow flames and dropped into a disintegrated heap on the palace steps. The other council members set themselves to hurling shards of ice at Azir, which he nimbly dodged.

Below Theryn, the Wyvern let out a shriek.

It inhaled, drawing in a large breath that threatened to cover the whole Astral Palace in a deadly sheet of ice.

"No!" Theryn screamed. The serpent would kill them all, and Theryn didn't wish to see anyone else get hurt.

He reached deep inside the Wyvern's mind. It let him in, with little care, seemingly concentrating on the battle. He felt the anger, white hot, seething hatred that had been planted there by Azir. Theryn tried to ease it. He tried to show the beast times in his own life when he had been angry, and it had only made matters worse. The Wyvern paused for a moment, regarding the memories. Theryn tried to emphasize that more violence wouldn't end the creature's suffering. The Wyvern remained still.

I did it, I connected with it.

Theryn held on tight as the Wyvern reared back its head and sent forth an icy burst.

Oh Seluna Above!

Azir, who was dueling another sorcerer with his ice blade, ducked and slid across the staircase on his knees. Two of the council members let out blood-curdling screams as they were frozen in place.

Theryn tried to steady himself and control the Wyvern, but the battle on the palace stairs proved to be too distracting. He couldn't center his thoughts long enough to stop the death that rained down from the beast.

"You were a hero to these people, Azir! Now you will destroy us all!" Fyladreus called, still sending sparks streaming towards his foe.

Azir ignored the words and lunged forward. Fyladreus screamed and dove to meet him. The robed man swung his scepter. From its gem, arcs of tetra-colored energy shot forward. Azir dodged low and sprung up with his sword. Theryn held his breath, wincing at what he thought would be a gruesome finishing blow.

Fyladreus disappeared.

The upward slash should have cut right through the Chief Astrologer, but the man was no longer there. The crystalline blade passed through thin air, and Azir looked as baffled as Theryn felt. Theryn searched for any sign of the man on the steps. He thought he spotted a faint shadow hovering across the pale marble. The shadow shifted, and moments later, the Astrologer reappeared behind Azir. Fyladreus' skin had paled slightly... he looked more like a cross between a Summerborn and a Winterborn now. The Chief Astrologer swung and caught the tattooed man on the shoulder with his scepter. The energy from the gem burned through Azir's hide armor, leaving a spot of charred skin. Azir let out a pained yell and backed away.

"I *knew* it!" Azir bellowed, gripping the gnarled flesh on his shoulder. "You stole the weave of a Shade. You toy with the powers of the Nocturnal Realm. You have been aiding its expansion all along!"

"We weave it away from Winterborn for the safety of Lunathal and its people," Fyladreus defended. "Being a Shade is not natural. This power is not of our world, Azir! It is not a gift from Seluna, it's a curse from an evil Goddess... and to defeat it, I must understand it!"

Below Theryn, the Wyvern signaled its intent to lunge forward. He could feel its anger, so raw and primal. It even wanted to strike at Theryn and Azir. Theryn attempted to calm the beast, trying to figure out why it was so bent on attacking. Theryn felt something strange, as if his thoughts were small waves in a vast pool. He was ripped from the mind of the Wyvern, and at the same time, the beast lurched and sent him sprawling to the ground. Theryn rolled to the side of the column, feeling a sharp pain in his side where he landed.

Theryn rose to his knees quickly to make sure he was out of harm's way. In front of him, the winged serpent reared back its head and exhaled. A deluge of ice exploded towards the Chief Astrologer. Fyladreus quickly tapped his scepter on the ground and summoned his shield again. The sparks and ice collided in a rainbow of light. Illumination shot out from the impact. Theryn covered his eyes as he became blinded from the bright collision. He could faintly see Fyladreus holding his shield against the Wyvern's icy breath.

"We could have made Lunathal a better place, Azir!" the Chief Astrologer called as he struggled to hold back the impending blizzard that threatened to swallow him. "Now look at what you have become. You are delusional. You yearn for what you cannot possibly control. I do what I must to protect Lunathal. You do it for power!"

"Your lies won't save you, Fyladreus!"

Seeing their leader occupied by the Wyvern, the remaining council members moved in on Azir. With a flourish, Azir jumped from the stairs in an arc, deftly avoiding the icy blade of an attacking council member. Azir spun as he landed and sliced the side of the council member who had attacked him from behind. The man dropped to his knees.

"We can't save the surface, Azir! I know why you want the Teardrop, I know your intentions. You are delusional!" Fyladreus roared as he held his shield against the Wyvern. He screamed the words over the crackling sound of two powerful energies colliding.

Azir approached the council member he had cut down. Theryn watched in horror as his mentor's hands formed a claw shape over the wounded man. Azir began to suck up the arcana of the dying council member. Energy swirled from the old man's mouth as he gasped a final breath and dropped to the marble steps. The spindling translucent wisps swam into Azir's palm, and as it did, the icy blade gripped in his other hand grew. He turned and leveled its long jagged point at the struggling Chief Astrologer with both hands.

"Don't do it, Azir!" Theryn tried to call. The exhaling breath of the Wyvern and the high speed winds emerging from the breached cloud wall swallowed up his words. He had to do something. Surely all this death wasn't necessary.

Theryn slammed his hands onto the side of the Wyvern.

Stop!

His thoughts echoed in the endless void of the Wyvern's mind. To Theryn's surprise he felt a thought return.

Why?

Theryn pressed his emotions forward.

Because you are better than this. You don't have to be his slave.

The Wyvern stopped its attack and cocked its head at Theryn. Its huge silvery eyes blinked as if surprised. Then its expression calmed. The dancing lights from the collision of arcana stopped. An eerie silence fell over the Astral Palace; the only sound was the wind whistling by them through the boughs of willow leaves.

Theryn was on the ground, hand on the Wyvern's tail, frozen in place like a statue. On the staircase before him, Azir raised the long blade and cut down another council member with two clean swipes. Fyladreus turned to face Theryn with a confused look, as if noticing him for the first time. The whites of his eyes were wide and wild, like a frightened animal. "Don't follow him, boy! There is no controlling the power in the Nocturnal Rea—"

The words were choked off as Azir drove his icy blade through the man's chest. Crimson blood began to well around Fyladreus's wound, and he gasped for air as his knees buckled. The Chief Astrologer dropped to his hands and knees, blade still piercing through. Azir loomed over him.

"Your tyranny has ended. I offer these people far more than you ever could. I offer them the world. Goodbye, old friend." Azir ripped the blade from Fyladreus's chest and dropped it to the ground. It shattered into hundreds of tiny shards, scattering on the white marble stairs. The Chief Astrologer lay limp, eyes sightlessly locked on Theryn.

Theryn's body went cold in a shiver so violent he had to stop himself from shuddering. What had Fyladreus been trying to tell him? The Wyvern pressed into his malleable mind.

You see? There is no resisting him. We are the same. Puppets for his use. Tools for his rise to power. This is only the beginning.

Azir made his hand into a claw shape over the dead Astrologer, but nothing happened. Fyladreus only lay still, no energy released from his lifeless corpse. Azir seemed to give up, brushed off his clothes and shot Theryn a commanding glance. "Come, grab the scepter, we will need it." The man's shoulder was still burnt and cracked, but he ignored it as he began to walk up the palace stairs.

Theryn approached the dead bodies of the council members. Some had been cut down by the icy blade while others had been frozen solid by the Wyvern. Their haunted expressions stared sightlessly, hands outstretched like statues pleading for their lives.

Theryn approached Fyladreus's body. These were the men who had threatened his parents. He should have hated them. He should have wanted Fyladreus and all the council members to die, but as he stood over the dead Astrologer, Theryn felt nothing but pity. The uncertainty of his death loomed over Theryn… What would it mean for the future of Lunathal? Theryn pushed the questions away as he grabbed the scepter and cautiously followed Azir.

I see the aspirations in the mind of the Rider. He believes great power awaits him beyond that Rift.

The thought had come from the Wyvern. The ancient beast sat on the Astral District Square, serpentine head bowed in a resting position.

Speculation sparked inside Theryn as the Wyvern's words tossed around in his head. *What was this great power everyone seemed to know about?* At times, it was hard to discern whether Azir was doing the right thing or not. Azir seemed to genuinely want to stop the Blight and close the Rift, but his methods for doing so proved to be less than moral. If Theryn was braver, he would have used the scepter against Azir. He would have tried his best to stop the man before more people died or anything else terrible happened. But Theryn was not the Hero of Lunathal. He was scared, and he was being torn apart by confusing ideology. On one hand, he hated how the Winterborn were treated—He hated how everyone was forced to live in Lunathal without a choice, oblivious of the immense world below. On the other hand, he loved Lunathal; it was his home, and he had always felt safe there, despite his parents' disappearance. At this point, the Blight posed an imminent threat, and Azir seemed to be the only one who could stop it. Theryn needed to keep playing along. Just enough to figure out how to close the Rift.

They followed the spiral staircase up to the observatory atop the Astral Palace. The large room had a dome ceiling layered with glass. The glass acted like lenses that allowed the astrologers to peer out beyond the clouds. In the center of the observatory, stood a giant marble carving of the Moon Goddess. Seluna's matronly visage was shrouded in robes, and she leaned against a milky crescent moon. In front of the statue, on a pedestal of white stone and surrounded by blue glass, was a single vial. It was small, about the size of Theryn's pointer finger. It was topped with a cork that was dry and cracked from age. Azir's face was smiling, mad with lust. He grabbed the scepter greedily from Theryn's hands and leveled it at the glass. There was a cracking noise as the amethyst gem that topped the scepter split. A crackling beam escaped from the gem as it disintegrated, turning to a sparkling dust. The blue glass shattered and fell away from the pedestal, exposing the single vial. They took a careful step forward.

How could something so small be so important? At the vial's bottom, a drop of moisture glistened. It looked like any other water droplet, except possibly a bit more… luminous?

"The last Teardrop of Seluna," Azir said with wonder.

He picked up the vial and held it close, "This is the key to everything, Theryn. Do you know how powerful this drop of water is?"

Theryn remained silent.

"From these tears, the Old Willow grew. From these drops, infinite floods came to an end. The Summerborn drank from pools of these tears, and it gave them their arcana. But their bloodlines have weakened as the power of the Old Willow fades. It is why our arcana strengthens while theirs dies away."

"That is a teardrop from a Goddess? It's been here in Lunathal all these years?" Theryn asked, staring at the miniscule amount of liquid in the vial.

Azir ignored him; instead, he continued to think out loud. "We will bring this to the surface and use it when the time is right. "

He brought the vial close and examined it with his icy blue eyes.

"Our one-way road between realms just became a two-way street."

Before Theryn could question what he meant, the tattooed man took off back the way they came. Theryn struggled to keep up as they exited the palace and made haste down the marble staircase. Azir continued to think aloud as they descended. "The ancient Moonfolk searched for power beyond our world to aid in their fight against the Men of Evaria. They unlocked a Rift, and Seluna closed it."

"So we can use this to stop the Blight and close the Rift," Theryn said as he huffed behind Azir, "just like you wanted." A sense of relief washed over Theryn. They held the power that would save them. Fyladreus had only been concerned with saving Lunathal... The Chief Astrologer seemed to think the surface had been a lost cause. Theryn thought that made Azir a little better than the Chief Astrologer. The lesser evil. At the very least, Azir cared about saving the surface.

They reached the bottom of the stairs, and Azir leaned over and picked up his dark jacket from where he dropped it.

"I'll do even better than closing the Rift," Azir stated, putting the vial into his chest pocket.

What?

What did Azir mean by that? Theryn gave him a concerned, questioning look.

"I'll enter the Rift and defeat the evil it holds. When it is destroyed, I will claim its power as my own. No one will dare to threaten us again."

The man's gaze turned to Theryn, determined and unyielding.

"With that power I can close it and stop anyone from ever opening another Rift. Humans, Half-Men, the Imperium... It doesn't matter, they won't dare attack us. The Moonfolk will rule Evaria. We could control all of Tellis if we wished."

Theryn's heart felt like it dropped into his stomach.

So that's what it had all been about.

Azir had wanted something to ensure he could enter the Rift. The man wanted to take the power of the Blight for himself. Theryn felt anger boil inside him at his own stupidity. How had he trusted this monster? How had he ever believed the Hero of Lunathal was a righteous and just man?

They faced each other on the stairs of the palace. At the bottom, the Wyvern rested its head on the platform, waiting and watching.

Theryn came to a halt as he cried out, "This was never about saving Lunathal or Evaria or the world! This was all about you." Theryn took a step back, the Wyvern raised its head as if sensing an impending conflict.

Azir leveled those crystal blue eyes on Theryn.

"You poor thing. So beaten down by the tyranny of the Summerborn that you don't even realize the utopia we will build. Theryn, when I am done, we will all live as equals, in harmony. Summerborn, Winterborn, Men, Half-Men, Sun Elves, animals. We can make this place a heaven on earth. It will be this way because I will be in control. I can ensure no one threatens what we create." The dark-lined tattoos at his chest trembled as he spoke. Azir's voice was so intimidatingly serious about his vision that it made Theryn's hair stand on end.

"Oh, and what about Orlo?" Theryn yelled, his voice shaking. "I saw you weave away his arcana and kill him," Theryn's eyes began to well with tears, his face hot despite the howling wind of the high platform. "What about my mother and all the people who died believing you were actually doing this to save them... to make the world a better place. Is that supposed to happen in a perfect world?"

"A few lives is a small price to pay to save the millions on Tellis, Theryn. Don't you see the potential? Your father sees the vision. He sees what civilization could be if good people ruled."

Theryn wanted to pounce on the man, but he knew that was hopeless. Like he told himself before, he was simply a pawn in this game. "Liar! My father only followed you because he believed you were doing the right thing. He believed you would bring my family back together!"

Azir looked at Theryn, a shred of disappointment in his eyes as he shook his head.

"And I have, Theryn, I have brought your father back to you. Do you know what *my* father once told me? He told me, '*If you want to right the wrongs in the world, you have to do your part to fix them. Never rely on others to do it for you.*'" Azir's eyes grew dark, and his sternness was replaced with a seething intensity. "Perhaps I was wrong about you, Theryn. When I looked at you, I saw so much potential... the loyalty of your father... the courage of your mother... the raw power of myself, a young Hero of Lunathal."

His eyes were hard chunks of ice, and his silver ponytail wagged behind him as he shook his head in disapproval. "It seems the faith I have placed in you is flawed. I, unfortunately, do not have time to sit here and discuss philosophy."

Azir leveled his hands and expelled a stream of crystallized moisture.

The Wyvern let out a shriek behind them.

Theryn didn't have time to react. The ice coated the stairs in front of him and crawled to his position. Theryn's legs froze to the palace steps. His arms were stuck tight against his torso. In a few struggling moments, Theryn was covered to his neck in a frigid shell of frost. Theryn let out a sharp breath as the skin touching the ice began to lose feeling. Just as the ice threatened to cover his face, Azir stopped and stood back, observing his work. "Luckily for you, I won't kill you. Your father has been a loyal captain, and your mother gave her life for my cause. No, it will be much more satisfying to return here and show you how wrong you were." Theryn's whole body seemed to twitch as the man spoke. Azir flicked up the collar of his jacket and checked his pocket before approaching the Wyvern at the bottom of the steps.

"I'll see you again, Theryn. In the new world."

Azir leapt onto the Wyvern's back in a clean sweeping motion. As Azir settled on his mount, he began checking his pockets and readying himself to fly. A strange sensation aimed from the Wyvern flooded Theryn's mind—Theryn had been so caught up in trying to break out of his frozen tomb that he had ignored it. Struggling against the solid restraints was a hopeless effort.

Sapphire light streamed from Azir's hands into the Wyvern.

The beast locked eyes with Theryn. Theryn swore he could see silver tendrils of light lazily floating his way. For a moment, Theryn felt oddly warm. The strange sensation dissipated.

Theryn tried to bridge the Wyvern's mind.

Help.

The creature just blinked for a moment. It gave Theryn a sorrowful look and took off in flight.

He is too powerful. He controls the winter now—He is the master.

A ripping sensation followed as Azir tore the Wyvern and Theryn away from their Soulbridge link.

Numbness washed over Theryn. The Wyvern and its Rider disappeared in a dive towards the hole in the cloud wall.

Theryn was left there on the palace stairs frozen from the neck down. He tried to escape. He tried to bridge the mind of anything nearby to help him. Moonfolk began to gather and shout up from the lower districts. Some had wandered up to the Astral Palace and began to cry and scream at the sight of their dead leaders.

They will kill me.

The Summerborn would execute him, claiming he had been a part of this. Theryn would be blamed for the death of the elders.

Although he couldn't feel anything on the outside, Theryn's insides swarmed with panic. Something stirred within him. It was dusk now, and the moon in the sky overshadowed them. It twinkled, its light piercing through with swirling blues and purples that cast around the clouds. Theryn's skin began to lose its feeling under his frozen cage. Inside the Wyvern's mind he had felt something. He reached inside himself, searching. There was seemingly nothing. Just the same endless black void he saw inside all the minds of others. *Soon, this is what the world will be like,* he thought. If Azir fails and that Rift is released, the whole world will be endless nothingness, just like the one he currently stood in. Theryn sat down in his own mind, the abyss a perfect setting for his internal despair. He sat there, inside his own mind alone when… it started to snow.

First it was small flakes. Then icicles began to form out of the black liquid on the ground. Soon, the winds picked up; larger snowflakes began to litter the obsidian floor. A feeling he had felt inside the Wyvern swirled inside him.

It was a churning blizzard.

Theryn screamed out, willing this power inside his mind to explode forth. Theryn was jerked back into reality, still entombed in front of the Astral Palace. The ice around him splintered and cracked before shooting out in all directions. Theryn stood there, his chest heaving from the effort of shattering his icy cage.

A group of gathering Moonfolk stared at him, bewilderment and confusion on their faces. Theryn ignored them. In his hand swirled a single snowflake. A single fragment of hope.

Theryn took off towards the edge of the platform, hands outstretched. He forced the blizzard inside himself out of his mind and through his hands. Ice began to form in front of him. He steadied himself as he aimed the frost downward in jagged steps.

Theryn hurried forward, ice spilling and shaping from his hands in front of him. His hands shaped crude spiraling pathways downward. He passed each district, gaze locked on the perforation in the cloud wall. The area where the enchantment had shattered, wide open. His icy staircase continued to layer on the air in front of him as he willed it downward. Theryn ran faster down his makeshift pathway. He ran as fast as he could.

He ran to save Lunathal. He ran to save the surface.

Chapter XVII
The New King

The Wyvern flew on. It had no choice. The Rider was too strong, and each thought of resistance that formed was quickly vanquished from its mind.

But the Rider wasn't perfect—He had missed something crucial.

The Winter Wyvern had shared its gift with the boy. The serpent had done it sneakily. Giving him just a sliver of winter fury.

The truth was, although the aged beast cared little for Humans or Elves, it still carried a shred of hope. Perhaps that empathy had been a gift from the Mother all those centuries ago.

Mercy, however, could be fleeting. History had told all the Wyvern had needed to know about most of Tellis's inhabitants. They had hunted its kind for centuries, seeking Wyrm treasure hoards and strong scales. Humans and Half-Men killed the Wyvern-kin and eventually drove them from their nests. The only respect the Wyvern held for the Elves of the Moon came from the fact that many shared faith in a similar Goddess. It was what attracted the Wyvern to Lunathal in the first place. It was what made Lunathal seem like it could have been a potentially safe place to nest.

It had been so very wrong about that…

The Elf boy was the lesser of the two evils. The boy had been the first to look at the Wyvern kindly—with sorrowful eyes. The boy had looked into the beast's feelings with innocent curiosity. The boy had asked, not demanded. When the Wyvern had peered into the boy's mind, there were no wishes for riches or power to be seen. Only the will to survive… much like the beast.

Unfortunately for the Wyvern, that had mattered little. The Rider was too powerful, and now he held the artifact they sought. From scent alone, the Wyvern could tell the vial contained something old, older than even the winter beast itself.

As they flew, Azir kept his thoughts hidden. The only thoughts able to be sensed from him were his surface level emotions. The Rider was clearly disappointed the Wyvern had stopped attacking his enemies at the palace; he was disappointed it had not found the girl; he was angry they had let the young ones escape in the first place from their fall. He thought of the beast like an untrained hound rather than the ancient mythical creature it was.

They flew halfway across Evaria. The Wyvern was exhausted by the time the faint castle town appeared on the horizon. The large castle was surrounded by white stone houses and red roofs. Sturdy buildings like these would be difficult to destroy.

Surprisingly, the Wyvern cared little about destroying the homes of Men today. It was hungry and wouldn't mind eating a few of them, but there was no lust for battle raging inside. Only a blanket of sadness, leaving that dampening, empty feeling. A feeling a creature might feel when realizing it was truly the last of its kind left in the world.

The Rider urged them forward, ignoring their shared exhaustion.

Watchtower bells rang as they glided past the castle town and over the city walls. The Wyvern hovered into the Castle Evaria courtyard and landed with a *thud* in the middle of the gardens. They had made it there rather unopposed, although now soldiers began to file onto the walls around them.

The Rider jumped from the Wyvern's back.

In a moment, they were surrounded by gray and blue clad men. The soldiers wore metal scales as if to imitate the Wyvern. It was a pitiful attempt, those pieces of armor wouldn't save them from the raging storm of the Winter Wyvern.

The Rider called for their king. The Wyvern shrieked with rage at what it saw.

Azir had removed the round glimmering orb and was holding it aloft. The swirling meteorite with rings of light. The relic the Wyvern hated so very much.

You promised we would destroy that. It's unnatural... It only brings pain to the world.

Azir ignored the Wyvern.

Guards on the walls leveled their longbows at them, readying themselves to release a volley. The Wyvern let out a shrill warning to the Rider.

We will die here. We will both be killed.

The man ignored him still, palm outstretched, displaying the meteorite to the gathering crowd.

A regal-looking bearded man entered the castle gardens from the double doors of his throne room. He wore a thin golden crown on his head and a flowing blue cape. The Wyvern had seen his face a thousand times throughout history on different men. Kings and Emperors. Royal Blood. Audacious, dangerous, and stupid men.

The sight of this king filled the Wyvern with a burst of fury. It boiled inside, tempting it to dive at the Man-King. It was unclear whether this was the beast's own urge or if it had been planted by the Rider.

Perhaps they shared it? The Rider and the Wyvern were similar after all. Yet, so was it and the boy.

"So, you are the one who killed my uncle and took his fortress. I was just mustering my legion to deal with you; it seems you have saved my men a great deal of marching," the king called with a complacent voice from behind his ranks of soldiers.

Azir gave the king a dismissive wave. "Don't try to fool me. Your legion is currently dying on some Imperium battlefield in Goldfyre," Azir laughed. "I'm not here to talk to you anyway. Where is your court magician? The one who used this to open the Rift in the north and release the Blight."

The strength of their Soulbridge link allowed Azir's intentions to become clear to the Wyvern. Azir intended to kill this man—this king and his bloodline were responsible for much turmoil in Tellis. The Rider would be doing the world a favor by ridding it of him.

The guards around the Evarian king leveled spears over their square shields in an attack position. Their king only waved them to stand down.

"I ordered him to seal it, and he never returned. He was consumed by the Rift as he tried. His apprentices told me it tore the flesh from his bones and turned him to smoke before their very eyes."

The Wyvern could feel the Rider's mind absorbing the information. Although it did not completely understand what was happening, there was an understanding within the beast. The Rider felt *he, himself,* was the predator. The Rider was in control. He always was.

"Then the fool got what he deserved," the Rider called. "You all deserve the same end. You opened that Rift with this meteorite I hold in my hand. You toy with powers you cannot control."

"And you can?" the king replied cynically. "Wasn't it the Elves who opened the first Rift all those years ago and flooded the world?"

"They were fools to use this, and they have been dealt with," Azir snapped back. The Wyvern readied as the Man-King waved his hand. Instead of an attack, the men directly in front of the king parted, allowing him to step forward and speak clearly.

"You are a hypocrite, Wyvern Rider. I am no fool. You are after the same prize we were... but the unlimited well of arcana trapped inside the Nocturnal Realm is not meant to be contained in the hands of a mortal. No Man or Elf can hold that power and live. We have learned this, and it is why I have given up hope of entering the Rift. It is why I ordered it to be sealed."

Azir seethed at this response, pacing, hand still outstretched and gripping that otherworldly ball of light.

"You sit by idly," Azir shouted, "while the mess you made consumes the world! You and this rock have caused enough damage. It's time for the new age to begin. Men are too dangerous to be in control. It's time for a new king."

With a sudden jerk, the Rider's fingers illuminated blue.

My promise has been fulfilled... Destroy it.

The Wyvern didn't hesitate. The Rider dropped the meteorite onto the ground, and the Wyvern's armored tail followed. It slammed with the strength only hundreds of years of hatred could conjure. There was an explosion of light. The illuminated air seemed to rip and fold around them before resettling. The expanding brightness blinded the Wyvern for a moment. There was screaming as the soldiers called out. A cacophony of whistling noises surrounded the Wyvern.

Pain. Small deep pinpricks of pain.

Arrows were set loose, and they struck the Wyvern. Most bounced off its scales, but a few found exposed flesh in between the natural armoring and pierced its hide. It shrieked in agony as the dozen or so arrows ripped into soft hide. The Wyvern slammed its tail into the ground in pain and sprayed a cloud of ice in the direction of the upper walls. When its vision was regained, the beast could see a courtyard in pure mayhem.

At the throne room doorway, the King of Evaria lay lifeless. Two jagged icicles stuck from each of the king's eyes. Men were shouting frantically, searching for the pale Elf who slew their king. The Rider was already climbing on the back of the Wyvern. Arrows continued to whistle by them and clink off scales. One arrow caught Azir in the shoulder. The Wyvern shared that pain. It was excruciating.

The pallid Rider set a hand on him in command.

Head north, towards the Rift. Make this place a frozen waste on the way out, but don't kill them all. We need some to tell the story of what has happened here today.

The Wyvern shrieked its disapproval. It tried to tell the Rider it was tired, and it didn't have the energy. It tried to tell him it was wounded. The thoughts hit a wall, and instead, the Rider burned any idea of resistance from the Wyvern's mind.

Do it now. The last piece of the puzzle has fallen into place. Take me to the Rift, and when I emerge, you and I will be unstoppable.

A group of legionnaires dropped their weapons and curled down in fear near them. Azir ripped the arrow from his shoulder and called out to them.

"In two days, my army will arrive with many great war-beasts. You will yield the castle to them, or I will return and personally feed you to the Wyvern. Tell the king's heir to be ready to kneel for his new ruler. The Wyvern Rider."

A lifting sensation hit the Wyvern and urged them upward. The Wyvern was so tired it was unsure if it could even carry them out of the courtyard. The urging continued—it had no choice. The beast took off in flight, but not before leaving ranks of soldiers frozen to the castle walls. They shrieked and cowered behind their shields as the violent torrent of snow fell upon them. The Rider's determination on its back inspiring it to dole out more deadly volleys. There was satisfaction with every Human who was hit by the icy blasts. The Wyvern could tell this was Azir's, not its own thoughts.

Something finally dawned on the ancient Wyrm at that moment.

That well of power inside the Rift. The one no mortal was supposed to have. Azir was going to fly them right to it. He was going to use the gift from their Goddess, and he was going to try and seize it. Azir was going to try to do something impossible.

Men died below them as the Wyvern whisked itself and its Rider away from Castle Evaria. They headed back across the country, towards the Rift and its insatiable hunger. The place where Azir would try to dominate an unstoppable force... a force in the form of a sinful deity from the void.

Chapter XVIII
The Infiltration

They sailed for almost two days. The Hyena rode the coast, sails whipping in the wind with haste whilst narrowly avoiding a few of the king's ships.

Lyra's hands ached from holding the line. Being a crew member was a lot more physically challenging than she thought it would be. It was no wonder Aranna and Black Eyes were so tough. They were seasoned veterans and had probably spent more time at sea than Lyra had been alive.

It was hard work, but as they sailed, Lyra felt her worries ease. The anxiety was still there, it just seemed to burn less intensely inside her than normal. She was free, just the cool sea breeze in her curls and the sounds of flapping sails. In all honesty, it was possibly the most at peace she had been since arriving on the surface.

Sailing with the odd crew had actually been enjoyable. In the evenings, Pimbo would tell stories of their failed heists. Helfi would interrupt to correct his boasts. Aranna would sing tales of Black Eyes' adventures during his youth. The elderly captain would sit back listening and smiling beside her, occasionally taking drags from his long wooden pipe. When the others slept, and it was Lyra's turn to take the helm, Helfi would sit up with her and help her train. At first, it seemed wrong; Lyra's instincts told her to be cautious, which inhibited her abilities to use her arcana effectively in front of Helfi. Her whole life, Mother had warned her not to let others know she was a Shade. Now, the crew encouraged her to practice. Sometimes Lyra even caught them watching eagerly from the main deck. With Helfi's encouragement, Lyra had managed to blink from one side of the ship to the other two times the previous evening. The crew had cheered as if they had the Wyvern's treasure already in hand. Pimbo claimed she would be the greatest thief who ever lived.

Black Eyes Barnett stood at the helm, steering the ship's wheel. The rugged captain was eager to reach their destination before the sunrise could make its appearance. Aranna ran around the deck frantically—as she did practically the whole voyage. The brigand woman was doing the work of a full crew while showing Pimbo and his team how to man a ship at the same time.

"I see it! Big stone building on the cliff! Up ahead!" Helfi called from the crow's nest through the midnight air. Lyra peered out over the netting of the ratlines. The moon shone brightly on Tellis, allowing her to see relatively clearly despite the fact that it was night. On the ridge, a dark stone castle sat upon a black sand beach. Dots of earthy green moss lined the craggy cliff nestled atop the shore.

"Our riches await!" Pimbo cheered, slapping a beaming Stringbean on the back.

"You mean our friend awaits," Lyra retorted with a bit of obvious irritation. Pimbo gave her a guilty look.

"Oh yeah and Theryn! We're coming to save you, kid!" The Gnome screamed a cheer into the wind as the ship cut through the water towards their destination.

Something felt wrong. There were no lights or torches coming from the Stronghold. In fact, the whole place was completely dark, save the halo of moonlight that shrouded it. Beyond the shoreline, Lyra could swear the color of the valley was receding.

"Prepare to anchor! No, not that one Stringbean, that's a buoy!" Aranna commanded.

The dock outside the stronghold had been completely destroyed, so the crew was forced to take a dinghy to shore. Stringbean had managed to get everyone on his side soaking wet within the first minute of his paddling. Aranna let out labored grunts as she did most of the rowing. Black Eyes stared at the dark stone Stronghold from the bow of the dinghy, a small cylindrical lense is his hand.

"I see no guards or fortifications," the aged pirate rasped. "Once we hit shore, we should be posting up along the west side wall until your critter has done his part of the deed."

Alongside the boat, Slip was weaving in and out of the water in graceful arcs. Eventually, the otter must have gotten tired because he just held onto the side, floating along with the dinghy.

"Freeloader!" Aranna grunted through oar rows.

The new crew of the Hyena reached the black sand beach. The Duke's old Stronghold loomed over top of them on the ridge. They pulled the dinghy in and ran across the grainy beach. Their shadows danced along the black sand in the sunset.

Lyra steadied her breathing. She could do this. She had to do this. She had to find Theryn and stop the sickness.

They huddled against the side of the castle next to an arm-sized sewer pipe leading out of the ground. The pipe had a sturdy metal drainage grate.

Lyra's practice on the Hyena had been useful, but the most crucial discovery she had made was the limits of her arcana. It seemed that the dimmer the sunlight was, the more effectively she was able to use her arcana. Luckily for her, the sun was currently nowhere to be seen, and she could feel the power coursing deep within her. Lyra touched the drainage grate and willed it to turn from solid to vapor.

Her hands went numb. Within a moment, the drainage grate vanished, only its faint shadow remained.

This place is huge. How is this little otter going to find Theryn in this big castle?

Lyra turned to Slip who was now nibbling on a small fish he had picked up along the way.

"You want to find Theryn, right?"

Slip nodded.

"You need to go in there and find him. When you do, come back out and lead us to him. He won't be able to fit in this sewer pipe."

Slip nodded.

"And try to remember where you see anything shiny," Pimbo interrupted.

Slip blinked at him.

"You know, coins and jewels, and stuff like that."

Black Eyes chimed in, "It's part of the deal, lass, we bring you to that scorched earth in the north *only* after we have been paid for our services. That means finding the Wyvern's treasure!"

Lyra tried to hold back her mounting frustration. She didn't care about stupid gold or stupid jewels. She just wanted to get Theryn and stop the people she loved from dying. She patted Slip on his fuzzy white head. "And if you see anything shiny or valuable, try to remember where it is."

Slip nodded. He stared at her for a long second. His beady eyes blinked. At that moment, Lyra thought he actually looked cute, his little whiskers twitching with anticipation. Then Slip took off through the narrow sewer drain.

"The future of my wealth is now in the hands of a fish-eating fuzzball," Aranna groaned.

"That fuzzball will pull through. Just you wait and see! He's full of surprises." Pimbo leaned against the wall and kicked out his feet in a lounging position. The funny little man began slathering his arms and face with mud.

"What in *Seluna Above* are you doing?" Lyra asked, disgusted.

Pimbo only shrugged, "What? It worked for Matty!"

An anxious hour passed. Lyra tried her best to practice her abilities subtly while she waited. She was able to make the drainage gate disappear a few more times, but it wasn't helping to distract her.

What if she couldn't find Theryn? What would she do?

A jolt of fear hit her as Lyra imagined Slip face-to-face with the Wyvern. She stood up briskly.

"I'm not waiting anymore! Slip is probably lost. I'm going in after him."

Stringbean and the mud-covered Pimbo were leaning against each other snoring softly. Helfi was cleaning her fingernails with her knife. Barnett had set himself to strapping pouches and sacks under his belt in the event they needed to carry out large amounts of valuables.

Aranna returned from her own scouting, "I found a larger sewer drain we could probably fit through along the northern wall."

"I can blink through solids with my rotten powers, you think I seriously wanna smell like sewer? I'm using the front door."

Lyra made up her mind to walk away, passing Black Eyes and trying to avoid his gaze.

"Aye lass, if that be what you want to do, then have at it, but I'll be coming along to make sure you don't pocket any treasure for yourself."

Lyra hugged the winding wall along the ridge. She tried her best to creep alongside it, but it was so dark, and the moonlight couldn't pierce stone. She stumbled a few times, but it was nothing compared to her follower.

Black Eyes had a more than difficult time keeping up with her. The man seemed to fall down with every other footfall. His aged legs folded and buckled a few times under him as he misstepped again. The old pirate always cursed under his breath and rose to continue following Lyra.

After a few more stumbles and tumbles, they reached the main gate. Solid wooden bars in vertical and horizontal patterns blocked off the world from the fortress entrance. It was sturdy wood, supported with metal spikes. The gate would be difficult to break down.

Lyra turned and faced the captain, "I'll meet you back here after I've found my friend."

"That wasn't the deal, lass. I'm to come with you and make sure you make good on your word."

Lyra didn't intend to stick around to argue. Her mind entered that dark void, and her form burst into smoking shadows. Her vision warped, and sound was sucked from her ears. Lyra could see from her smoking form that the pirate was yelling at where she had stood, yet no sound could be heard in her current state.

How had she never noticed she couldn't smell in here either?

It was like each of her senses was completely muted. All except for sight. She couldn't see colors, but at least she could see her surroundings.

Lyra pushed herself in the direction of the gate. The sensation of going through a solid was weird. A bit like having running water flow on you, but also all through your insides. It was a feeling of relief when she was finally through. Lyra let go of her tension, releasing her mind from the abyss in the process. Her senses returned to her body as she rematerialized. Still tingling, Lyra rubbed her eyes to help with the sensory overload. Her hands came away from her eyes and vision returned. The world was colorful again. She was inside the courtyard and beyond the wooden gate.

"You had better come back with some gold, Lyra... Or you will be walking home!" Black Eyes threatened hoarsely from the opposite side of the gate.

Lyra gave him her best arrogant salute and entered the courtyard.

Only a few moments of exploring told her she could drop her guard a bit.

The place was clearly abandoned.

She walked through corridors and halls. Nothing but animal droppings and basic household items. It was clear whoever owned this fortress had terrible hygiene.

Lyra searched through studies and common rooms. The whole place seemed as though it had been hastily packed up and left. All that remained were old banners, suits of armor, portraits, and statues. She found a single copper coin on a dresser, which she picked up.

In one room, however, she did find something interesting. Moonfolk clothing... woven ponchos and britches from the willowmoss of the Old Willow. There were a lot of them, in varying sizes and styles, and they had all been discarded. Some seemed like they had been folded and tucked away without being worn in many years.

What has been going on here?

Why was the Duke collecting Lunathal clothing?

Lyra pressed on down the corridors, encouraged to figure out why the person who owned this fortress was so interested in itchy fashion.

Occasionally, she would accidentally step on animal droppings of various sizes, far too large to be Slip's. She wiped her feet on an expensive looking rug outside a large room.

Lyra entered the room, noticing it still faintly smelled of wood smoke. This place seemed important; it was one of the biggest spaces in the hall besides the courtyard. Three banners hung from the mantle. Two she recognized instantly; they were common in Lunathal. The first was Lunathal's own banner, a silver tree covered in clouds. The second was the purple crescent moon of Seluna, the Goddess. The third was new to her—a blue winged serpent perched on a brown mountain.

A handful of books lay scattered around the bed at the corner of the room. Lyra studied some of the titles. Although they were written using a few different characters than what she was used to, she could still make out the titles. She was grateful at that moment that her mother had forced her to learn notation symbols in homeschool. She picked up each book and sounded out the titles.

History of the Great Flood

Evarian Studies of Alternate Planes

Research of the Nocturnal Realm

Lyra tossed each book over her shoulder as she read the titles. These were too long and boring for her, plus they barely had any good pictures. The last book was on the bedside table and had no title. Instead, a thin piece of charcoal rested on its leatherbound cover. Lyra picked it up and opened it.

To her surprise, the characters were written in the same exact style the Moonfolk used. Even by the inflections of the words, it was plain to see someone from Lunathal had been the author. The person used the same sentence structure as most Moonfolk writers and even dotted certain vowels like she had been taught to do. Lyra read a few of the early pages to herself.

When Fyládreus dubbed me the Hero of Lunáthàl, it was just à formálïty. He hàs found à wày to twïst ït to hïs benefït; however, my exïle hàs proved most enlïghtenïng. Todày I hàve leàrned à terrïble truth. Our àncestors càused the greàt flood. They used the relïc from ànother world to open the fïrst Rïft, then begged theïr Goddess for à wày out of the mess they hàd creàted.

Now I understànd why Fyládreus ànd the councïl hàve càst me àwày. He must hàve knöwn I would eventuàlly dïscover thïs. He knows my love for the surface, yet despïte àll we could àccomplïsh here, he retreàts bàck to Lunáthàl. He ïs à cowàrd ànd no better thàn the Humàns of Evárïä... He ïs no longer à frïend, but àn enemy.

The handwriting was neat and organized, but the charcoal was smudged as if it had been written long ago. Lyra knew the name Fyladreus, the Chief Astrologer, but she drew a blank on the meaning of the rest. Lyra continued to flip the pages to some later entries.

I am not the only one who this happens to. The arcana is called Soulbridging, and it is not a gift from Seluna. I have found a monastery of those able to Soulbridge with a master to teach me. They may be more learned, but i am the one with a Wyvern at my command. Perhaps, I will be able to control the wretched thing.

This was the Rider's journal. She continued to scan the pages. There were so many. This guy liked to write. Lyra flipped a few pages and continued reading.

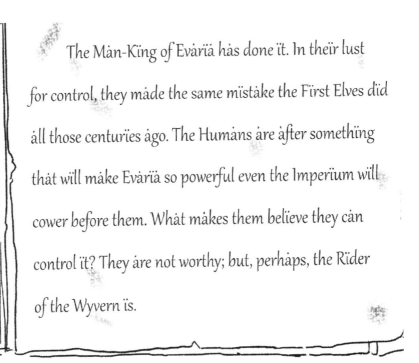

The Man-King of Evärïä has done ït. In theïr lust for control, they made the same mïstake the Fïrst Elves dïd all those centurïes ago. The Humans are after somethïng that wïll make Evärïä so powerful even the Imperïum wïll cower before them. What makes them belïeve they can control ït? They are not worthy; but, perhaps, the Rïder of the Wyvern ïs.

A few more page swipes. The handwriting became messier with each page, scribbled out more and more frantically.

I have learned something great today from the Duke's libraries. I have learned what my ancestors were after when they opened that first Rift. The Humans' texts theorize the First Elves were communing with a demon or shadow. The translation is unclear. Our ancestors were losing the battle with the Humans of Evaria, so they became desperate. They were promised a mighty power locked away in an eternal void. Instead of reaching the realm they sought, they used the relic incorrectly and were sent an endless flood. That knowledge, and the relic I have captured here, makes today a great victory.

A great victory? Lyra thought the man wrote with an indulgent self-importance. He seemed to believe his thoughts were undeniable truths. She read on, to one of the latest entries.

The amount of ▓ death the Rift has already caused is astounding. The Humans were ▓ foolish to try and control it. Evaria, the Imperium, the council... they will all yield to me. I can sense it and so can the Wyvern. I will be better than they were. Now I know the errors of my ancestors. They left the ability to ▓ open Rifts on the surface, and the Humans found it. It will be destroyed when I am sure it is of no further use to me... No one should hold the power except me. Surely the Hero who can tame the most ferocious beast in all of Tellis can trick a trickster God.

Especially once I obtain the last Teardrop of Seluna.

The Rider wanted something inside that Rift. Was this the same thing that was making people sick? Was this Rift the thing that was killing her mother?

Clang!

A suit of armor in the corridor hit the stone floor with a resounding echo. Lyra pocketed the book and ducked behind the bed.

"It's too late, Slip, the Acolytes are already gone!" a familiar male voice called out from the corridor. A figure appeared in the doorway. Slightly short. Round face. Black hair. Curved ears that came to a point and pale skin.

"Theryn?"

Lyra poked her head out from behind the headboard. Her eyes weren't playing tricks on her. There stood Theryn. Messy hair swept back, wearing purple robes with a white otter hanging from his shoulder.

Her face lit up and she ran at him. Lyra tackled him in a hug.

"I never thought I would be so glad to see you, bird boy."

He hugged her back tightly.

"I knew you would be here. I could feel it," his voice choked a bit as he talked. "Slip led me right to you... Lyra, so much has happened." He released from her grip and stepped back, holding out a wooden stick.

"Azir, the Rider, has gone completely crazed. The whole reason he had the Wyvern capture me was to help him with his insane plans. He wanted me to control the Wyvern for him." Theryn's eyes grew dark and serious. "Lyra... he killed the council, and he took Seluna's last Teardrop from Lunathal."

The boy tossed the wooden stick to the ground; the faint emblem of Lunathal had been branded into its side. Lyra was barely able to form words. *He went back to Lunathal?* She looked at him astounded. "You were there? You were in Lunathal?"

Theryn nodded.

"It wasn't the homecoming you think it was. The Old Willow is dying. A Rift from another world is eating away at the surface. Azir's trying to get inside and take the power for himself!"

"I know, I read about it. This guy likes to write down his feelings," Lyra held out the journal in front of him. "So, someone was really riding that Wyvern when we first fell... He really thinks he is the Hero of Lunathal?"

Theryn ignored the book and gave her a serious look. His usual lighthearted optimism was gone. Where there was once a nervous boy, now stood a determined young man. He spoke sternly.

"He was the Hero of Lunathal. But that's not important."

Theryn spoke quickly and intensely. "Lyra, I've learned what being a Shade means. It means being able to partially cross over to the Nocturnal Realm. It's why your powers are so strong at night. It's when the distance between our realm and the endless void is closest. Your abilities aren't from this plane of existence."

It made sense. Somehow, Lyra had always known this, considering she couldn't recall a single time when she was able to use her power during the day. All the information about different realms and endless voids, however, was a bit too much for her to wrap her head around in the current moment.

"I think my powers aren't from here either. It's why they took away arcana like ours in Lunathal. They aren't gifts from Seluna like the Summerborn. They thought our powers were dangerous."

Theryn placed a hand on Lyra's shoulder, "They may be right about our powers being from another realm… You might be the only one who can close the Rift and stop Azir. He needed you. One of the reasons he grabbed me in the first place was because he thought I was the Shade!"

Lyra's head swam. The Hero of Lunathal needed her? Was she supposed to help him? She couldn't in her right mind assist someone so narcissistic and power hungry, of course… but if it meant healing her mother…

How could Theryn expect her to do this? She was a petty thief, a lower class musician, a rotting *fruit fly*! Not a hero!

"What about the Wyvern?" she asked.

"I can handle the Wyvern."

"Where's the gold, *boy*?" A new voice rang out in the study. Hoarse and menacing. Theryn, Lyra, and Slip whirled in unison.

At the doorway stood Black Eyes Barnett, soaking wet. He wore his old hat. The plume Pimbo had sewn on now plucked off. Behind him was Aranna, also damp and dripping, her curved sword drawn at her side. The intensity their faces held made Lyra's skin crawl.

"Where's Pimbo and the crew?" Lyra questioned.

"Disposed of... Dead weight," Aranna smiled deviously. "You should know better than to trust a pirate."

Lyra paled further at the sinister words.

"We will be having that gold now, lad," Black Eyes rasped. "Bring us to the Wyvern's hoard, and we will grant you your lives."

Fury welled inside Lyra. How could she have trusted these double-crossing woodrats? How had she seen Aranna kill Tate before her very eyes and still thought, *oh yeah, let me just hop on a ship with these guys. She just murdered her longtime crewmate for basically no reason. It will be fine.*

Lyra felt stupid for believing they would help her. She had been betrayed, and now her only friends had been killed, just when she was starting to like them too.

They would have to surrender. There was no fighting these two.

"Stand back," Theryn said as he pushed Lyra gently to the side. She watched in astonishment as the air around them began to swirl. There was a sudden chill, like the temperature in the study was dropping. Water seemed to appear from nothing. First, as small drops, then as crystalline flakes that stacked together. The flurry picked up, and from it formed a long pointed spear of ice in Theryn's grip. It was made from pure, translucent ice, and each side carried a deadly sharp tip. The pirates took a step backward in surprise. Theryn walked forward, placing himself between Lyra and the pirates. "We need to get north and stop that Rift or there won't be any place left in the world to spend gold."

Black Eyes unsheathed his own sword, undeterred by the deadly icicle in Theryn's grip.

"I'm not afraid of your fancy sorcery, boy. The world ain't ending. Cataclysms come and go, and we keep on living. I've been on this rock a long time, and I know the world will spin on long after I'm gone."

Theryn turned to face Lyra. His nervous brown eyes were trying their best to look confident. "Get to the ship and sail towards the Rift. I can feel the Wyvern. They are flying to it now. I'll meet you there."

"Are you crazy? I'm not leaving you! And since when can you do that?" Lyra pointed at his hands incredulously. Theryn opened his mouth to protest, but it was too late, she didn't wait around for an answer.

Lyra dove forward, hands outstretched and summoning her arcana. With a blink, she was a vaporous shadow. The endless void around her swirled as her smoking form went right through the pirates. It was unpleasant as usual, but she didn't care about that right now. She blinked and reformed on the other side of Aranna, grabbing at her sword. The woman was stronger than her, but Lyra had a well-positioned grip. The blade jostled around them as the pair struggled for its possession.

"You should be helping us, skinny. Do you know how rich we could make you?" Aranna sent a knee into Lyra's abdomen. The shock of the blow knocked the air from her lungs, but she continued to hold the sword hilt tight. Aranna readied her stance for another kick.

Lyra's hands began to tingle as she pushed her arcana into the sword. With a sound like a candle being snuffed, the sword burst into smoke. Aranna's hands went up, and she was knocked off balance as the weight from the blade dissipated. The sword reappeared a moment later in the same spot it had vanished. Lyra snatched it out of thin air. She held it up to the neck of Aranna.

The brigand woman let out a groan and raised her hands in surrender. "That was cheating!"

Behind her, Theryn was dueling Black Eyes with ferocity. Shards of ice flew through the air as the pirate's blade hacked at Theryn. The spear was being chipped away, unable to withstand the durability of a tempered-metal blade. With each blow Theryn repaired the spear with moisture from the air around him.

The moon hung in its usual heavenly aura outside the stained glass windows. The dueling pair's shadow danced beside them as they exchanged blows. The captain was old and past his prime, but Lyra could see his years of experience in the way he finessed his blade. Theryn was on the defensive for the most part. He was untrained, and his motions were too wide and slow. Soon, Theryn was being beaten back towards the corner of the room. Black Eyes delivered an overhand strike. Theryn blocked with his spear hastily and the ice shattered into hundreds of crystalline fragments as they made impact. He fell back to the corner.

"The Wyvern's hoard is here somewhere, boy. And we will be finding it with or without you!" Black Eyes raised his blade for the final strike.

"Don't do it, I have your *First Mate* hostage here!" Lyra screamed.

Black Eyes didn't seem to care. His blade was set to fall on Theryn with a deadly strike. Those onyx eyes burned like charred coals in his bloodlust.

What could Lyra do? If she moved, Aranna would be on her in a moment. But she had to... Theryn would die if she didn't. Lyra readied herself to blink towards Theryn when a blur in the corner of her eye distracted her.

Slip dashed across the room and launched himself over the bedside table. He soared through the air and landed on Black Eyes' head. The otter began biting and scratching. Theryn saw his chance and kicked up, catching the old captain in the crotch. Barnett let out a howl, dropping his sword. He tried clawing at Slip, but the otter was too slippery. Theryn rose to his knees and grabbed at the captain's feet. He held the man's ankles and tensed his face. Icy water began to pool at the ground. It climbed up his ankles all the way to Barnett's waist. The moisture began to freeze over.

"Floods and the seven hells!" the captain bellowed as the frost crawled up his body. Slip launched himself from the pirate and landed on Theryn's thigh. The ice continued to climb. The old pirate howled in discomfort, the same way someone would howl if he got a bucket of ice water thrown on his head. Just as the frozen shell threatened to cover Barnett's face, it stopped.

Theryn released his grip from the captain with a smile.

Aranna shot Lyra a nervous glance. "You won't be able to sail without me! Take me with you!" She made a motion that looked as though she wanted to run, but Lyra only pressed the tip of the blade closer to her neck.

"Hold still... you look a little sweaty. Theryn help her out with that issue."

Theryn approached from behind Aranna and set his hands on her shoulders.

"You need me!" Aranna pleaded.

"I'm sure we will manage without you. You're '*dead weight.*'"

Flakes of ice flew from the air around them like a contained blizzard. They surrounded Aranna and lined her body, freezing her in place up to the neck. Theryn froze her in a position that made her eye-to-eye with Black Eyes. Lyra actually let out a breath of amusement. These two would be getting a lot of prolonged eye contact until the weather decided to melt their new frozen shackles.

"Don't you dare touch my ship, you pointy-eared fiends! You haven't seen the last of Black Eyes Barnett!" The pirate captain grunted as he struggled beneath his cage of ice.

"Thanks for the ship," Lyra winked at him and plucked the captain's hat from his head, placing it on her own. "At least you guys can have plenty of staring contests to keep yourselves entertained. Maybe you can explain to Aranna why you were going to let me kill her!"

Lyra took Black Eyes' sword and placed it between them with a mischievous smile. The pirates eyed it, their expressions fuming. Lyra then sheathed Aranna's curved sword through the loop of her belt and turned to face Theryn. "I didn't know you could do that!"

He grabbed Slip by the paw and hoisted the otter onto his shoulder. "Until very recently, neither did I. It seems to be a recent occurrence. I think it was a gift…"

Black Eyes screamed at them to return his hat as they hastened from the study. They left the frozen pirates there, with nothing to do but wait for the ice to thaw and stare into each other's eyes.

Slip led them through the sewers and out a child-sized storm drain on the opposite side of the wall. They barely managed to squeeze through. It was amazing to her that Aranna and Black

Eyes had been able to weasel in this way. They ran in the night across the beach, soaking wet and smelling like sewer water. Moonbeams of purple and white faintly illuminated the coastline.

"There's a dinghy around here some—"

Lyra cut off as she spotted the dinghy on the beach where they had left it. Inside was the silhouette of three figures. Lyra felt her stomach turn. The murderous pirates had dumped the bodies right in the dinghy. The thought of seeing her three deceased friends made her nauseous. Theryn ran up close and waved her over.

Pimbo, Stringbean, and Helfi.

Lying face down on the boat floor… tied up at the hands and feet with a long rope… cloths shoved into their mouths and… breathing?

Pimbo jerked to the side, his eyes shot open as he began to wriggle about. His yells were muffled by the cloth tied around his face.

"They're alive!" Lyra exclaimed. She ripped the cloth from Helfi's mouth.

"Who's this one?" Theryn asked, pointing to Helfi.

"Pimbo's sister, and the only one of them with a shred of common sense."

"Hey!" Pimbo groaned, spitting out his gag, "I have plenty of common sense. I knew those stinking sea dogs were going to double cross us. I just didn't know Stringbean was going to get knocked out so fast!"

Lyra went to cut Stringbean free, but Theryn had already begun. He held out his hand, and in a moment, a translucent knife of ice appeared. Theryn cut the cloth and rope from Stringbean with the icy dagger.

"They snuck up behind me, Pimbo! They bonked me on the head so hard everything went blurry. I still don't think I can smell."

"Oh, you're fine, you big lug. We'll take you to the medical donkey after we get out of here."

Pimbo eyed Theryn. "I see you found the kid, and I see he found a way to make ice come out of his hands. Very interesting. Should have done that when we were first locked up..." He gave Lyra his best pathetic look, "Please just tell me you found some gold."

Lyra flicked him the single copper coin she had found. "Sorry, just this coin and this journal."

"One measly copper? No gold? So all this was for *nothing*? Stringbean lost his sense of smell, and I had to spend *quality time* with my sister. All for *nothing*? I sold my father's dingy and wore fancy clothes, and covered myself in mud, all for *nothing*?"

"You can have the ship," Lyra said. "We need to sail north to that Rift. It's leaking an endless void that's going to kill everything if we don't stop it. We need to beat the Wyvern Rider there. After all that is done, the Hyena is yours. If there is anything left of the world, that is."

Pimbo's eyes lit up.

"Helfi, imagine the look on Ma's face when I bring a whole stinking ship home!"

Lyra placed Black Eyes Barnett's hat on the Gnome's mud-crusted head. "Lead us to your ship, Captain."

The little man let out a squeal of delight. He smoothed out his shirt, straightened his hat, and tossed an oar to Stringbean. "Row, you limey bilge rats! *Row! We set sail for the endless void!"*

Chapter XIX
The Rift

They sailed through the mist-shrouded night. Theryn had tried to read the journal during the sunrise, but any attempts at focusing became agonizing. From what he read, it seemed Azir believed their world had not solely been created by the Moon Goddess, as most Moonfolk thought. The Men and Elves of the surface had believed Goddesses had done it… multiple Gods and Goddesses, not all of them as loving and nurturing as Seluna. Theryn tried to read on, but he started to feel feverish.

He could feel it in Slip first. The little otter spent most of his time sleeping through the morning and afternoon instead of swimming along the ship. The sunlight became obscured by billowing ashy clouds, and the fog thickened, which only served to diminish any signs of good cheer amongst the crew.

As they drew closer to the Rift, the water began to lose its blue hue, and the grip of Theryn's fever strengthened.

The sickness from the Blight was upon them.

It started with a dampening of emotions. The crew of the Hyena started to complain of exhaustion. They began showing signs of lethargy. Helfi napped longer. Pimbo stopped making jokes. Stringbean still couldn't smell and complained of sore muscles. Theryn could feel his own mind become drowsy after the efforts of trying to do any thinking. It was the exhausted feeling of someone who has stayed awake too long. He felt a desperation to sleep. They were wracked with little appetite and little motivation to do anything beyond curling up in a ball and wasting away. A day or so ago there had been wailing in the brig below deck by the man, Matty, who had stayed locked up. Pimbo had tried to set him free on their trip to the Stronghold, but the man had refused to leave the cell. The man's sanity had clearly fled. Matty claimed if he left, the beast would find him.

As they sailed towards the void, Matty began writhing in pain, skin green and veins black like dark spider webs woven through his body. The crew had tried to help him. He began screaming for them to turn around; he was a blabbering, frothing mess. The crew tried to give him food and water. Matty, however, had gone wild in his eyes, and his face was a mask of pain. A day later, he gasped his last breath with a sickening wheeze. The color had been completely drained from him, all that was left behind was a pallid corpse. The Blight was slowly eating away at all of them.

Then there was Lyra. She no longer trained, her energy for that long gone. She stuck to the helm, completely concentrated on getting them to the Rift as if she had a personal vendetta with it. Her skin grew sickly in hue and her veins darkened, but she steered the ship on.

The sea that surrounded them became a sludgy gray, as if heaps of ash had been poured into the waters. The wind blew furiously away from the Rift as if it was the heart of a monstrous storm. Because of that, the Hyena could only crawl forward at a painfully slow pace. The closer they sailed to the Rift, the more and more tired they became and the more the landscape darkened around them. Theryn watched his own skin go from its typical alabaster white to an anemic green.

In the distant valley, beyond the field of dead trees, Theryn could see a smoking rip in the earth.

"I can't take it," Theryn said, as Lyra steered the wheel of the ship while Pimbo napped on the helm deck beside them. "We won't have enough strength to get there, let alone stop Azir."

Theryn reached out with his feelings. His fingers glowed the normal shining arcane sapphire. It was a relief his arcana still worked. He searched the landscape for the Wyvern. Quick pulses next to him echoed in his mind... that was Slip.

He stretched further, searching in that endless void for any sign of the low booming heartbeats the Wyvern's connection produced. The Wyvern's pulses were so different from the pinging noises of the pigeon or the sharp staccato rhythms of the coyote.

Theryn heard it. First, the low beats to the south. Then the shriek in the distance. The Wyvern was approaching rapidly. It and its rider would reach the Rift far before the ship did.

"Lyra, you have to get us to the Rift." Theryn said, the desperation in his voice trying to convey how dire the situation was.

"Azir will reach it before us. We need to travel through the Nocturnal Realm to get there first."

Lyra looked at him, bags under her tired eyes. "But it's so far. I've only ever done a few meters before."

Theryn gripped her arm. He squeezed with his remaining strength and met her eyes.

"You can do it. You have to do it, Lyra."

The Wyvern let out another shriek in the distance. Tired and labored sounding. Lyra seemed as though she had heard it, too, because she turned to Pimbo and kicked him awake.

"Huh?" The Gnome woke up, groggily rubbing his eyes. "*Boiling Grasshoppers*, I feel awful."

"Take the helm, Pimbo. You've done your duty. Get the ship out of here." Lyra helped Pimbo up with an extended hand. "Thank you for everything, now get your crew to safety."

Pimbo's head swiveled to each of them. "Oh, you can't be serious? You guys are headed into *that? Alone?*"

Theryn nodded, "We have to. Get the ship out of here, and sail for the Castle town. There will be a group of Elves in purple robes with animals camped outside the city. Ask to speak to Tarvin and tell him Theryn sent you. He must not invade the city. If I live through this, I'll return to him. Please tell him I love him. Have him tell Bub that I love him."

Pimbo looked at him strangely before nodding somberly. "Ok, kid, you got it."

Theryn looked to Slip. The white otter had risen from his nap and was now gazing at Theryn with sad eyes. Theryn scratched the little otter behind the ears. "Don't worry, friend. I will always be with you. We are a part of one another. I will see you soon."

The otter held out his paw. Theryn took it delicately. He held it for a moment, staring into those beady eyes.

For one fleeting moment Theryn forgot his aches and pain. The whole world zoned out around him. It was just Theryn and Slip, in an endless void. Theryn saw something inside of Slip. The reason he and Slip were so close. They respected one another because Theryn had given him a choice… a choice to complete their Soulbridge that Slip and Theryn had made together. There was no master and no servant between them. They were partners, and from that partnership, there was love.

The world came back into focus, and the frailty returned to Theryn's body. Theryn patted the otter on the head and returned to Lyra.

It was time, and she knew it. Theryn could see it in her. Behind those tired eyes, there was intensity and determination. They were ready, ready to give it their all to save a world they had just discovered together.

A black dot moved in the distant skyline. The Wyvern was coasting through the air towards the ashen valley.

"We have to go. We have to do it now."

Lyra held out her hand to his. "We will have to run fast. We need momentum."

They locked hands and took off towards the bow at a run. Theryn used his last strength to push himself into a sprint. They sprung from the edge of the bow towards the murky waters. As they lifted into the air Lyra let out a cry of effort. Her hands erupted with a purple light and began to smolder. There was a faint grabbing feeling on Theryn's robes behind him. The world around them warped and sound left Theryn's ears.

They were smoking forms, sailing through the air towards the Blight's origin. The gray waters and shore around them had shifted into that endless black void. The only light came from a rip in thin air ahead.

The Rift.

It was a sliver of substance in a world of the non-physical. Theryn thought he could see the moon on the other end of it, obscured by the black smoke that poured through the gateway. They sailed through the air, Lyra's ethereal hand still outstretched, anchoring them towards the Rift.

The oil-slicked ground began to bubble beneath them.

Seluna Above. What was happening?

Theryn tried to call out, but his words couldn't form in the vacuum of the void. The liquid was massing, shaping together. It appeared almost solid, yet still swelling and rippling like waves in the sea. The nocturnal ooze began to amass into the shape of a woman, easily three times the size of the Wyvern. It formed near the Rift as if it had been peering through like a child with a spyglass. The matronly figure turned its attention to them and held out a terrible hand.

It pointed at Lyra with spindling tendrils.

Lyra's smoky eyes widened. Theryn tried to shake her but his hands passed through her incorporeal form. He felt a sudden snapping as they were ripped from their shadowy state.

The pair fell back to physical forms with a *thud*. Theryn rolled along the graying ground and lay face down in the cracked earth. The feeling of rematerializing had totally disoriented Theryn. He pushed himself up, trying to tame the sensation of vertigo.

Right in front of them, hovering just above the ground, the Rift vibrated.

It looked as though someone had cut into the world with a shadowy knife. It was about half the size of Theryn and impossibly black. It cast no shadow and hummed loudly. Its edges waved as though it was made of liquid, like a flag blowing in the wind. Above them, thick gray clouds obscured the sky. All around them, the ground was a colorless stain, covered in a thin layer of black smoke that leaked from the Rift's narrow opening.

There was a tugging feeling on Theryn's sleeve, followed by a tickling on his face. Slip stood there, face so close to Theryn, one would think the otter was trying to get in his mouth and hide. The little otter had followed them in and had been with them when they pushed through the Nocturnal Realm. Theryn was about to reprimand his friend for coming along when he heard Lyra's voice.

"It called to me…"

Lyra was huddled in a ball on the ground next to him. The smoke began to crawl up her body and envelope her curled up form. She was holding her knees close. "It thanked me for using its gift."

She gazed at Theryn, her tired eyes carrying a haunted look. "I felt its hunger. It wants to consume everything—It called on me to set it free."

The Wyvern came in for a landing on the other side of the Rift. Azir's jacket billowed behind him in the wind as he rode the neck of the Wyvern. The winged beast had arrows jutting from between its purple and blue patterned scales. Small trails of deep burgundy blood had dried down the side of each wound. Slip ducked behind Theryn's leg. Theryn sat up on one knee and held out his hand. He reached out to the Wyvern. The beast welcomed him into its mind, there was no strength left to resist.

Such exhaustion... it had been flying since they abandoned Theryn in front of the Astral Palace.

This will be the end, Theryn... A life of servitude is no life at all.

The beast tried to roar, but it had no strength. Instead, it collapsed to the ground. The brilliant scales of the Wyvern were losing their amethyst and sapphire shine. Its breath was shallow and labored. The Blight was killing them all... even the mighty Wyvern.

Azir flung himself off the side of his mount. He landed nimbly and approached them beside the Rift. Behind a face of forced confidence, Azir tried to hide his surprise at seeing Theryn.

"Have you come to witness the Hero of Lunathal save the world?" Azir called over the humming of the Rift. "I've come to close this gate and ensure no one has the power to ever open it again."

"You mean you intend to seize that power for yourself. I've read your journal. You could kill us all in the process!" Theryn screamed.

Azir ignored him and took a step forward to regard Lyra. "You brought me the girl. It seems you weren't completely useless after all, Theryn. For the loyalty your mother showed me, I offer you this final gift. I'll tell your father you died a hero."

Azir held out his tattooed arms at Theryn. If Theryn stayed still, he would be frozen alive or impaled by ice shards. Summoning as much strength as he could, Theryn jumped out of the way, tumbling backwards over his shoulders away from Azir. Slip followed him, dashing to his side. Theryn expected to see a line of frost where they had been kneeling.

There was nothing.

Theryn rose, trying to take advantage of the moment. He extended his hands and called for the blizzard inside himself. The air around him didn't even stir. No spear of ice emerged from his hand, not even a flake of snow appeared. The air around them was completely devoid of moisture.

Azir looked at his hands with annoyance and put his arms back down at his side, realizing the futility of his efforts. "Lucky boy, I will have to deal with you after I seize the power in the Rift. Unfortunately, it will be more excruciating for you then."

He pointed at Lyra, "You are coming with me."

Azir made a running dash for Lyra. Theryn half expected her to still be curled in a ball, unprepared for the attack.

She wasn't.

Lyra was up, on unsteady feet, but she was up nonetheless. The curved blade of the cutlass she had taken from Aranna was extended in front of her.

"I'm not going in there. Not again!" she screamed, fire in her eyes.

Azir charged her. Lyra swiped at the air in front of him, but he ducked and slid under the blade. The curved sword cut a single lock of his long hair. The silvery strand fell to the ashen earth and burned away. Azir whirled from his low position. He kicked Lyra's legs out from under her. She fell on her back, landing hard.

Theryn was already up and running forward to help, trying desperately to summon any ice he could.

Nothing came.

The only arcana inside him was the low heartbeat thud of the Wyvern. It was slow, but Theryn wasn't focused on that—He had to help Lyra. The creature was dying, it was true, but they all were. The Rift was sucking the life from them as they faced off in front of it, and Theryn realized it would soon be the only victor if they kept battling.

"Azir, Stop! There's a monster in that Rift. We've seen it! If you go in, you could release it." Theryn dove to tackle Azir, but the man simply side-stepped and sent him sprawling to the smoky floor. Azir's tattooed arms reached down and grabbed Lyra by the neck.

"I either need you or your arcana. You choose, girl!" He lifted her up to a standing position. She gagged and choked from the force of his grip. Lyra tried to jab the sword into Azir's stomach, but he caught the hilt with his other hand. They wrestled with it for a moment before the sword went flying and clattered to the ground next to them. Behind them, the Rift hummed loudly, smoke continuing to pour from it and layer on the ground. Azir raised his hand in a claw-like shape. The same shape he had used to weave away Orlo's arcana... and his life.

Theryn dove forward for the blade. Azir kicked at him as he reached down to grab it. The blow caught Theryn in the side and knocked him to the ground just out of reach of the sword. Azir continued to try to weave away Lyra's arcana. He choked her with one hand, the other right in front of her face. As he did, the Rift seemed to vibrate and expand... Something in the Rift was stopping him. Azir gave up and gripped her neck with both hands.

"Bring us in, use your arcana!" he demanded. Lyra clawed at her neck frantically, her feet now dangling from the ground. Theryn reached for the sword again. As he grabbed the wooden hilt, a flash of purple light blinked Lyra out of existence in front of him. In a moment, she was on the other side of Azir. Behind them, the Rift osculated and widened. Smoke began to billow out stronger. Azir turned and kicked at Theryn again. Pain ran down his back as the booted foot knocked him to the ground. Smoke filled his lungs, and Theryn began to cough and sputter. He flung his arms upward in a desperate attempt to cut Azir. The silver-haired man dodged nimbly to the side and ignored him—regarding Lyra instead.

"Don't you see? You fuel this. Your power and every Shade before you only widens the portal to the Nocturnal Realm. If I pour the Teardrop onto the void's Goddess, I may be able to harness its power! Don't you see? Seluna has abandoned us, she won't save us. I have to!"

Theryn was up again and ready. In front of him, Lyra shook her head, rubbing the red marks on her neck that were already bruising. She was trying to catch her breath, panting quick and shallow. Where was Slip? Theryn didn't know if the otter could help, but they were running out of options. He was just so exhausted. If only he could just lie down and close his eyes, maybe the pain would go away...

"We have to stop it, girl!"

"No, not your way. I've seen what is in there. It's an endless hunger. You can't possibly control it!"

Azir smiled wickedly. His cold glacial eyes sparkled with cunning as he reached into his jacket. Azir pulled out the small vial with a single crystalline drop in it.

"With this, divine miracles are within my grasp."

Azir lunged forward and pummeled Lyra. Theryn could tell the sudden force caught her by surprise, and they staggered backwards towards the Rift. Theryn watched in horror as Azir grabbed her by the waist and heaved her into the otherworldly gateway. She screamed out as the opening in the air swallowed her. The sound was sucked away and Theryn saw half her form turn to smoke as she entered the opening.

"Lyra!" Theryn's hands extended, trying with all his might to conjure ice to seal the Rift before she could disappear into it fully. The blizzard inside him was still, no winter arcana showed signs of even a single drop of moisture to freeze.

There was only the low beat of the dying Wyvern.

The Rift let out a gelatinous wriggle, and it widened further as it consumed Lyra. Azir eyed the vial, making sure it was unharmed. He gave Theryn a curt smile before turning to step into the Rift.

Theryn felt so alone on the smoking field, surrounded by a burnt landscape of ashen grays and charred blacks. Hope left him.

If the Blight didn't kill him, then Azir surely would if he was able to harness its power. Somewhere in the distance, his father marched to war; somewhere in the clouds, his grandfather believed him to be dead. He was truly alone… No one was coming to save them.

Theryn looked at the Wyvern from the other side of the Rift. A small white dot was next to the mythical beast. Slip was standing in front of the winged serpent. His eyes locked on the exhausted eyes of the Wyvern. They were dying, together, having life slowly bled from their bodies, yet, they gazed at each other. Slip even held out a paw and stroked the Wyvern's snout. Theryn tried with his last strength to reach out to them with his mind.

Slip yielded and willed him towards the Wyvern's mind. It was a sensation like having your hand held as you jumped into cold water. The beast let him in, and Theryn's vision blurred. As he entered, there was a jarring feeling like being elevated at a rapid pace.

The next thing Theryn knew, he was standing in the mind of the Wyvern. Everything around him was black except for the ancient serpent and the countless stars that dotted the sky. There was something else above the yonder of the Wyvern's mind. A crescent moon casting a purple light down on them. The Wyvern raised its head from its curled position. It sent its thoughts to Theryn.

The Goddesses created the Wyverns long ago. Before there were Men and Elves. There were some for each season. I am all that remains. The last of the Winter Wyverns of Seluna… and now oblivion is upon me.

Theryn crawled forward, his muscles aching. He rested a hand on the Wyvern. The creature was cold, colder than usual. It's sadness was insurmountable.

I came to Lunathal to find a resting place. A place where I could be free from the tyranny of my hunters. Instead, I found my own enslavement.

"I'm so sorry," Theryn said, tears streaking down his face as he gripped the Wyvern's sorrow as if it was his own. "I'm sorry for everything… but we need to do something. We need to stop him."

The Wyvern looked at Theryn, its oval eyes half closed and cloudy. It sent him a question.

Why should I save a world that has treated me so poorly? The world of a Goddess who has abandoned me?

Theryn placed another hand on the Wyvern. The beast blinked slowly, waiting for an answer.

"Because life is a gift. You have lived so many magnificent centuries because Seluna wanted you to. Centuries filled with life, death, glory, pride, strength, and weakness. All things must come to an end, but that doesn't mean it has to for everyone."

Theryn took his hand off the Wyvern and positioned himself so that he was now eye level with the creature's bowed head.

"I'm not Azir—I won't force you to do anything. But please, we can't just give up. Tellis needs you. Life is too precious to just let it fade away like this."

Theryn's mind burned with memories. He pushed them forward onto the Wyvern.

Memories of his mother, holding him outside their home in Lunathal. Joyful memories of his father teaching him to climb branches. Sad memories of his parents' funeral ceremony after they had jumped. Memories of Bub holding him close at night when he had nightmares. Proud memories of when he taught a rook to do tricks in the air. The memory of when Theryn first locked eyes with the creature, not so long ago. They gazed at these visions together as they lit up the void that surrounded them.

Theryn wept as he watched them. They were so beautiful, even the sad moments in his life. The thought that there would be no more memories made his heart ache. After they were done, the Wyvern regarded him for a moment. Theryn wiped away his tears as the Wyvern insisted that Theryn look above them. Its head raised to the sky where a single vision flickered, sent forth by the Wyvern himself.

In it, a single blue egg cracked. A claw fractured a piece of the shell from the inside. A dull blue serpentine head appeared, small and infantile.

A motherly figure with flowing white robes hovered over the egg. Her face was obscured by small clouds except for the crescent moon on her forehead, which glowed with an amethyst light. Her eyes were sparkling diamonds, like two full moons glimmering through a cloudy sky. They watered with joy at the sight of the newborn Wyvern. The motherly figure wiped away a sparkling tear and held it forward.

"I offer you this single Teardrop. It is my love incarnate. It contains the essences of life. Happiness, joy, pride… but also sadness, fear, and pain. This is the balance all things must endure."

A single finger holding the Tear touched the head of the hatchling. The newborn's scales began to crystallize. They shimmered as if being polished into tiny flecks of gems. The motherly figure spoke again, the sound of a thousand female voices rang out in unison as it did,

"I give you the gift of winter. Harsh though it may seem, winter is an important part of the cycle of our world. Some will call you a monster. A brutal creature. But to me, you are

beautiful, as all my creations are. Life is about balance, and I give you the gift of life."

The tiny Wyvern let out a proud roar.

The vision faded, and the void around them began to retract. Before it did, the Wyvern sent one last thought to Theryn's mind.

Life is a gift.

Chapter XX
The Nocturnal Realm

Lyra soared through the air towards the Rift. It swallowed her up eagerly. Crossing over felt similar to using her arcana. The only difference was instead of pushing herself to become a shadow, the gateway seemed to pull her in and do it for her, like a hungry force of gravity.

Her mental exhaustion remained, but her physical ailments melted away as Lyra's body became a vaporous shadow. The world emptied, all that surrounded her was the thin layer of black liquid that lined the ground. There were no stars in the sky, no moons, not even a single cloud. Just infinite darkness.

Behind Lyra, Azir drifted in, his own shape a hazy mist. His long silver hair floated upward as if this realm was devoid of gravity.

It was complete silence. Lyra could feel herself being pulled away from the entrance. She held out her hands trying to wade through the air to get back. Lyra just continued to float away from it. The only solid thing in the void was the vial Azir had carried in. The glass of the vial had turned to smoke, but the Teardrop inside was now a single solid crystal. A gem of brilliant rainbow colors that sparkled in the limitless abyss. Azir tried to reach for it, but his hands passed through. His usual stern face was panicked, and he pointed frantically to Lyra trying to communicate with her to do something.

Lyra felt a stab of panic. If her skin was able to, it would probably crawl. In the distance, the liquid on the floor was beginning to bubble and pull together.

Lyra held out her hands, willing something to happen.

In a matter of moments, that wicked feminine figure had formed from the black liquid. It looked like a woman that had been covered in melted wax and sap.

Come forward, former children of Seluna. I offer you a power greater than she ever could. Give me that Teardrop, and you shall be rewarded.

The voice was high pitched and shrill. It echoed out in the void, impossibly loud.

I've already gifted your kind with a sliver of my potential. Come and seize the rest. Take your place by my side. You are my children now.

Lyra reached for the inky liquid that covered the ground and slammed her smoking hands into it. To her surprise, she felt her fingers tingle. The black liquid retracted and was replaced with the smoking cracked earth of Tellis.

Around Lyra, a bubble expanded, and she felt herself remateralize. Azir fell to the ground with a *thud* as he too became physical. A shell of energy blossomed out of the ground as she pushed. The bubble connected to the Rift entrance. Behind her, the world came back into view. Lyra looked at her tense hands in wonder. She was straining, and it took all the force she could muster, but she was actually holding the void back. It felt like she was holding back an entire ocean. Lyra had created a pocket in the Nocturnal Realm. She was now the gateway between the world she loved and the destruction that threatened to swallow it.

The gurgling liquid withdrew for a moment, staying away from the bubble.

The Teardrop fell to the earth, back to its liquid form in the vial. The vial bounced on the stiff dirt but did not break. It rolled to Azir's feet, just under the layer of smoke.

"Empty it on the Rift!" Lyra screamed. "We can close it now!"

Azir bent down and picked up the vial. He eyed it closely, intensity in his gaze.

"No... you are right. I was foolish to try and trap its power. It doesn't want me. I cannot possibly contain this void."

He uncorked the vial.

"But this... the blessing of Seluna. This power should suffice."

The liquid monster screeched and sent tendrils shooting from its form towards the bubble. Lyra braced herself for the impact. The tendrils beat against the shell. She held on tighter, every muscle in her body straining to keep the shield up.

To the side of her vision, Azir opened his mouth and lifted the vial over it. He stuck out his tongue, intending to consume the liquid Teardrop. The vial turned, and the Teardrop slid to the edge of the glass vial.

Time seemed to still as Lyra's mind raced for a solution—but what could she do?

She thought to break her grip on the bubble she had created, in hopes that the Teardrop would crystallize and pass through him, but she couldn't. The liquid monster's tendrils were battering at the edge of the bubble, trying to break in and grab them.

The divine Teardrop was about to fall from the lip of the vial when a fog of winter wind billowed through the entrance behind them. The Rift hummed loudly and jostled, splitting open more.

The Wyvern came ripping through. On its neck sat Theryn and Slip, each holding on to a spike. The beast shrieked and released a blast of ice right at Azir. The man turned and held up his hands. Some of the ice reflected away, but the Wyvern was too powerful. In a moment, the man was covered in the blast.

The frost settled, and Azir was enveloped in ice, eyes wide and frozen solid in place. The Teardrop still clung to the edge of the vial in his now frozen statuesque hand. It had resisted the sudden frost and stayed locked in place, still a sparkling singular drop of liquid.

The Wyvern landed next to Lyra in the safety of the bubble she had created.

The tension of holding the bubble was threatening to overwhelm her. Every muscle burned and ached. Pain coursed through her already tired and sick body in ways she didn't think was possible.

Lyra could feel her life draining away. She didn't know where she found the strength to hold back the inky tendrils, but she did. The monster continued to batter its long limbs against the bubble, seeking desperately to break through. Lyra thought of doing this for her mother, and that was enough to hold on a bit longer. She yelled through clenched teeth to Theryn.

"Get the Teardrop! Empty it on the Rift!"

Theryn jumped off the Wyvern and headed for Azir's frozen body.

The ice flew away in thousands of pieces.

A shard caught Theryn in the stomach and he toppled to the ground. Azir fell to his knees, gasping for air. The vial bounced to the ground once again.

"You useless lizard!" Regaining his footing, Azir screamed at the Wyvern, "Kill him!" Azir's hands erupted with sapphire light which flew towards the Wyvern. The beast shrieked, and its silvery eyes went so cloudy Lyra couldn't even see the pupils. The beast opened its wide jaws and snapped at Theryn.

Theryn rose, still gripping his stomach, which had been cut by ice. Slip was on his shoulders, tapping frantically, encouraging him to get up. Lyra could see he was bleeding. The young man gripped his wound with one hand. The other held Aranna's sword.

"Kill him!" Azir demanded again…

Lyra watched as Theryn locked eyes with the Wyvern and dropped the sword.

"What are you doing!" Lyra screamed.

Theryn held up the bloodied hand that had been covering his wound.

He'll use his powers. He'll try to control the Wyvern.

But there was no sapphire light. Instead, Theryn called out.

"There is one thing that you never truly mastered, Azir!"

"Kill him!" Azir shouted again, this time with eyes wild.

The Wyvern reared back its head to snap again. Theryn gripped Slip's paw, the little otter clinging onto his robes.

"A bond is strongest when you trust your partner. You have to both want the same thing. It's a partnership."

Theryn turned to face the Wyvern who was about to bite down. "This is your choice, and your choice alone. My soul is a part of you just as his is—and I want you to be free!

"*Life is a gift!*" Theryn screamed the final words.

The beast stopped in its tracks. Azir tensed and pushed his hands forward, willing the beast to follow his order.

The Wyvern's silvery eyes regained clarity.

It closed its jaw and whipped around in a quick sweeping motion. The tail of the beast crashed into the side of Azir, sending him flying towards the edge of their contained space. He crashed through Lyra's bubble and into the void. The Rider let out a scream as his physical shape transformed to smoke. Azir floated there beyond the bubble for a moment before the hundreds of inky tendrils grabbed at him. Lyra could see his expression; though hazy, his eyes went wide with fear as the undulating monster pulled him forward. It consumed him, swallowing his cloudy form. Azir disappeared into the liquid.

"The Teardrop!" Lyra screamed. She couldn't hold for much longer. Her head swam, and her vision was growing blurry. If she continued to tense like this, she would black out in a few moments.

Theryn picked up the vial, the Teardrop sat at the edge, threatening to spill out to the ground. Theryn eyed it for a moment.

"Drop it on the Rift, seal it off!"

"We will be trapped in here!" He called back.

Beyond the bubble and through the opening of the Rift the night sky's moon shone. It cast a moonbeam of silvery light down onto them. Lyra had just noticed it for the first time since she put up the arcane shield.

The light was warm.

It was as if the light wanted her to keep fighting. The Wyvern cocked its head to look up at the crescent moon. Lyra continued struggling, she was going to collapse any moment. The Wyvern lowered its head to Theryn and extended its forked tongue.

"What are you doing?" Lyra tried to scream.

Theryn turned over the vial. The drop fell and landed on the Wyvern's tongue.

There was a pause… then the creature began to glow. The dull hue of the Blight completely washed away from it. Its scales shone brilliantly, and it let out a proud roar.

It was the last thing Lyra saw or heard before her body gave out and her mind went black.

Chapter XXI
Choice

The protective shield Lyra had conjured was falling. The edges of the physical realm began to retract as Theryn watched Lyra hit the ground. She had done the best she could. She was unbelievably strong and had given her last ounce of strength. Theryn was so proud of her.

Lyra looked so frail now. Her hands were burnt and charred. Theryn's eyes welled with tears at the sight of her huddled form. The ink creature's tendrils forced themselves through the fading bubble shield and grabbed hold of Lyra by the leg.

Theryn looked to the Wyvern in panic. Its eyes, now shining brilliantly.

Life is a gift.

The winged beast dove forward towards the void and its monster. The Wyvern's scales sparkled in the moonlight, bathing the abyss in dazzling tricolored light. Theryn felt himself become the vaporous form of the Nocturnal Realm. Lyra's unconscious body was being pulled towards the dark mass. Next to Theryn, the bubble shield's edge vanished from existence as the Wyvern passed through it.

To Theryn's surprise, the Wyvern retained its physical form.

Just as the Teardrop had.

The moonlight surrounded the Wyvern like a spotlight. The ethereal beam of light followed the Wyvern as it extended its long wings. The ancient beast dipped and dodged as violent tendrils shot forward to strike it. The Wyvern approached the mass and opened its jaws.

Instead of snow and ice, liquid light flooded from its mouth.

A moonbeam formed of sparks so bright, Theryn had to avert his eyes.

The mass writhed as the radiant light made its impact. Sparks of oranges, silvers, and purples flew all about the void. Behind them, the moon shone brighter through the Rift. The moonbeam covered Theryn and bathed him in warm light. He felt himself become whole again, dropping to the ground. A small pocket had been created in the void. Another beam of light shone through. It outlined the unconscious body of Lyra, on the ground in front of him.

Hope flooded Theryn's heart. Slip chittered next to him. The sickness washed away from his body. He found the strength to run forward. The light followed him, outlining a safe path for him to weave forward. Tendrils darted out at him. He reached Lyra and hefted her limp body over his shoulder. An inky limb tried to grab at them, but it retreated back as the moonlight seared it with a sickening sizzle. The void monster echoed with a deafening chorus of shrill voices.

"Seluna!" the mass from the abyss swore in its screeching tone.

Theryn reached the Rift entrance and turned back. The Wyvern was locked in battle with the monstrous mass. Light and sparks burned through the oozing, inky monster. The onyx blob of tendrils shot out sharp liquid thorns in all directions. The obsidian darts pierced through the scales of the Wyvern, drawing long lines of blood. The serpent, however, did not stop; instead, pressing its attack with increased ferocity. Theryn could feel its focus, its incredible strength and determination to protect life. Slip tugged at Theryn's shoulder and pointed frantically—Behind them, the Rift began to seal.

Theryn held out his hand towards the Wyvern.

"Come with us, we need to go now!"

The Wyvern ignored him, instead whipping its tail at the void mass and slicing off a few of its writhing limbs.

"Please! We need to get out of here!" Theryn begged.

The Wyvern turned and faced him.

You never commanded me, Theryn. You were the only one who ever gave me a choice. Today, I will make Seluna proud. Today, I choose to preserve life instead of taking it.

The Wyvern turned its head and dove into the mass. The shrill voice cried out in a thousand blood-curdling screams as the Wyvern exploded with brilliant light. It punctured the inky body of the monster. The collision caused a flash that blinded Theryn, followed by an extreme push. The force of the wind sent Theryn, Slip, and the motionless Lyra toppling through the Rift.

Theryn hit the ground and collapsed. His eyes felt heavy. He tried to open them, but they were so weighted he could barely see.

Brown dirt. A single blade of green grass waving in the wind.

A gentle breeze filled his ears. He tried to catch his breath. It felt much like it did when he had first landed on the surface after his fall from Lunathal. Surprisingly, he no longer felt feverish.

After a few moments, Theryn heaved himself up. Slip was next to him, curled in a ball, breathing slowly and peacefully.

The ground around him was no longer ashen gray. The trees were still dead and bare, but the cracked earth was no longer covered in smoke. The Rift was completely gone. The only light shone down from the twinkling stars and the deep purple aura of the moon in the sky.

The light bathed Theryn in warmth.

Lyra lay across from him, eyes closed, body limp. Her skin was its normal porcelain color, but she carried no signs of life. Theryn rushed to her. He picked her up and laid her out over his legs. He was crying now. Hot tears and breath leaking from his face. Theryn didn't have it in him to accept that she was gone.

She looked so peaceful and serene in the starry light. That only made him weep further. Slip sat next to them, his head buried in his furry paws.

Theryn held Lyra. He held her tight, not able to control his weeping. A single teardrop fell from Theryn's eyes and landed on her forehead. It glistened down her face in the amethyst moonlight...

Chapter XXII
The Crescent Moon

The last thing Lyra remembered was her legs giving out from under her. She thought she could recall the sensation of being grabbed by the monster and pulled towards its maw.

From there, everything had faded away.

She simply didn't have the strength to hold on any longer. She wasn't sure where she had found the strength to push back the void in the first place.

Now she was in that void—surrounded by an abyss.

How was it possible that she felt no despair?

In fact, something felt oddly serene.

Her surroundings were the typical darkness she felt when she used her powers. It was pitch black. All except for one thing. Above her was a crescent moon. Curved and silvery with an amethyst aura, it bathed her in its illumination. Its luminescence rippled down and blanketed the abyss around her. The light was warm. She felt like she was being cradled by someone who loved her.

Lyra blinked and rubbed her eyes. When she opened them, she was surrounded by stars as well. Little dots of twinkling oranges, blues, and purples, just like the light bugs back home. That same moon was now impossibly close. Its grand shape hovered just overhead.

There was a woman here too. Kind eyes gazed down upon Lyra. The woman had her arms wrapped around her and was hugging Lyra close.

Pink freckles, same as Lyra's, dotted the woman's nose. Her long curly white hair fell in beautiful locks around her face. She had the same cheeks as Lyra, but they had a few aged lines. The woman's skin was pearly with a faint illumination to it as if she was glowing.

"Mom…" Lyra said in a weak voice.

Her mother smiled and nodded.

Lyra tried to reach up to touch her mother, but the hand passed through her. It was like touching a warm reflection in a pool of bathwater. Lyra could feel it in her heart what this meant. Somehow she had known this would happen.

"You're gone... aren't you?" Lyra asked, through choked tears.

Her mother nodded, her expression gentle and caring.

"It's ok, *keeko*," her mother said tenderly. She wiped away the tear that fell down Lyra's cheek. Her touch felt nice. Comforting.

Lyra shook her head in disbelief, "I was too late. I couldn't save you."

Her mother lowered her face closer, giving her daughter the same look someone might give a toddler who says something silly.

"No, Lyra. You saved me. You saved us all. You did something with our power I didn't think was possible."

Lyra's face contorted, trying to understand the words without breaking into tears. Her mother continued.

"I'll always be with you. As long as the moon is in the sky. I'll always watch over you."

Lyra shook her head, her face no longer able to keep its composure.

"I can't live without you. I'll be alone!" Lyra pleaded.

This time her mother shook her head, still smiling, "But you won't. You have found purpose. There is a whole world on the surface to explore. There are people who care about you there. Enjoy the gift of life. When you need me, look to the moon, and I will be there for you... always. You have so much life left to live, Lyra."

Her mother leaned down and kissed her on the cheek. Lyra's face was hot with tears. She reached forward and held her mother. She didn't know if she was actually holding her, or if the warmth just made it feel that way, but she held on desperately. After a while, the warmth faded. The light of her mother flickered, and the moon overhead began to retreat back into the sky. The stars blinked out one by one until everything was pitch black. All that remained was the moon, nothing but a tiny speck of light in the distance. It released a single drop.

The glowing droplet of moisture fell towards Lyra. She winced as it plopped lightly on her forehead.

When Lyra next opened her eyes, she was greeted by a sunrise. The pink and oranges in the sky hung over the northern mountains. She was lying on something soft. Around her were small blades of grass. Little sprouts of life that persevered through the waste of the Blight and were being reborn. She looked up and Theryn was there. He was crying. His eyes shut and his face a mask of despair and seemingly… blue.

"What's wrong, bird boy?"

Theryn opened his eyes in shock. His gloomy expression melted away as his smile widened.

"Lyra!"

He clung to her, clutching her tightly in an embrace. "You were gone… and then your breathing… it was so faint at first… I didn't know—"

He gave up trying to explain himself. They just sat there in an embrace. Surface birds sang around them, and the sun continued its laborious ascent over the valley peaks.

After a few moments, they released each other, and Lyra sat up to take in the color that surrounded them. It was accompanied by a sigh of deep relief. The valley was a mosaic of vibrance. The water was its normal shimmering blue. The distant mountain peaks restored to their earthy tones. The clouds that wafted through the sky had their normal pillowy texture. The place in the air where the Rift had been was gone.

The moon in the sky was faint, giving way to the sunrise, yet still watching over the world. Theryn leaned his head back and let his head go limp, basking in the light of the spring sunrise. Lyra tried to do the same... Something inside her felt different. She looked at her hands and her skin had turned a tinge of blue. The same color as the Summerborn. She rubbed her eyes and looked again.

No, her mind wasn't playing tricks on her. Slip was sitting next to them grooming himself, and he was still that same milky white. Lyra observed her hands again. There was just the faintest hint of blue to her skin, as if a clear day's sky had smudged onto her.

She looked at Theryn. She had been so preoccupied with the valley, she had barely noticed his skin actually *had* turned blue.

"Are we?"

"Blue, yes," he answered, "I am not sure why. It happened as the Rift closed, I think." He held out his hand and a small blizzard materialized. "I can still summon ice, but I can't feel Slip anymore, even though he's right next to me. It's like someone has weaved that arcana away. It's just gone..."

Lyra held out her own hand. There was no tingle. No numbness. She focused. Steadied her breathing. Searching inside herself for that blank canvas.

There was nothing.

Wait... yes there was.

There was something faint, but it didn't come from its usual place. It didn't come from the darkness of her mind. It came from lower, like a fluttering in her heart. She tapped into it. Sparks began to crackle wildly from her hands.

As the sparks danced in her open palms, they pooled together causing her outstretched hand to light up with radiance. It felt warm, like holding a heated stone. A small figure appeared, forming together from wisps of light.

"Lyra... what are you doing?" Theryn stammered.

Her mother's voice spoke to them.

"There were never Winterborn or Summerborn. We have been the same all along. Some of us just lost our way. You have restored Seluna's faith in her children—all her children—even the most ferocious of her creations."

The radiant figure in Lyra's palm continued to speak, casting out thousands of miniature sparks as she did, like a tiny contained sun.

"*You and Theryn have shown Seluna that life is truly a gift.*"

The light faded, and the matronly figure of sparks melted away, like a water fountain running dry. Theryn relaxed and pushed his hands through his dark hair, taking it all in.

They didn't speak for a few minutes after that. The cool breeze through the pines of the valley was the only noise that whistled by them.

Finally, Theryn spoke up, "You know… I take it back. You aren't such a rotten *fruit fly* partner after all."

Lyra laughed and nudged him on the shoulder.

"Yeah, well, I guess we could have done worse when it comes to partners. I'm glad I fell from that tree with you, bird boy."

He placed his hand on hers.

Slip nestled between them, and the three sat there in silence, watching the sun rise over the distant Old Willow. Its bark was a healthy brown, and the pillowy cloud wall floated loosely around it. Strangely, Lyra didn't long to return as she had before… The surface was her home now.

A whole world to explore.

With people she cared about.

She gripped Theryn's hand tighter. "What now?" she asked.

Theryn smiled broadly.

"Now?" he pointed towards Lunathal. "We build the world we always wanted to live in."

Epilogue
1 year later...

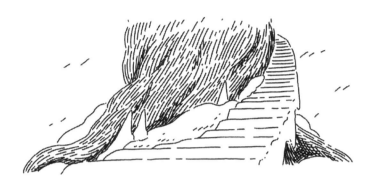

"Looking good, old man!" Tarvin called. "Not bad for an ancient relic!"

"Would you be quiet!" Bub called. "I'm not so used to this magic mumbo-jumbo!"

Theryn stood next to the Crabber's lake. Around them, a busy village wrapped up the day's work and returned to their homes.

"Show him again, Theryn. He's still not understanding!"

Theryn repeated his motion, moving his hand upwards in a sweeping arc. A cool line of snow traced in the air after his fingertips and fell gracefully to the ground. He laughed as Bub tried to mimic him.

The old man was waving his hands in wild shapes, noodly arms flailing. After a few frantic spasms, a single snowflake popped from his hands.

"Look!" Bub shouted. "I did it! One hundred and fifty-six solstices later, and I finally have arcana!"

Theryn beamed as his grandfather, now blue, danced around happily. From his seat, Tarvin laughed and clapped against his leg with his only hand.

Bub stopped and put his arm around Theryn.

"This magic stuff ain't so bad. I don't like being blue though. I could do without looking like a songbird's egg."

Around them, the lower city of Lunathal settled by the lakeside summit. A year ago, only the Crabber's shack stood here. His shack was now replaced with a sprawling manor, which he governed as mayor of the lower city. Now there were circular homes of wood and stone littering the mountainside. Large spiraling staircases of ice crawled up the side of the mountain and ascended the trunk of the Old Willow. Moonfolk could be seen climbing and descending as they pleased as well as some Humans and Sun Elves from Goldfyre.

When Tarvin had returned with the Acolytes, they had helped him build the staircase, linking their world to the surface. Their Soulbridging was gone, but now many held the touch of winter along with Seluna's other gift: sparkwielding. When they had reached the city, the enchantment around the clouds had dissipated. They were greeted by the leaderless Moonfolk, with whom they shared tales of the surface and invited any who wanted to come and see for themselves. No one had stayed behind. Both Summerborn and Winterborn had come down the frozen stairs to see the surface of Tellis. The only difference was that you could no longer tell who was Summerborn and who was Winterborn. In Lunathal, every person's skin had changed to that tinge of blue.

Theryn sat down on the log next to his father. Slip jumped from the pool and shook himself dry. The otter jumped into Theryn's lap.

"Slip! You're still soaking wet!"

Slip ignored him, instead, curling in a ball and closing his eyes. An eagle landed and perched on Tarvin's shoulder. He stroked its head absently, running his hand through its majestic feathers.

"I'll never understand why they stuck around, even after our Soulbridging faded."

Theryn stroked the snoozing Slip on his lap. The white otter was napping peacefully. "It's because we gave them a choice. It's a partnership, Dad. We want to be with them, so they want to be with us."

His father considered the words, "I guess that's one thing Azir never got right. He was powerful, but his need to be in control blinded him."

The eagle took off, soaring through the air, as if showing off for them. At length, Tarvin spoke, "I should have never followed him. He was wrong about so much. I still believed in what he promised though. He used to speak of how Winterborn and Summerborn were meant to be the same. How our ancestors had been abandoned by Seluna. He was going to close the Rift and prove to her that Moonfolk were good people."

Tarvin clapped Theryn on the back. "You did what he could not. Now we get to build the world he promised us… only better."

"Hey, bird boy!"

Lyra approached them. Next to her, stood Pimbo in a wide-brimmed captain's hat. "You ready?"

Theryn placed the sleeping Slip in his shoulder satchel. He rose and hugged his father.

"You sure you don't want me to come with you?" Tarvin asked.

Theryn patted his father on the back. "They need you here, plus, someone has to continue Bub's training." Behind them, Bub flailed about frantically, trying his best to replicate his single snowflake.

His father laughed. "Alright, alright. But be safe, ok now? I've lost you once, and I can't do it again."

"Don't worry about him," Lyra cut in. "He'll have me watching over him. I'll save him if we fall from anything."

Theryn scoffed, "No you won't! You're not a Shade anymore."

Lyra put her hands on her hips, "I'm something better now, moss brains. Only problem is, I'm still poor."

Next to her, Pimbo cleared his throat.

"Don't you worry about that! We'll be remedying that issue real soon!" Pimbo held up a leatherbound book from his back pocket.

"I've been reading up, and after confirming with some historians and geographers, I am confident I know where Azir had the Wyvern hide its treasure hoard. We are going to be so rich, Ma will be cooking from a *golden* cauldron!"

Lyra rolled her eyes at the Gnome, "Stringbean does not count as a geographer *or* a historian."

"We consulted maps, I swear. Helfi even agreed. The treasure is somewhere north. Past the Hailing Peaks. The old nesting place of the Wyvern! You'll be thanking me when you return to Lunathal in a golden chariot."

"We'll see about that. For now, I'll just be satisfied with seeing more of the surface." Theryn looked out beyond the lake. "There's a whole world there waiting for us to explore."

Pimbo straightened his cap and tugged at Lyra's poncho sleeve. "Can we get going now? Helfi will be done with the repairs, and I wanna get to Oar's Rest before the markets close. Gotta make sure we got plenty of stew before we set sail."

Theryn bid Bub farewell with a big hug and a promise to return soon. He took one last look at the new Lunathal. The cloud wall had opened for them, and although it still protected Lunathal, it no longer sealed them away.

People now had a choice.

Theryn realized how important that was—to have a choice. Some people didn't have the choice to do the things they did. Life simply dealt them what it did, and they had to overcome what they could. That is why he was incredibly grateful for the life he had been dealt. Every time he looked at the crescent moon in the sky, he realized how lucky he was.

Theryn looked up, checking on the crescent moon at that moment. It hung in the sky like a ripe omela slice, ready for picking. As he gazed at its magnificence, an echo, almost cerebral in nature, sounded out. Whether it echoed in the depth of Theryn's mind or the actual valley before them, Theryn couldn't tell. It was a proud roar, the call of someone or something who had made the right choice.

Theryn also thought it sounded like the call of someone or something who understood that life was worth protecting.

Theryn took Lyra's hand and set off towards the coast. Towards a new adventure. It was his choice to do so. He wanted to. Life was a gift, and he wasn't going to waste it picking fruit all day.

Acknowledgements

The world of Tellis was first created as a Tabletop Game world, which I had the pleasure of shaping and leading amazing friends through. Three cheers for the brave adventuring parties whose own tales and exploits helped pave the way for Theryn and Lyra's. My partnership with Petar Kovacevic, also known as Extellus, helped motivate me to create the world of Tellis. His artistry and collaboration is matched only by his friendship.

Oftentimes, we can set our minds to something with unyielding determination, and it can still never come into fruition. Life seems to find a way to upend progress even when we are most passionate about completing a project. Yet, other times you build yourself a community so inspiring and amazing that you just have to see the final product blossom. Without the following people the world of Tellis simply would not exist.

First, to my editor, Michelle Baird of Baird Books, who took this book from an uncut gem and polished it into a beautiful jewel with the power to transport readers to other realms. Without her, the book in your hands would be vastly different, for the worse, I fear.

Secondly, to my beta readers: Jacob Burney, Ren Burkhardt, Mia Carlone, Tyler and Tanner Gillis, Craig Johnston, Mairead Leahy, Wesley Marchena, Rose Martin, Francesca Panunto, Stephen Rianhard, Shiori Sameshima… and last but not least, Emily Lavins, who helped breathe life into this story in many different, amazing ways.

And finally, for my mother, Susan Carlone, whose love for reading was taught to her by her own Bub. Thank you for letting me keep my head in the clouds.

About The Author

Christopher S. Carlone is an author, composer, dungeon master extraordinaire and educator from Connecticut. He has composed award-winning music for over one hundred games, films, videos, and series. He is also a life-long creative writer who, until only recently, felt music was his only way to express himself.

He kept his books hidden.

Recent adventures with friends both in real life and in fantasy worlds have led him to the creation of the world of Tellis.

You can find out more about Tellis, and its Moonfolk heroes at www.ChristopherCarlone.com

ISBN 979-8-986963-90-7

9 798986 963907

90000>

Made in the USA
Middletown, DE
27 October 2023

41383088R10224